SILVER MOON

GREAT NOVELS
OF
EROTIC DOMINATION
AND
SUBMISSION

NEW TITLES EVERY MONTH

www.smbooks.co.uk

TO FIND OUT MORE ABOUT OUR READERS' CLUB WRITE
TO;

SILVER MOON READER SERVICES;
Barrington Hall Publishing
Hexgreave Hall
Farnsfield
Nottinghamshire NG22 8LS
Tel; 01157 141616

YOU WILL RECEIVE A FREE MAGAZINE OF EXTRACTS
FROM OUR EXTENSIVE RANGE OF EROTIC FICTION
ABSOLUTELY FREE. YOU WILL ALSO HAVE THE
CHANCE TO PURCHASE BOOKS WHICH ARE
EXCLUSIVE TO OUR READERS' CLUB

***

NEW AUTHORS ARE WELCOME

Please send submissions to;
Barrington Hall Publishing
Hexgreave Hall
Farnsfield N22 8LS

Silver Moon books are an imprint of Barrington Hall Publishing.

All characters and events depicted are entirely fictitious; any resemblance to anyone living or dead is entirely coincidental

FRUIT OF SUBMISSION
(A SEQUEL TO SEED OF SUBMISSION)

By

Robin Ballantyne

CHAPTER 1

'Cynthia?'

Silence. David Arundel sighed, and called his daughter again.

'Cynthia!' And, after another pause: 'The cab's here. Yves is waiting!'

'Coming!' There was the sound of hurried movement from upstairs. David turned to the tall young man at his side and shrugged. Yves shrugged back.

Moments later, Cynthia Arundel flew down the stairs, a full-length cape trailing after her. She was tall and slim, with pale skin and long hair of dark reddish-brown, and not for the first time David noticed how she looked very like her mother had, at that age. He smiled at his memories, and then kissed his daughter on the cheek.

'I hope you have a wonderful evening,' he said. 'Where are you going?'

She laughed. 'I haven't told Yves, and I won't tell you either. It's a surprise!'

Yves looked put out, and Cynthia took his hands. 'Please, darling! You did say I could go anywhere I liked, and you'll find out in a little while anyway.' She squeezed his hands then turned away. As she did so, David saw her expression change. Just for a second, he thought she looked almost calculating, but the look was gone as soon as he had noticed it. Then his daughter spun round, took Yves by one hand and pulled him towards the door.

'Come on,' she told her boyfriend. 'We'll be late!' As David watched, she dragged the bemused-looking Yves out of the house, and few moments later there was the sound of a car pulling away.

David listened as the sound faded. Then he shook his head, and closed the door. There was work to be done. Not unpleasant work, to be sure, but a duty all the same. He turned and walked back along the hall, up the sweeping flight of stairs that led to the upper floor of the handsome apartment, and into the drawing room where his wife was waiting for him.

At thirty eight years old, Julia Arundel was still a striking woman. Her waist, which would anyway have been trim, was pulled into a stern hourglass by the corset he made her wear. Together with the close-fitting red dress she wore over it, it emphasised the feminine curves which had been hers from adolescence, and which had been filled out delightfully by childbearing. Her auburn hair, not yet touched by grey, fell to the small of her back in a thick straight torrent.

Even after eighteen years of marriage, David found her deeply attractive. He allowed his gaze to roam over her for a moment, feeling himself stiffen at the sight of her. To his pleasure, she blushed slightly. Then her eyes fell to the collared girl who kneeled, naked, beside her. David followed her gaze, and smiled.

'Yolanda,' he said to the girl. 'You have not been good!'

She looked at the floor. David reached down and lifted her chin so that her eyes met his. 'In fact, you have been bad, haven't you?'

She nodded.

'You have become lazy and disobedient, haven't you?'

She nodded again, and a tear sprang from the corner of one eye.

'What happens to lazy disobedient girls?'

Her eyes slid away, and she whispered something. David tightened his grip on her chin. 'What did you say?'

He felt her stiffen for a moment. Then she repeated: 'They must be punished, Sir.'

'Exactly! They must be punished.' David let go of her, and she sagged forwards. He turned to his wife. 'Julia,' he said, 'fetch the new martinet.'

Yolanda gave a little gasp of horror, but Julia only nodded, and walked over to a tall cupboard in the corner. She unlocked it, took something out, and carried it over to David. He took it, and held it out.

It was a whip, of twelve thongs bound to a short thick handle. Each thong was about three feet long, made of a single slightly flattened leather strand with a thin hard knot near the end. David ran his hands through it.

'I know you've heard of this,' he told Yolanda. 'It's a sort of a cross between a birch and a cat o' nine tails. Now it's time you felt it. The French believe in it completely, and as we are in France we'll take their advice.' He paused, and then added: 'Of course, this one is rather longer and heavier than the French version.' He looked up at Julia. 'Take her, and put her over the writing desk.

Her face expressionless, Julia took Yolanda by the hands, drew her upright, and led her to an elaborately carved writing desk that stood near one corner of the room. She pushed the girl over it and, without being told, walked round to the other side of the desk and took a wrist in each hand, pulling Yolanda forwards until she was bent fully forwards, her small childish breasts flattened against the leather surface.

David allowed himself a moment to admire the view. Unlike his wife, Yolanda had never borne children, and her hips were still slim. Her duties around the house had kept her behind almost as taut as a boy's, and the firm globes parted as she bent forwards to reveal a small, tight cunt framed with a straggling hint of hair – an animal signal that David enjoyed enough to preserve, although he would never have permitted it in his wife. Despite the girl's apparent fear of punishment – or perhaps because of it – the neat lips glistened with moisture, complementing the smooth, dark shiny skin around the puckered hole above them.

It was an inviting sight, and as always David fought a brief battle with himself. What a pleasure it would be to shaft the girl, immediately. Why not?

The answer was obvious. I'll be shafting something soon enough, he thought. Plenty to enjoy before then.

He ran his hand through the twelve lashes of the martinet, combing out their tangles. When he was satisfied, he drew the whip back. 'Now,' he said, and brought his arm round fast.

The knotted thongs hissed through the air and landed on Yolanda's neatly presented bottom.

She arched her back and gave a high, genuine, cry of pain. There was a note of surprise as well – Yolanda had not enjoyed her first taste of the martinet. David examined her behind. He wasn't surprised. None of the thongs had landed between her cheeks – something he must correct with the next stroke – but her right flank bore a row of purple spots where the knots had bitten. He adjusted his aim, and struck again, the leather making an angry hiss.

Much better! He had aimed a little further back, and this time most of the thongs had landed between those firm little globes, drawing a wail of pain.

Certainly a result. Dark pink weals tipped with purple dots had appeared between the girl's cheeks, covering the full compass from that delightful little quim to the top of the crease and all points in between. He stepped back and aimed again, sending in another two strokes that landed low, and the tips of the lashes wrapped sharply round the inside of the girl's parted thighs. Across the table, Julia's arms tensed as she held the struggling girl in position.

David grinned to himself, and changed sides. Wherever he stood, it was still a wonderful view – the already-tight buttocks tightened further by Yolanda's posture, and then beautifully animated by the twitching and straining of the girl's muscles as she suffered under the lash. Her anus twitched, too – a lewd little wink with every movement of her bottom, that caused David's throbbing cock to strain against his pants until he could almost have groaned aloud. He raised his arm and lashed again.

Yolanda gave another desperate howl of pain as the thongs curled into the depths of her cleft. Even after only five strokes, her lower bottom and the insides of her thighs were scored with angry weals, each one tipped with a livid purple dot where those evil knots had done their work.

The whip curled viciously around the pale flesh, three times in quick succession. Yolanda squealed and cried out: 'Ahh! Oh, God…'

How many strokes should he give the girl? She had taken eight so far, and the effect was certainly impressive. The globes of her bottom were covered with weals, several of them tipped with dark dots where the hissing knots had bitten. David could have flogged her until he had flayed her, but enough was enough and besides, he had other plans. He laid his hand on her bottom, feeling the starting heat of the raised skin under his fingers. Yolanda flinched at his touch, and his cock jerked. His eyes met Julia's, and he saw that they were shining with excitement. Your turn soon, he thought. Then he turned his attention back to Yolanda.

'I think,' he said deliberately, 'that twelve strokes should be enough, for your first dose of the martinet. Do you agree?'

She nodded quickly.

'Good. Another four, then.' He drew back the whip and brought it lashing down.

He had put more force into the stroke, and Yolanda rewarded him with an outraged scream of pain. Even though her behind was already well marked, the fresh weals stood out, almost glowing. He raised his arm and thrashed her again, drawing another agonised scream.

'AAAHHHH! Aahhh! Oh, please…'

David could tell that he had almost broken the girl; once again the tips of the martinet had nipped in to land on her most sensitive flesh, and she was sobbing continuously now. Her muscles had the relaxation of defeat, and he knew his instinct to end the whipping at twelve was correct.

The eleventh stroke sizzled in, laying yet more damage over the flogged flesh, and Yolanda cried out, but not so loudly this time. The girl was quietening; another sign that the flogging had almost done its work. David had always prided himself on his ability to time a punishment properly, and it was time to end this one. He raised the martinet for one last time.

It was a perfect stroke. Half of the lashes had landed on the girl's lower bottom, just above the crease. The other half had wrapped round the searing skin of her inner thigh.

Yolanda howled. Then she collapsed against the table, her body shaking with sobs and her muscles limp. David looked up at Julia and nodded, and she released her hold on Yolanda's arms so that the girl slid to the floor and lay there, curled up and quivering.

David let her lie there for a moment. Then he reached down, took a handful of her hair, and pulled upwards.

'Come one,' he said. 'On your knees, where you belong!'

Slowly she raised herself until she was kneeling by the table. 'That's better,' he said. Then he turned to Julia. 'Now you've had the pleasure of watching the girl's punishment. Is there something we should do for you as well?'

She nodded.

'What is it? Speak up!'

Julia licked her lips. 'I want to be made a good girl too, please,' she said, in a small voice.

David's cock raged, and for a moment he thought he would lose control and take his wife there and then. Instead, he seized her arm, spun her round and shoved her roughly over the table, pinning her down with one hand while her reached down and hauled up her dress with the other. Then he stood back and took a long look at his wife.

She was still magnificent. Her generous bottom was smooth and round. It swept down from that tiny waist to a pair of firm, white thighs, sensually indented by the tops of the hold-up stockings which, apart from the ever-present corset, were the only underwear he usually allowed her. Without needing to be told, she had parted her legs as she bent forward, revealing a grown woman's full moist lips, and above them the puckered rim of her most secret sex, still small and neat despite all the use he had made of it over the eighteen years of their marriage.

And would again, soon enough! But not quite yet; there was another pleasure, almost as great, to savour first. He reached out and ran his hand over the proffered bottom, exploring the ghostly hint of an almost-faded weal.

'When did I last punish you?' he asked.

She answered promptly. 'A week ago.'

'Ah, yes.' He smiled. 'Remind me what you got.'

'Twelve strokes of the cane.'

'Hmmm.' David stroked her bottom again, and her skin twitched slightly. 'Twelve is a good number,' he said. 'Twelve with the martinet, though, I think. Do you agree?'

'Yes, sir,' she said faintly.

'Good! Let's begin, then.' He stood back, ran his hand through the lashes of the martinet once more to separate them, and then brought them whistling sharply down across the centre of the delicious target in front of him.

They landed with a greedy snap.

He had to admire his wife's self-restraint. The twelve hissing thongs had landed across her lower bottom, splaying out to cover fully half of the span from the crease to the top of her cleft, but the only sound she made to give away the pain was a slow indrawing of breath.

He would soon see about that. He changed sides and delivered the next stroke backhand, sweeping the whip across her bottom in a flat arc that ended with a sharp flick of his wrist.

Julia raised her head and gave a long, quiet moan as the lashes bit. David watched the marks blooming across the pale skin. He noted with satisfaction the way several of the knots had nipped into the outside of her thigh, leaving a neat line of blue-black dots. He began to alternate, forehand and backhand, delivering his strokes in pairs.

The strokes fell across the right and left of the out-thrust hemispheres, scoring the tender flesh just above the crease.

For the next two, David lowered his arm, and most of the lashes flew in to plant their wicked kisses on the tops of Julia's thighs. Now he was getting through to her; she stamped her feet, one after another, with the searing pain, and every breath was let out with a quavering 'Aaaahhhhhh!'

Time for another change of aim. Standing slightly further back, David whipped the eager knots straight into Julia's cleft, and now she raised her head and squealed. It wasn't surprising – every inch of her skin, including those inviting lips, was scored with the effects of the martinet. But despite his wife's obvious pain David noticed that she was moist, and more than moist – a trickle of wetness was running down the inside of her thigh. David felt himself tightening unbearably at the sight. His heart thumped, and he almost feared his arousal would overwhelm him. For a few moments he teetered on the brink, but then he managed to draw back. There were still four lashes to go, and he meant to make the most of every one of them. He raised the whip and sent in another pair of strokes.

This time he had moved his attention upwards. The leather landed on the top half of Julia's rump, scoring pale skin that had so far escaped. The unexpected pain made her draw a whistling breath and then yelp with outrage. David nodded to himself, and then repositioned himself for the last two strokes. He raised his arm high and brought the whip down diagonally so that it landed across each cheek in turn, spending its force from right and left in the dark, glistening gash at the base of her bottom.

His aim had been perfect. Julia wailed with pain and then lay supine, sobbing quietly.

It was time; David could restrain himself no longer. He ripped open his trousers, and his cock flipped out and stood high, hard and ready.

'Now,' he said thickly, 'for the rest of your discipline.'

Even as well thrashed as she was, Julia clearly got the message. She managed to shuffle her feet even further apart, and pushed out her richly scored bottom towards him.

He entered it, ignoring the obvious moistness of her quim for the tight little bud which he felt to be more his private property that any other part of her. He felt the ring of her muscles open for him, and then he was in, pushing himself to his full length as she relaxed her expert behind to admit him. Within seconds he was at full stretch, thrilling as he always did to her heat and the way her body embraced him so closely, and to the deep animal grunt of pleasure that she could never conceal when he took her this way.

He held himself at full length for a long moment, then began to move. As he withdrew, her muscles gripped and caressed him, only to relax as he thrust back in to her. It was one of her exceptional talents, learned during her training at The Grange all those years ago, and David gave thanks for it every time he buggered her. As he moved faster she matched him, following his rhythm, so that far from being in a human back passage, he felt as if he was in the most subtle, complex machine, designed to give the greatest possible pleasure (and part of him whispered that it was the same thing, that what else was a woman's arse if not a machine for a man's pleasure?). The scent of her rose to his nostrils, a complex blend of sweat and quim and musk, and his pleasure mounted with his effort until he was slamming himself home in a frenzy of lust, his balls slapping against the lips of her sex in an echo of the force his cock was inflicting on her anus.

His pleasure climbed to an unbearable peak and then exploded, and he grunted and growled with pleasure as he pumped his seed deep into her belly, and even through the mist of his orgasm he noticed how her contractions matched his own. It's like telepathy, he thought, and then for a little while he thought nothing at all.

When he came to his senses he was lying along Julia's back, his skin joined to hers by a film of sweat. With trembling muscles he eased himself upright – God, he ached! – and withdrew his softening manhood from Julia's behind. It made an obscene bubbling noise, and he looked down to see a trickle of his juice running down her cleft. He turned to Yolanda. 'Clean her,' he said, and the kneeling girl shuffled forwards and began to lap at Julia's bottom. Julia moaned a little, and pushed her hips back to meet Yolanda's tongue.

There really was a strong resemblance between Julia and her daughter, David thought. He wondered what Cynthia was doing, and if she was having fun.

CHAPTER 2

It had been a half-hour taxi ride from the Arundel's apartment to the discreet frontage of L'Histoire d'O, which lay in a quiet street off the Rue de Rivoli. Now, standing on the pavement outside, Yves was looking doubtful.

'What is this place?' he asked.

Cynthia couldn't help giggling at his stiff concern. 'It's just a night club,' she said. 'Just a bit of fun, that's all. What's the matter?'

He still looked doubtful. 'It's more than just a night club really, isn't it? I mean, The Story of O? Come on, Cynthia!'

'Why, have you read The Story of O, then?' Cynthia knew she was making him uncomfortable, but she couldn't stop herself.

Even in the dark she could tell he was blushing. 'Read it? For God's sake! Of course I haven't read it.' He paused, and then said in a calmer voice: 'I've heard about it. It's an obscene book.'

Cynthia burst out laughing. 'Obscene? Of course it isn't. It's about sex.'

'Exactly! And, and…' he tailed off, and she couldn't resist completing the sentence for him. 'And whipping, and hand-cuffs, and people being naughty?'

He nodded, and she realised he was already far outside his comfort zone. Well, she thought, if that's a problem, it's not going to be my problem. At least, not for long. Out loud she said: 'Look, I know you're uncomfortable. Maybe you're right. But let's give it a try, shall we? Please, darling? After all, it is my birthday. And the beginning of my gap year.'

She put her arms around him and kissed him gently on the lips. Briefly, he stiffened, but then she felt him relax, and he returned the kiss, as gently as she had given it.

'Okay,' he said. 'As it's your birthday.'

'Oh thank you!' She hugged him hard, then turned and hauled him towards the door. 'Come on then! Let's see what this place is like!'

What it was like, was huge. There was an entrance lobby which led on to a very plush bar in a fifties retro style, with what looked like a darkened dance floor beyond. Soft, complex music thumped.

Cynthia handed her cape to an attendant and turned to Yves. 'What do you think?' she asked. She saw his eyes widen.

She had taken a long time over her clothes. In the end she had settled on a black basque, pulled in at the waist by some complicated laces that had taken a while to get right. Below it she wore black silk French knickers, rather tight, with hold-up stockings peeping out of a long pair of boots, also black and shiny.

She felt very sexy. To her secret delight, Yves looked shocked. She ignored his expression, waiting while he shrugged out of his overcoat. When he had finished, she took hold of his unresisting hand and drew him towards the dance floor. Where she stopped, her mouth open and her heart banging.

Although there were a few people dancing, it really wasn't a dance floor. As her eyes adapted to the dim light, she realised that the polished parquet was dotted with pieces of equipment. There were A-shaped frames, and things like step-ladders, and stools, and one very complicated thing that looked a bit like a padded operating table, if you could get operating tables made from mahogany and iron and black leather.

A few of the things were occupied. As she watched, a tall man in evening dress led a naked woman over to one of the stools. He pushed her forwards so that she bent over it, and then reached down to fasten her wrists and ankles into slim cuffs that were fixed to the base. The posture parted her legs and pushed her bottom back, so that she seemed to be offering her sex to the watchers, and Cynthia resisted the urge to let her fingers wander down to her own crotch in sympathy. Then the man turned and took something long and thin from a stand nearby, and Cynthia's mouth went dry.

It was a cane. An old-fashioned school cane with a crook handle.

Ohmigod, he's going to cane her! She barely had time to finish the thought before the man stood back, tapped the cane a couple of times against the woman's bottom as if taking aim, and then drew it back and lashed it down.

The cane whistled through the air and landed with a crack.

'Aaaaaaahhhhhh!' The bent woman threw her head back and gave a wail of agony, and her body writhed over the stool, making the muscles in her bottom dance against each other. Like most girls of her era Cynthia had never been caned but she had read of it many, many times, mostly with a hand between her legs, and all the stories agreed that the pain of a cane stroke built up to a peak over several seconds. It certainly looked like it, if the squirming victim was anything to judge by.

Then the woman brought herself under control, and spoke. 'Est-ce que je peux avoir le prochain, s'il vous plait, cherie?'

The voice was low and breathy, but clear. The rather formal French words rearranged themselves in Cynthia's head. 'Please, darling, may I have the next?' Oh God, that's sexy, she thought. She watched eagerly as the man whipped the cane down, and the woman screamed and began her writhing dance of pain. The weal from the first stroke had darkened to a livid purple, and the second began to appear just below it, a little above the crease at the base of the woman's rounded twitching bottom.

Cynthia found herself gripping Yves' hand tightly as the superb spectacle continued. Each stroke drew an agonised wail from the pinioned woman, growing louder as the weals that blossomed across her skin began to overlap, and each time she wriggled and squirmed until she was able to speak. Then, the husky request for more, and another whistling lash would begin the process again until the cane had scored her dancing bottom a dozen times. With every stroke, the shuddering of her behind exposed the lips of her sex which, even in the soft light, looked swollen to Cynthia.

After the twelfth stroke, the whipped woman lay quietly over the stool, while her tormentor stood to one side, tapping the cane against his foot. Eventually she raised her head and said: 'Merci, cheri,' and Cynthia thought there was a note almost of joy in her voice. Perhaps her man thought so too. In any case, he seemed pleased with his work. He took the woman by the shoulders and raised her from her stool. Then he put his arms around her and kissed her, hard, in a way that Cynthia found almost as exciting as the caning that had led up to it. She turned to Yves.

'Oh darling, wasn't that beautiful?'

He looked at her, his face disbelieving. 'It was barbaric,' he said. 'Surely you can't want that?'

'Why not?' She was stung. 'Lots of people do! Why shouldn't I?' He looked away, and she reached out and caressed his shoulder. 'Come on,' she said, more gently. 'At least let me try it. You French have such beautiful words for it. How do you say it? Veuillez me fouetter? Please whip me?' She spoke the last words in a breathy whisper, her eyes on his.

For a moment his face remained frozen. Then the corners of his mouth turned up a little. 'Oh, alright,' he said. 'If that's what it takes to get you through this.' He paused, and added: 'What shall I use, and where do you want to be?'

Cynthia ignored the part of her that was screaming, tell me what to do! He was doing his best. She walked over to the stand from which the man had taken the cane and ran her hand along the rows until she reached a soft, many-tailed whip.

'This,' she said, holding it out to him. 'Please whip me with this.' She allowed herself a slight emphasis on the word whip, and felt her belly tense with excitement.

He took the whip and ran it through his hands. 'And where?'

She nodded towards the stool. 'There,' she said. 'Just as she was.'

He nodded, and she walked over to the stool. She wriggled her knickers down and stepped out of them. Suddenly very aware of her public nakedness, she bent herself over the padded top. It preserved a trace of warmth from the body that had just left it. As she bent herself over, she felt her thighs being drawn apart by the cunning design of the thing.

When she was settled, she turned her head back to Yves. 'Please, darling,' she said, 'bind me.'

At first he hesitated, and she wondered if he was going to back out. Then he seemed to make a decision. He stepped forward and fastened the soft leather straps, first around her thighs just above the knee, then over her waist, and finally around her wrists.

Cynthia tensed her muscles and pulled against her bonds. They were firm, but not quite unyielding, so that she could wriggle without the slightest chance of escape.

Perfect, she thought. Out loud she said: 'Now, darling. What are you going to do to your girl?'

He said nothing, and again she wondered if he was going to desert her. Then she heard the faint sigh of leather moving through the air, and the leather thongs landed across her eager behind in a gentle explosion of pleasure tempered with a little tingling pain.

Wow, she thought. And then, I want more!

She was tempted to say it out loud, to plead for Yves to treat her as she had seen the other woman being treated, but she was certain that if she did, Yves would lose the rest of his fragile confidence. So she held her tongue, except for allowing herself a grateful moan every time the caressing lashes swept across her haunches.

Ten strokes, and then twenty, and her skin was warming to the kiss of the leather. The trouble was, warming was not enough! It was like having an itch that you could only scratch with your gloves on. She wanted more, and it was time to say so. She drew a breath.

'Excuse me, Monsieur?'

She let the breath go. Who was this? She turned her head.

Someone was standing next to Yves. A tall someone, taller than Yves, and wearing evening dress. A handsome someone.

The someone spoke. 'Monsieur, I congratulate you both on the subtlety of your technique, and the beauty of your target.'

Yves looked nonplussed. 'Thank you,' he said. And then, rather formally: 'Who are you?'

The tall man smiled, and the smile sent a wave of wetness through Cynthia's loins. 'I am José Mestré', he said. 'And, before you ask, I'm here because I particularly enjoy whipping beautiful women, and I see a beautiful woman who is being whipped. I would love to take your place for a while. Have I your permission? Or, indeed, her permission, if it is needed?'

If it is needed? Arrogant swine, thought the public part of Cynthia's brain. Another more private part wriggled with pleasure at the thought that perhaps some men didn't have to ask.

She was sure Yves was going to refuse. Would he be angry? She held her breath, and then let it all out in a whoosh of astonishment when she heard Yves saying: 'Why not?' He paused, and then added: 'Maybe if you show her what it's really like you'll do me a favour by curing her of the whole stupid idea.'

'Who knows?' José sounded amused. Cynthia heard a faint rustle, and guessed he was running the tails of the whip through his hand. Then he spoke again, addressing her directly for the first time, and some of the amusement was gone. 'Your boyfriend hasn't asked your permission, so usually neither would I, but it would feel rude to flog you before we have even exchanged a word. So, if you will, you may now ask politely for your whipping in whatever way pleases you best.'

Cynthia's heart raced. It was going to happen! This complete stranger was going to whip her! She ran through a handful of phrases in her head (phrases she had whispered to herself how many times when there was no one to hear?) and finally settled on the simplest. 'Please whip me,' she said. And then, daring herself, she added: 'Sir.'

'Very good.' José sounded pleased. 'So, let's see how you respond to my caress.' Then, almost as soon as he had finished the words, she heard the hiss of the leather, much louder than before, and the lashes landed.

Cynthia squealed.

José watched the girl's reactions. The lashes had spread wide as they travelled, marking the taut orbs of her behind from top to bottom with fine red lines that stood out against skin which the half-hearted efforts of her boyfriend had only made slightly pink. The girl was obviously unused to the whip; he had not struck particularly hard but she had still made plenty of noise, and her bottom was wriggling delightfully.

He struck again, drawing another yelp, and watched the fresh weals blooming. Her buttocks clenched and relaxed as she rode the pain, opening to give brief, beautiful glimpses of the flesh that lay between them. God, but she was a prize, and god, he longed to claim her. His manhood swelled and ached at the thought, but he controlled himself. This was a catch to be played gently.

'What's your name, girl?' he asked.

'Cynthia, Sir,' she said, and his cock swelled even more at the sound of that sir.

'Cynthia,' he repeated. 'Well, Cynthia, I intend to whip you until you cry. When I have finished, you will thank me. Yes?'

She gulped, but then nodded, and closed her eyes.

The lashes whistled down. He had lengthened his arm, landing the first real stroke, and the girl gave a husky cry of pain as the thongs bit into her lower bottom.

'Aaaahhh!'

Again the dance of agony animated her delicious behind. He waited until she had stopped wriggling. He was determined to prolong his pleasure as much as he could; what was the point of whipping the girl to tears in a few minutes? Besides, the sight of her pretty little chat flashing in and out of view was worth savouring properly.

Finally she was still, and he changed sides and let the whip sing through the air.

'Aaaaahhhh!'

And the pattern was set; the whistle of the leather, the sharp crack as the hungry lashes bit into the ever more brightly scored skin, the cry of distress, and the sensual writhing and clenching of what, he was sure, was the best young bottom he had ever seen.

He was not sure how long he had been whipping her when he realised two things. First, that the boyfriend had gone, and second, that his victim was sobbing softly, and her eyes were wet with tears.

He dropped the whip and laid a hand on the girl's wet cheek. 'There,' he said. 'You are crying, and so it is over. What do you say?'

She moved her head a little so that her cheek pressed his hand for a second. 'Thank you, Sir,' she said. Then she looked up. 'Where is Yves?'

José clicked his tongue. 'Is that his name? Well, he has gone.' He paused, and added: 'Do you count that as much of a loss?'

She shook her head.

'Good,' he said. 'Now, you took that well. Do you think you have earned a reward?'

She nodded, looking a little watchful.

'Well, then...' He let his hand trail gently down her back, running his fingers across skin that was damp with sweat and noticing how she arched up a little. He drew his hand down her spine to her behind, cupping and squeezing each hot thrashed globe in turn so that she wriggled and hissed. Then he laid the tip of his finger against the wet lips of her sex, and paused, pulling away slightly as she tried desperately to thrust herself onto it.

'Eager for your reward?' he asked.

She nodded quickly, still pushing herself back against her bonds so hard that the straps bit into her flesh. He grinned to himself, and let the tip of his finger describe a couple of gently circuits of her labia.

'Well, then,' he said. 'I think… yes, I think it's time you went home.' And he withdrew his finger.

The combination of shock and anger on her face was almost comical. She opened her mouth but he held up his hand. 'Ah, ah, little Cynthia! Let me explain. I don't do things by halves. I would love to reward you in all sorts of ways, and to do many other things to you too, believe me, but I can't do it here. So I'll do you a deal. Interested?'

She looked cautious. 'I might be,' she admitted.

'Well, Miss Might Be, when we have got you dressed, my driver will take you home, and you can take my card with you. If you decide to claim the rest of your reward, and everything else that goes with it, come and find me. Agreed?'

She stared into the distance for a moment. Then she said: 'I don't need a lift home. I'll get a taxi. But I'll take your card.'

'Fair enough!' José reached down and undid the restraining straps and the girl stood up, picked up her cape and swirled it around her, and held out her hand. He took a card from his pocket and dropped it onto her palm, and without looking at it she closed her hand, turned, and strode off.

José watched her for a moment. Then he shrugged to himself, and strolled out of the club.

His car was waiting for him. As he sat down, the older man at the wheel turned towards him. 'A success?' he asked simply.

José pursed his lips. 'I believe so,' he said. Then he turned to look out of the window, as the car surged forwards.

CHAPTER 3

It was full daylight, with the sun well on the way towards noon, when something woke Cynthia. She wasn't sure what it was – some brief, passing sound down near the limit of her hearing. She would listen out for it.

She stretched. Her skin moved against the sheets, and she realised that she had a sore bottom. She reached a hand down to explore, and memories of the previous night rushed back.

Yves had whipped her, rather unwillingly. Then, José had taken over – a man she had never met before, and it had hurt, but it had been good. She turned over and ran her fingers over the slightly ridged surface of her behind and replayed a few of the swifter strokes in her mind. Mmm, yes. Definitely.

Her fingers strayed into the soft warmth between her legs, and at that moment she heard the sound again. Like a distant click and then a voice. It seemed familiar, now. Where had she heard it?

Her fingers began to dance faster over the moist velvet flesh. She imagined they were José's, and then that he was whipping her, and then that he was using a cane, as she had seen done so beautifully when they had first entered the club. Then the sound came again, and memory crossed over with reality and she rolled over and sat upright, her pulse racing.

It was the sound of a cane, heard at a great distance. Somewhere at the other end of the apartment, someone was being caned. The idea was utterly erotic, and Cynthia slipped her hand between her legs again. As her pleasure began to mount, she wondered dreamily who it was. Yolanda, she supposed. Surely it couldn't be anyone else?

But although she couldn't know it, Cynthia was wrong.

In his private office at the other end of the apartment, David stood back and admired the four livid purple tramlines he had planted across his wife's writhing hind quarters. Exactly parallel, and so close as to be almost touching each other, they began halfway down her taut bottom and ended just above the crease at the top of her thighs.

She was a perfect picture. Her skirt, lifted up over the severe blouse he liked her to wear, revealed her tightly corseted waist. She wore no underwear, again at David's instruction, so that she should always be immediately available for either pleasure or punishment. Hold-up stockings stopped a hand's breadth below her bottom, their elastic biting a little into her thighs in a way David always found extraordinarily erotic.

He brought himself back to the job. Should the next stroke land above, or below, the first four? He allowed himself a moment of thought. Then he flexed his arm and whipped the cane down so that it landed exactly on the crease, drawing a hoarse wail from Julia.

David felt a surge of pride. Partly in himself, in that even after years of marriage he could still wring such sighs of genuine anguish from his wife. And partly in her; he had set out to whip her severely, and despite his skill and the agony she must be suffering she was still keeping to her position, bent over his desk with her legs spread far apart. Yolanda, watched, naked and wide eyed but ready to hold her mistress if necessary, but apart from her moans, the only signs Julia gave of the torment he was inflicting on her were her knuckles, whitened by her desperate grip on the far edge of the desk, and the involuntary twitches and wriggles of her lashed hams.

He changed his aim a little, and the rod blurred through the air and landed across the top of her left thigh.

Julia rewarded him with a piercing shriek, and drummed her heels desperately on the floor. By the look of it, the tip of the cane had nipped in to taste the sensitive meat between her thighs – meat which had already been looking dark and engorged as her body responded in the ancient way of all submissive women. Above the reddened quim, the tight pucker of her anus quivered, causing David's cock to swell painfully. What a sight, he thought. But I used that last night. It's your cunt for me, this time. That's where I'll enjoy you, when I've finished thrashing you.

It wasn't time yet. He changed sides, shifted the long, thin cane into his other hand, and brought it hissing down on to the top of her right thigh, in a stroke that was the mirror image of the last one.

Julia hooted with the pain of another direct hit on her snatch, and David adjusted his raging cock inside his trousers. He couldn't wait much longer; it was time to complete the thrashing.

'Five strokes to go,' he told the sobbing Julia. 'And don't think I'll hold back. You won't be sitting down for a day or two.'

She gave a little whimper and tightened her hold on his desk. He raised the cane and brought it lashing down across the centre of her bottom, three times in quick succession. The last two strokes had landed across skin that had already felt the cane before, adding the fresh pain of the new weal to the reawakened sting of the old, and Julia's head rolled from side to side at the scalding pain.

Time for the grand finale. David swished the cane through the air a few times, noting with pleasure the way Julia flinched at the sound. Then he brought the cane down hard, in two swift stokes, one on the forehand and another on the backhand, so that the rod angled down from the top of each cheek, crossing all the previous strokes and ending with two final, wicked bites at the suffering woman's open flaming sex.

The breath whistled out of Julia as if she had been winded, and she lay limply over the desk, gasping and sobbing. Then, after a few moments, she raised her head from the polished timber and gave a long, low moan, and as she did so a trickle of fluid made its way down her thigh and collected in a little puddle at her feet.

Thrashed beyond endurance, Julia had wet herself.

David handed the cane to Yolanda, who took it as if it was red hot and scuttled away to replace it in its cupboard. While she did so he looked reflectively at his wife's extravagantly marked cheeks. How many times had he written his mastery of her across that skin? And every time it had the same effect, of reinforcing yet further her deep, unquestioning submission and her helpless desire for more.

More she would have. He unzipped his trousers and allowed his aching shaft to stand free.

'Yolanda,' he said, 'to me, and kneel.' The girl obeyed, trotting up to him and dropping to her knees in front of him. Seeing her glance flick to the swollen manhood that swayed before her face, he nodded. 'Moisten me,' he said.

She leaned forwards and opened her mouth to admit him. Since he had commanded moisture rather than pleasure she did not linger, but encompassed the full length of him as quickly as was comfortable. He shivered a little at the delicate brush of her lips, but stood firm as she gathered saliva in her mouth to warm and wet him. Then he tapped her on the head and she pulled away, leaving his cock wet and glistening.

'Very good,' he said. 'Now, the Mistress is wet where she should not be wet. Clean her.'

She shuffled round on her knees, and bent down so that her face was close to the floor, reaching out her tongue towards the puddle between Julia's legs. Before she had a chance to begin, David caught hold of her hair and drew her back.

'No,' he said sharply. 'We will deal with that later. Your job is to clean the Mistress.'

She nodded, and began to lick at the trickle of urine that had wandered down Julia's ankle. David watched as she worked her way up her mistress's leg, lapping like a cat and occasionally drawing back as if to check that all was well. Eventually she reached the cleft, and Julia sighed as the busy tongue worked into her abused lips, but David was prepared. Once again he took hold of Yolanda's hair and pulled her back.

'Not there,' he said. 'I'll deal with that – it doesn't need making any wetter than it already is. But you can lick her hole when I've finished, as you've been so helpful.' She shuffled back, and he laid a hand on the small of Julia's back. 'Now,' he said, 'for the reckoning.' He rested the tip of his rigid tool against Julia's punished lips, and then thrust forwards as hard as he could.

Her flesh resisted him for a fraction of a second, and then expanded quickly so that he almost fell forwards with the speed of his entry. Julia gave a grunt of pain but stood her ground as he invaded her, his shaft forcing her further and further open until he was at full length, the hot walls of her flesh holding him in a tight embrace. He rested there for a moment, then began to ram into her impatiently, making her gasp with pain. Despite this, her long training and her astonishing skill with her muscles did not desert her; he could feel her relaxing as he thrust forwards and then tightening as he withdrew, just as she did when he used her arsehole. My God, he thought, Someone ought to write a paper about you! And then he stopped thinking altogether, so that for a long time there was just his cock rocking in and out of a world of pleasure. At last, with a shout of triumph, he forced himself to his full length so that his groin was jammed against her, and came, pumping bolt after bolt of his seed deep into her belly.

He wasn't sure how long his orgasm lasted - he never was – but it seemed a long time. When he had savoured the very last twinge of pleasure he withdrew himself brusquely, and gestured to the still-kneeling Yolanda.

'Clean me, and then clean her,' he told her, and she obeyed, shuffling forwards on her knees until she could take his juice- and sperm- streaked organ in her mouth. It was a task he demanded often, and although he gave her no choice in the matter, it was something she did at least without any sign of disgust, and in fact with every sign of pleasure, no matter which hole he had used. He closed his eyes and let himself relax as the warmth of her tongue relaxed his hypersensitive shaft, reflecting that Julia might excel with her anus and her vagina, but Yolanda's oral skill had no equal.

When he felt clean he pulled himself from the girl's mouth, and turned her head with his hand so that she was facing her Mistress.

'Go on,' he said. 'Clean her, and then lick her as you like best.'

Yolanda obviously needed no encouragement. She shuffled up to Julia's out-thrust bottom and plunged her face between the parted thighs, and from her quick breaths and the sound of slurping David judged that she was applying herself to her Mistress's sperm-filled crack with hunger and enthusiasm. She lapped at the moist sex and the surrounding skin with quick cat-like strokes, cleaning every square inch of skin, while Julia moaned appreciatively and gasped when the girl's tongue touched one of the sore spots where the cane had landed.

David watched the performance. Even after his recent orgasm, the sight of the kneeling girl with her tongue flicking and lapping at his wife's haunches was enough to stiffen him again, and for a moment he toyed with the idea of a second course. Then reality asserted itself; he had things to do, and Julia was showing signs of getting carried away, and besides, there was always the evening to look forward to. He grinned to himself. 'Yolanda,' he said. The girl froze. 'I think that is enough of that particular pleasure. You may lick your favourite hole, now.'

The kneeling slave let out a quiet sigh. Then she straightened slightly and angled her mouth up towards her Mistress's anus, and Julia moaned again and pushed herself back on to the probing tongue. David watched almost admiringly. He knew from frequent experience just how good Yolanda's tongue could feel on that part of the body, and Julia's body language was bearing it out again. Her vividly marked cheeks embraced Yolanda's face as she squirmed with pleasure, and David's flesh stood harder than ever at the sight. And Yolanda obviously felt the same way – her kneeling position exposed her own sex, which was looking distinctly swollen, and which glinted with moisture.

David let the two women have their pleasure for a few minutes. Then he took hold of Yolanda's hair for the last time. 'Enough,' he said, pulling her firmly back from her Mistress's chasm. 'Both of you – get dressed, and then serve breakfast. I have things to do and besides,' and he looked at his watch, 'it's time Cynthia woke up.'

There was a thought. Cynthia had gone out with Yves, but according to the taxi driver she had come home alone. Now what could that mean?

Cynthia was still dreamily fingering herself when she heard the breakfast gong. The sound snapped her out of her reverie. She threw back the covers, hopped out of bed, and grabbed a pair of jeans and a tee shirt – good enough for breakfast, and she could always change afterwards. She would have to, she realised, as the rough denim nestled into the wet hypersensitive flesh between her thighs. She couldn't spend all day like this, she'd end up sticking to the furniture.

She snatched a comb from her bedside table, ran it hurriedly through her hair and then slammed it down again. And then stopped, and picked up the card that was lying next to it.

It was the card José had given her the night before. She read it. Not much to go on; just the name, José Mestré, and an address near Perpignan. Way down south, in Catalonia, where France got mixed up with Spain. She looked at the card a little longer, and then shoved it into her pocket and strode out of her room.

When she arrived in the breakfast room, her mother and father were already eating. David looked up and smiled.

'Good morning,' he said. 'Did you have a good time last night?'

Cynthia nodded noncommittally, and sat down, intensely aware of the tenderness between her legs and a faint itching from her rump. She poured herself some coffee, and then, on an impulse, looked up at her father.

'Daddy,' she said, 'I thought I heard some funny noises this morning. Do you know what they were?'

She watched him intently, but his face gave nothing away. 'Nothing in particular,' he said. 'Just a domestic matter.' His tone was final, and Cynthia shrugged to herself. That was that, then. She glanced at her mother, and then looked again.

Julia was sitting upright. Her face was composed, but somehow she looked uncomfortable, and as Cynthia watched she shifted slightly in her chair.

My God, thought Cynthia. It wasn't Yolanda; it was you!

The realisation hit her like a slap. Her mother and father had some sort of master-and-slave relationship. Now that she thought of it, it made perfect sense! Her mother was always so polite and composed, and her father always so confidently in charge. No wonder they never exchanged a cross word; if there was any problem her mother probably paid for it in the old-fashioned way. Cynthia looked at her mother with fresh eyes. She wondered what it would look like, to see her father deal out a beating.

He was saying something. She dragged herself back to the present. 'Sorry, Daddy. What did you say? I was miles away.'

He smiled. 'The result of a late night, I expect. I was asking if you had thought what you are going to do with your gap year?'

Cynthia didn't have to think. She let one hand trail over the pocket of her jeans, where she could just feel the outline of José's card. 'Oh, that's easy,' she said. 'I'm going to go travelling.'

Her father nodded, and said nothing more. Cynthia smiled to herself. Two thoughts had struck her. First, that perhaps she had something in common with her mother, and second, she was pretty sure that Mestré was the Catalan version of Maitre. Or, in English, Master. Well, well.

CHAPTER 4

Nine hundred kilometres to the south, José Mestré stood in the courtyard of the Mas Gassac estate and looked down at the naked girl who knelt in front of him. He owned the estate, and for practical purposes he also owned both the kneeling girl and most of the onlookers who had gathered at his orders.

'Slave,' he said, and she raised her head. He was pleased to see her lip trembling a little, even though she was obviously doing her best to hide it. Fear was an excellent adjunct to punishment.

'Slave,' he repeated. 'You have been reported by Monsieur Pera, for disobedience and insubordination. He tells me that you have already been punished by your overseer for the same faults. Is that not so, Pera?' José turned and looked enquiringly at the old man who stood at his side. Pera nodded, and José turned back to the girl. 'Well, then, as your overseer has failed to drive out your faults we must do her job for her.' He clapped his hands. 'Horse her!'

Pera walked over to the girl and took her by the hair, pulling her firmly so that she winced and crawled quickly after him. He led her to a simple wooden stool, waist-high and elongated like a sawing horse. Then he hauled sharply upwards. The girl yowled and rose to her feet, but before she had time to find her balance Pera pushed her forwards so that she sprawled over the horse, holding her there with a heavy hand on the small of her back. One of the yard hands stepped forward and bound the girls wrists and ankles to the legs of the horse so that she was folded in two with her legs stretched far apart and her bottom raised and vulnerable. Pera checked the bindings, nodded, and stood back.

'She's ready,' he said.

'Good.' José strolled over to the horse and examined the girl. She was quite a recent arrival, a just-nineteen year old country girl, and her short strong thighs and muscular behind suggested that she came from good peasant stock. Southern, too, because her skin was naturally the colour of an almond, darkening erotically to chestnut brown in the exposed cleft between her cheeks.

The sight of the bound, spread girl was primitively sexual, and José found his body responding. He smiled to himself, then clapped his hands again.

'The whip,' he said simply. Pera handed it to him, and he shook out the eight long knotted tails. It was a chicote, one of the harshest forms of punishment on the estate, and he heard gasps from a few of the watchers. Good; let them share the fear, and the lesson! Out loud he said: 'The girl will be flogged with the chicote until I am sure she has learned. All of you, learn too – the same could happen to any of you.'

He drew back the whip, and for a few heartbeats there was complete silence in the courtyard. Then, using all his strength, he struck.

The knotted tails bit home.

The girl raised her head and howled. The thongs of the whip had spread a little as they flew, landing in a narrow fan shape that began at the top of her thighs and ended half-way up the swell of her bottom, which was already marked by vivid red wheals that darkened almost as José watched.

He listened to the girl's wailing for a moment, then changed hands and sent the lashes whistling in from the other side, drawing another animal howl of pain from the already-sobbing slave as the heavy knotted leather branded her dancing buttocks. She looked superb; her skin was already alive with a sheen of sweat that extended to the animal cleft between those suffering globes, and the enticing bud of her anus winked with the involuntary spasms of her muscles.

Another lash, this time with the hard knots whipping in between the girl's shaking cheeks. She squealed, and José saw her arms stretch as she tried uselessly to pull her wrists free. He grinned, and changed hands again.

Once again the lashes found their target, snapping home into the sensitive skin of the girl's cleft. The whipped slave let out a squeal that was so high-pitched as to be almost soundless, and slumped forwards on to the horse, sobbing steadily.

José looked over to Pera, who nodded slightly. They both knew the signs. The first stage was over; the girl's resistance had been broken, and now she would accept the rest of her punishment. José drew back his arm.

The whip struck again and again, scoring the conquered girl's haunches with lash after lash. The many weals on her punished flesh darkened from scarlet to purple, and spread up to the top of her mounds, and down onto her glistening thighs, and she sobbed and moaned, and her tears fell onto the dusty yard and left a scatter of dark spots that faded slowly under the hot sun.

Eventually José stopped. The girl lay supine, weeping quietly. The watching slaves and servants stood in respectful silence. They would remember the girl's punishment for a good while, thought José, although she herself would feel it for a lot longer.

He signalled to Pera. The older man looked a little surprised, but then untied the girl's wrists and ankles and drew her upright. 'Come on,' he said to her, roughly but not unkindly. 'Indoor work for you, today. Back to the fields tomorrow!'

He handed her over to another servant, who led her away into the house. Then he turned to José and raised his eyebrows as if to say, what now?

José winked. Then he turned to the watching crowd and raised his voice. 'We are not done yet,' he said. He heard indrawn breaths, and there were some fearful looks.

He ignored them. 'Where is the girl's overseer?'

There was a pause, and then a tall black-skinned woman stepped forwards slowly. He waited until she was standing in front of him. Then he said: 'You should have taught that girl a lesson long before now. If she needed punishing it should have been you who did it!' He paused, and then added: 'I have done your job for you. Do you expect me to be pleased?'

She shook her head.

'Exactly. I am not pleased. You will be punished as she was.' The woman gasped but he ignored her and signalled to Pera, who stepped forward quickly and caught her by the arms. He reached for the buttons on her short dress, but José shook his head. 'There's no need to be gentle,' he said. 'Strip her. She won't need her clothes again.'

Pera grinned, and then with a single quick movement, tore the woman's dress off her and threw it to one side. And then stood back in amazement. He heard the crowd whispering behind him, and no wonder.

The superb body seemed to make everything else in the courtyard fade. José moved closer and let his eyes wander over the smooth, glistening black skin. She was like a Greek statue, crossed with the action figure from a comic book – tall and perfectly proportioned, from the small feet and slim calves to the proud neck and the head held defiantly high. He walked round behind her to admire a pair of breath-taking buttocks, full and muscular, with a firm slim waist above them and strong thighs below.

José whistled, and turned to Pera. 'My God, old man,' he said, 'you've kept this one quiet! Where did she come from?'

The old man grinned. 'Traded in six months ago, and went straight out to the fields,' he said. 'I guess I was keeping her as a surprise.'

José took the woman by her chin and turned her head, admiring the high cheeks and strong chin, and noticing her faint female scent.

'Well, she's certainly that,' he admitted. 'I wonder what else she is.' Without letting go of the woman's chin, he quickly whipped his open hand down onto the side of her thigh, as hard as he could.

The smack rang sharply round the courtyard.

The black woman blinked, and held his gaze.

José stood back. 'Oh, we have a proud one here,' he said. Then he spoke directly to the woman. 'What's your name?'

'Princess,' she said.

'Princess, eh?' José picked up the whip. 'Well, I think it's time you were humbled, Your Majesty!' He signalled Pera, who grabbed her and shoved her over the horse. José watched while she was tied in position. As her legs were forced apart, the female flesh between them was revealed, slightly pinker than the rest of her body. The contrast was extraordinarily erotic, and José felt his manhood straining upwards.

He stepped back, and brought the whip hissing down.

The leather thongs snapped into the taut flesh with a sound like a firecracker. José watched to see how the overseer reacted. He was intrigued to see that she didn't react at all. The weals blossomed purple on mahogany skin that stayed quite motionless. She hadn't even blinked. José shook the lashes out carefully, and brought them sighing down again, in almost the same place. More purple weals bloomed, but still the prostrate woman showed no sign of pain.

A challenge was a challenge. José lengthened his arm and began to flog the black buttocks ferociously. He struck from the right and the left; he changed the length of his arm so that the knotted thongs curled round the impassive girl's flanks, and down her thighs, and on the tender girl-meat between her cheeks, and the purple weals darkened to black, and dots of blood appeared where the hungry knots had bitten, and still the wretched girl remained unresponsive, her eyes fixed on the ground in front of her.

After a while, José stopped. The sun was getting hotter, and he wiped the sweat out of his eyes. Then he looked down at the flogged slave.

She was still showing no sign that anything was happening.

He needed a breakthrough. He thought for a moment, and then changed his aim, standing a little closer to the vividly scored globes of his slave and extending his arm.

Swwwwwackkkk!

His aim had been good. The hissing lashes swept down across the woman's curved haunches, landing far beyond their centre so that the knotted tips whipped round her cheek, round her thigh, right round her whole body, to land with searing force on the swelling mound at the base of her belly.

The magnificent black body gave a single, tremendous heave against the pitiless bonds, highlighting every firmly muscled curve and depression so that the blood hammered in José's cock. Then the girl lifted her head and gave an animal wail of agony.

'Aaaaaaahhhh!'

It was the breakthrough he had been looking for. He raised the whip again and brought it lashing down on her over and over again, flogging her indiscriminately, and even as she howled and strained with every lash, in response to some ancient instinct she still straightened her back and thrust her bottom out for more, almost as if she had entered into some self-destructive pact with the leather that branded her flesh so cruelly.

Eventually José stopped. He was not sure how long he had flogged her, but his arm was tired and the blood was singing in his ears. He dropped the whip and looked down at the results of his efforts.

It was certainly impressive. Not an inch of the superb black globes was untouched. The first purple weals began at the top of the girls thighs. Her buttocks and flanks were striped and swollen, with dots of blood punctuating the ridges left by the whip, and the marks went all the way to the top of her behind and covered the delicate flesh in between. The slave's body glistened with sweat, and the split pink fruit of her cunt glistened with something else.

José grinned, and let his fingers hand down the open cleft into the hot wet meat within it. His slave moaned as his fingers brushed her swollen lips, and he saw her muscles tense as she tried to push herself back on to his hand. Her movement released a gust of the strong, sweetly rank scent of the aroused female, which drifted up to José's nostrils on the current of warm air that rose from her body. It inflamed him; his pulse hammered, and his cock, already hard, seemed ready to burst with tension. For a few seconds he was overwhelmed and he forced his hand hard against her, making her moan with mixed pain and pleasure.

Then his brain took over again, and he stopped his attack, withdrawing his fingers slowly so that the bound girl tried desperately to follow him, hissing with frustration as the thongs round her wrists and ankles prevented her.

He stood back, and raised his hand to his face, inhaling the rich perfume of the girl's juices. Then he lowered his hand again until it was just in front of the girl's face. She strained forwards, her tongue flicking out to try to lick his fingers, but he kept them just out of reach, laughing at her desperation. Then, abruptly, he swung his hand away, and turned to the watching crowd.

'She's hungry,' he said, and his audience laughed. 'Shall I give her something more filling?'

There was a buzz of approval, and José guessed that the former overseer had made few friends. 'Very well,' he said. He reached down his hand, still slick with the girl's juice, and unbuttoned his trousers. Released at last from captivity, his cock stood out high and hard. He reached out, took the bound girl's face in his hand, and forced it upwards until her eyes met his.

'It's time you made amends,' he said quietly. 'Are you ready to please your Master?'

She nodded, and he squeezed her cheeks a little before letting her go.

'Good,' he said. 'Do it well!' And he stepped forward so that the tip of his swollen organ brushed her lips. Her tongue flicked out to meet it, and he pulled back his foreskin to reveal his glans, shiny with pre-ejaculate, She began to lick it, and he shuddered with pleasure as the tiny contact inflamed him. Gradually, he allowed himself to drift closer so that more and more of the head, and then the shaft, of his aching manhood was enveloped in the hot velvet of her mouth, until at last he was at full length. She gagged a little as he entered her fully, and the rippling of her throat teased him almost beyond endurance. He gripped her head and began to rock in and out of her, and as the delicious sensations mounted his urgency increased, until he was slamming the whole of himself into her face, stretching her and bruising her with the force of his passion, and possessing her as only a true slave can be possessed.

Finally, his pleasure came to an explosive peak, and he strained and jerked as his seed pumped into his slave's mouth. Even through the fog of his orgasm he was aware of her licking and gulping at him, and a little part of him found time to think that she had indeed begun to make amends.

His spasms faded and he withdrew his softening cock, watching Princess's face for any dribble of sperm. To his satisfaction, there was none. The girl had swallowed everything. On an impulse he reached down and caressed her cheek.

'Good girl,' he said quietly, and she mewed a little and pressed her face against his hand. Then he stood up, buttoned his trousers and signalled to Pera. 'Release her,' he said, and the old man went up to the girl and began to loosen her bonds. José watched as the girl was pulled upright, wincing from the pain in her flogged behind. 'Take her back to the fields,' he said. 'She will begin again as an ingénue.' There was a muttering from the watching slaves; to add to the humiliation of her flogging and her subsequent use, the former overseer had been demoted from one of the highest ranks a slave could attain to the lowest, that of an absolute beginner with no rights at all.

José watched the humbled girl being led away. Then he turned to the assembled slaves and waved his hand. 'Off with you,' he said, and they quickly turned and left. Within half a minute José was left alone in the empty yard. He stood quite still for a while, staring at nothing.

After a while Pera returned. He walked slowly up to the younger man and stood by him in silence, until José turned to him resignedly.

'Go on,' he said. 'Out with it, whatever it is.'

The old man grinned. 'I've said it before, and you didn't lose your temper then, so I suppose you won't sulk at me now. It's all very well amusing yourself with the girls, to be sure, and long may you be able to do so, but I think you have greater needs.' He took a deep breath. 'It's time you took a wife, Mestré.'

José stared into space a little longer. Then he smiled. 'Perhaps it is, old man,' he admitted. 'But finding one, that's the problem.'

Pera shrugged. 'No more a problem for you than for any other man,' he said. And then, after a pause, 'What about the girl you met in Paris?'

José pulled a face. 'What about her? She hasn't been in touch. What shall I do – track her down and kidnap her?'

The old man nodded. 'It is a difficulty,' he agreed. 'Can you reach her?'

José shook his head. 'No,' he said. 'She has my telephone number, and that's all. She'll call, or she won't.' And the two men went inside, leaving the punishment horse, and its surrounding ring of dark spots of sweat and other fluids, alone in the silent courtyard.

CHAPTER 5

Cynthia had spent a couple of days preparing. She didn't call José, not yet. She wanted to be properly ready, almost as if that would bring her luck. She would need clothes, suitable for late summer in the south, so she shopped, buying light dresses, loose pantaloons and soft cotton chemises. She tidied her room, feeling a little strange and wondering why, until she realised that she was really leaving home even if no one was saying so. She drew two thousand euro in cash from her savings account, and she looked up the train times from Paris to Perpignan, and all the time she felt as though someone was looking over her shoulder. Sometimes it was José, and she imagined him staring appraisingly at her from those dark eyes. Sometimes it was her father, and in her imagination he looked proud but a little worried. Occasionally, but very intensely, it was her mother, but Cynthia could never read the expression on her face.

Then, the night she finished everything, her mother came to find her in the flesh. Cynthia was finishing her packing, and had to move her case aside so that Julia could sit on the edge of her bed.

Her mother seemed awkward, chatting in a slightly forced, brittle sort of way about nothing important. Eventually, partly out of sympathy and partly out of boredom, Cynthia sat down beside her, took her hand and said simply: 'I know you want to say something. It's either about sex or drugs, because you're embarrassed. I won't be embarrassed, so you needn't be. What is it?'

Her mother blushed – something Cynthia had never seen before – and then laughed softly. 'Alright,' she said, and took a breath. 'I know about the club you went to the other night.'

Cynthia waited, and her mother continued. 'You arrived at the club with Yves, and you left it without him.'

Cynthia concentrated on keeping her face expressionless. 'Ah,' she said. 'The driver?'

Her mother nodded. 'The driver,' she agreed. 'And the club was L'Histoire d'O, and I know what that means. And now you want to go travelling to the south. And I wonder.'

She squeezed Cynthia's hand, and both women fell silent. Then Cynthia disentangled her fingers. 'Alright,' she said. 'While we're exchanging confidences, here's one for you. The other morning I woke up because I heard something that wouldn't have been out of place at the club.' She looked at her mother. 'And now it's my turn to wonder.'

'To wonder what, darling?'

Julia held her gaze for a moment. Then she smiled. 'To wonder if you and I maybe have something in common?' she asked.

Her mother looked down. 'Perhaps,' she said quietly. Then she looked up at her daughter, and her eyes burned. 'If that's true, it's a gift and a risk,' she said. 'I've been lucky. I won't tell you any more at the moment, but believe me, I was lucky.' She looked away. 'You might be lucky too, but at least be careful.' Her hand found Cynthia's again, and squeezed it hard. 'Be careful,' she said again. Then she stood up, straightened her dress, and left.

Cynthia sat still for a long time. Then she stood up, patted her thighs as if to wake them, and finished her packing.

Then she picked up her phone, took a deep breath, and dialled the number on José's card.

It was answered after only a few rings.

'Mas Gassac?'

It was a man's voice, professional, and definitely not the one she was hoping for.

'Monsieur Mestré, please,' she said. And, after a moment's thought: 'Please tell him it is Cynthia, of Paris.'

'Very well. Please wait.'

There was a click, and the background noise of the phone line was replaced by classical music, sparse, cool and formal. It went on for a long time; either José was busy, or Mas Gassac was big enough that it took a while to find people.

Then, just when she was getting ready to be disappointed, the music clicked off.

'José Mestré speaking.'

It was him! A thrill ran through her at the sound of his voice. Keeping her own voice carefully level, she said: 'This is Cynthia, from Paris.

Was there a slight pause? She wasn't sure.

Then he said: 'Cynthia who arrived at a club with a friend, and who left alone?'

For the second time in a few minutes, Cynthia felt a faint touch of guilt at the reminder of how she had abandoned Yves. Then she reminded herself firmly that it had been Yves who had walked out on her, not the other way round. 'Yes, that's right,' she said.

'Ah. Hello, Cynthia. It's good to hear from you. What can I do for you?'

'When we met...' she paused, and found she was blushing, 'you talked about a reward.'

'That's right, I did. So?'

She took a deep breath. 'I'd like to claim it, please.'

He was silent for a few seconds. Then he said, slowly: 'You need to know that it might not be an easy reward to have. I don't play games.'

'I'd guessed that,' she said.

'Alright then. When can you come?'

Her heart leapt. 'Tomorrow? I can be at Perpignan by six o'clock.'

'That will be fine. Travel safely, Cynthia.'

The phone clicked and went dead. She sat staring at it for a moment, feeling rather dismissed, and thinking that she didn't know where to go from the station, or what she should take. Then she shrugged. Presumably there would be taxis, and someone would know where to find Mas Gassac, whatever and wherever that was.

In the end, she would just have to trust José.

In his study, David Arundel switched off the speaker phone and stared into space for a moment. Yolanda knelt naked next to him, her bottom liberally striped with weals from a caning he had delivered not half an hour ago, and her mouth stretched by a large ball gag which had muffled her cries to soft whinnies.

He toyed with Yolanda's leash. His first impulse was to march into Cynthia's room and forbid her from making the journey. He shook his head. She was eighteen; she had a right to her own life, and anyway at her age and with his encouragement, Julia had been about to start her own training as a slave. His slave, in the end. Even if he suspected his daughter had something similar in store, what was he supposed to do – deny her the fulfilment he had given to her mother?

He compromised. He switched on the phone and dialled a number. After a moment a voice answered simply: 'Yes?'

'I need some information. Tell me what you can find out about a place called Mas Gassac, and a man called José Mestré. I need it tonight.'

'One hour.' The phone went dead, and David switched it off. One hour – time to finish what he had started with Yolanda. He knelt behind her and roughly kicked her knees apart so that her scored cheeks parted. The sight of the whipped buttocks, with the angry stripes curling in to crease the puckered bud, inflamed him as it always did, and he hitched out his cock, spat on it perfunctorily, and forced it into the punished woman's anus, driving forward cruelly until he was at full length, savouring the tight spasming heat around him and the agonised sighs that were all his impaled slave could get out round her gag.

He hauled back on the leash, forcing Yolanda to arch her back until her hands almost left the ground, and buggered her brutally, his balls slapping against her with the speed of his thrusts. She grunted into the gag with each stroke, and the muscles of her rectum clenched involuntarily around his shaft as if she was trying in the most delicious way possible to milk him. Before long she succeeded; his thrusts rose to a peak he couldn't control, try as he might, and he climaxed with a long, animal growl of pleasure, holding himself deep inside her until his spasms had finished.

Eventually he withdrew his softening manhood, and as he did so he realised that Julia had entered the room and was watching them. He didn't know how long she had been here, and she made no comment; to do so would have meant instant punishment.

David left his slave where she was, on all fours. He buttoned himself up and turned to his wife.

'Cynthia is off on her travels tomorrow. I think she is going to visit someone she met the other night.' He explained the phone call he had overheard.

As he spoke, Julia nodded slowly. 'I see,' she said. 'It doesn't surprise me. I was talking to her a little while ago. It seems she overheard me – us – that morning. I think perhaps we inspired her.'

David drummed his fingers. 'Well,' he said, 'it wouldn't be surprising if she turned out to be her mother's daughter in that way as well as in others. Is that your instinct?'

His wife nodded again. 'I think so,' she said.

'Hmm.' David stared into the distance. 'Well, we'll know more about this man in a while. I've made enquiries.' He fell silent, and Julia reached out and touched his hand.

'Of course, we must be sure she will be safe,' she said. 'But please, darling, don't stop her unless you have to.'

David looked at her curiously. 'Why do you say that?' he asked.

To his astonishment a tear appeared at the corner of his wife's eye. 'If she is like me,' she said quietly, 'it would be cruel to deny her.'

David took her hand. 'Don't worry,' he said. 'If she is like you, it will be a matter of honour for me that she is placed with a man who can handle her properly.' He squeezed her hand for a moment, and then let it go. 'Now,' he said, in a brisker tone, 'get about your duties, wife. Starting with this!' And he handed Yolanda's leash to her, and she led the girl away, still on all fours. David watched them go, noting with satisfaction the way movement caused beads of sperm to trickle out of Yolanda's body.

As the door closed behind them, the phone rang. David picked it up.

'Yes?'

The voice at the other end spoke for several minutes. What it had finished, David said: 'Thank you,' and put the phone down. He stared at nothing for a little while. Then he smiled quietly to himself.

His informant had been detailed. It seemed that Cynthia was in for an interesting time.

CHAPTER 6

It is nine hundred kilometres from Paris to Perpignan. The best trains go via Avignon, and take around eight hours. Cynthia had boarded her train early on a close grey morning at the Gare de Lyon, which is not the most beautiful of the stations of Paris. When she left it, though, she walked into the hot Mediterranean embrace of a late summer evening in the south, with the sound of crickets in the distance.

She let the platform empty, and looked out for anyone who was obviously waiting, but no one was, so she walked out to the taxi rank. A single car waited there. It had no taxi sign, but the driver leaned across and opened the door as she walked up to it.

Cynthia leaned into the car. 'Do you know a place called Mas Gassac?' she asked.

He smiled at her. 'I come from there. If you're Cynthia, I'm to take you with me.' He looked at her appraisingly. 'If you're not Cynthia, I expect you'd still be welcome!'

She laughed. 'I'm Cynthia.'

'And I'm Pera. I look after Monsieur Mestré. In you get!' She put her case on the back seat and climbed in.

Pera drove quickly out of the centre of Perpignan and took the N116 route to the west, and after half an hour they left the main road and began to climb into low rolling hills patchworked with olive groves and vineyards. They turned on to smaller and smaller roads until at last they drew up in front of a pair of old wooden gates, bleached and sagging, but still somehow graceful and strong. The gates were set in a dusty stone wall, twice Cynthia's height, that didn't look sagging at all.

Pera had not spoken since they had left the station. Now he turned to her, and his lined face was serious. 'You are very trusting,' he said. 'You haven't asked me a thing. Do you want to ask me anything, anything at all, about what lies on the other side of these gates and this wall?'

She thought quickly. 'Is José there?'

He nodded.

'Then that's all I need to know.'

Pera looked at her for a moment, his face unreadable. Then he sounded a quick tattoo on the car horn, and the old gates swung inwards.

They drove through and the gates began to close behind them. Cynthia turned round in her seat to see what was moving them, and gasped.

Two girls, she guessed of about her own age, and naked except for strips of cloth around their loins, were pushing the gates to, their thighs straining as they shoved the heavy timber along. A young man wearing jeans and a white cotton shirt stood behind them. He had something coiled up in his hand, but it was only when he shook it out that Cynthia realised what it was.

It was a whip. As she watched, he raised it and flicked it out almost casually at one of the girls. At close range the snap of the whip and the girl's flinch as it struck her across the thighs were simultaneous. A scarlet weal appeared on the girl's skin, and now that Cynthia looked she noticed that both girls bore many similar marks.

The car had stopped. She looked over at Pera, who was grinning at her. 'Still want to go on?' he asked.

His humour annoyed her. She wasn't here to be laughed at! She turned away from him, and said, tartly: 'Why not? I didn't meet your José in a tea shop, you know.'

He shrugged, and drove on. 'Fine,' he said. 'As long as you're sure.'

She didn't answer, and they drove on in silence until the car drew up in front of a handsome old house, three stories high, with a wide courtyard in front of it and trees peeping out from behind. Pera stopped the car.

'Well,' he said. 'You've arrived. This is Mas Gassac. Among other things we grow grapes here, and we make wine here. As for the rest, you'll find out about it if you go into the house. Are you still willing?'

She didn't answer, but opened the door, took her case from the back seat, and marched up to the front door. She rang the bell. A moment later the door opened, and she marched through into a large, square hall.

It was empty. She looked round for a moment then turned to Pera, who had followed her through the door. 'Where is everyone?' she demanded.

'Put your case down,' he said.

She shook her head in confusion. 'Why?'

'Put your case down.' His voice was calm. 'Then remove your clothes.'

'What?' Cynthia stared at him. Obviously he had gone mad.

Pera walked over to a tall cabinet. He opened it, took something out, and turned to Cynthia. 'This is a whip,' he said, holding it out so she could see. 'It is one of the ways we keep order at Mas Gassac.' Cynthia shook her head again, but he ignored her. 'I told you we make wine here, and I told you we grow grapes,' he said. 'I gave you many chances to discover the rest, but you were too proud. Or too stupid.'

He paused, and Cynthia took the opportunity to study the whip which he still held out to her. It had a short stock and a long, thin lash which ended in a sharp-looking tassel. She had seen something like it before. It was a hunting crop, made to have an effect on the thick, hair-covered hides of hunting dogs. She tried unsuccessfully to imagine what effect it would have on human skin. She shuddered, and kept quiet.

Pera let the hand which held the whip fall to his side. 'I think you are beginning to understand,' he said. 'In case you do not, let me explain once more. You have left the present day, with all its laws and conventions, and entered a place which is worked by slaves. You have already seen two of them, at the gates. In the end, José is the master of all of them, and from the moment you walked through that door you joined their number. You have one more chance to revise your decision, now that you understand it. Take off your clothes, or leave for good. It is up to you.'

Cynthia stood very still for five, then ten, then fifteen seconds. Then she made a decision. Slowly, she put down her case and reached down to the hem of her dress. She lifted it up, drew it over her head, and dropped it on the floor next to her. She wore no bra, but only a pair of brief panties which she lowered, and stepped out of. Then she stood up uncertainly, her face burning.

Pera nodded. 'Well done,' he said. 'I think you have gone with your heart, not your head. Is there anything you would like to ask, before we begin?'

There was only one thing, she knew, and it could be expressed in a single word. 'José?' she said.

The old man nodded. 'He will be here,' he said,' and he is interested in you.' He grinned. 'After all,' he said. 'just as you told me, you didn't meet him in a tea shop. Have you any more questions?'

She shook her head. She had made her decision; now she would wait to see what Pera did next.

What he did surprised her. He held her eyes, and then lowered his head in a nod that contained a trace of a bow, almost as if he was offering her his respect. The movement was over in a second, and when Pera straightened up his face was cold and professional. 'Right,' he said. 'Now you are an ingénue – a new girl. We'll begin.'

Pera studied the girl who stood in front of him. She was certainly worth his respect, he thought. She had a very fine body indeed, smooth and taut without being over-muscled. Her breasts were high and firm, her belly very slightly rounded, and her thighs fell in perfect proportion to the curved hips which saved her from being too boyish. He walked round her. Her bottom was exactly as good as he had expected; his cock stiffened at the sight of the firmly rounded hams of a fit young female. He looked closer, and saw that her behind was marked with faint, fading lines, which were presumably the remains of José's handiwork from a few nights ago.

It was a good place to start. He raised the whip and swept it down across the trembling bottom. The whip landed, the thin lash curving round her body so that the tasselled end bit into her thigh. She flinched, but held her position.

The whip sighed down again, an identical blow from the opposite side. Again, the girl flinched but did not falter, and Pera sensed that she had the measure of the whipping so far. He was impressed, but they had only just begun, and for the first few strokes he had used only part of his arm.

Time to change that; he drew back the whip and brought it lashing down hard across the girl's lower bottom.

'Oooowww!' She gave a squeal of pain and her buttocks danced a jig as she hopped from one foot to another. Pera watched as a thin angry weal darkened from pink to scarlet at the base of her globes. As soon as the girl had settled he raised the whip again and sent the thong hissing in from the other side.

The girl rewarded him with a vigorous yelp and launched into another dance of pain, and Pera decided it was time to increase the tempo. He stepped forwards and took her by the hair. 'Kneel,' he said, pulling down for emphasis, and she sank awkwardly to her knees, looking up at him as if she was checking she had got it right.

He nodded. 'Good,' he said. 'Now, on all fours.'

He let go of her hair and she bent forwards until her hands were flat on the ground. Again she looked up, twisting her head round as if to check his reaction, but this time he shook his head. 'Further down,' he told her. 'Face on the floor, back arched, bottom in the air.

She did as she was told, and his cock hardened further at the sight. He reached out his foot and tapped at her ankles. 'Spread your legs,' he told her, and she shuffled her knees a little way apart. He clicked his tongue, and brought the stock of the whip down smartly across her thighs, using it as if it was a cane, and making her squeal with pain. 'Further,' he said, and she quickly spread herself so that he could see the tension in her thighs.

When she was in position he stood back a little and ran his eye over her. Her posture thrust her bottom up and out, tightening the cheeks and thoroughly exposing her sex – small and neat, but with full lips, he noted, which glistened slightly. He nodded approvingly to himself. The girl was aroused, either by her situation or by the physical pain of the whip. It was a good sign.

He raised the whip and lashed it across her bottom, giving her two swift cuts from either side. She squealed and trembled, and scarlet lines blossomed on her pale skin. Her bottom was getting quite well marked, and the sight was inflaming Pera's already aching cock. He grinned to himself. Some time soon he might get to enjoy her, but not until he had José's say-so. Meanwhile, there was plenty of pleasure to be had from his legitimate job of completing the girl's first whipping, and introducing her to the strictures of Mas Gassac.

First, the whipping. He changed his aim, and the lash sang through the air and bit into Cynthia's shoulders. She hissed with surprise, but held her position as if she was coming to terms with the pain. He began to strike regularly, moving his aim so that the weals spread down her back and the sharp tassel whipped round to nip at her belly and her breasts. Each quick, sizzling sssssssszzzack of the whip drew another hiss of pain, and the girl swayed a little with the rhythm of her thrashing. As the angry tracks of the whip gathered and joined she began to moan, and then to sob quietly, and Pera sensed that she was crying not so much with pain, as with release.

It was time to stop. He put the whip down, and squatted down by the girl's head. 'Welcome to Mas Gassac,' he said, reaching out to stroke her hair. 'You've had your first lesson. Now shall we go and find José?'

She nodded, her head pushing slightly against his hand in a way that reminded him briefly of a horse looking for a pat. He allowed her the comfort for a moment, then took hold of her hair and gently drew her upright. 'Come on,' he said. 'He'll be expecting us.'

He led her out of the hall and up two flights of stairs to the door of José's private apartment. He raised his hand and knocked, and after a moment José's voice said: 'Come in.'

Pera looked at the girl. She seemed nervous. 'Go on,' he said. 'You've come a long way, and gone through a thrashing, for this. In you go!' And then, when she still hesitated: 'I'll be right behind you, if it helps.'

Obviously it did. Her hand found the doorknob, and after a tiny hesitation, she turned it, pushed open the door, and walked into the private apartment of the man who owned Mas Gassac and everything in it.

CHAPTER 7

José did his best to conceal his fascination as he watched Cynthia enter his apartment. He knew that Pera would whip her – it was a standard welcome for newcomers to Mas Gassac – and he had heard it, too; the hiss-crack of the hunting crop and the moans and squeals of the girl had floated up to his ears like an erotic symphony, charging his body with hormones and making his manhood stand out like a tree trunk. Now came the test, though. How would she look? If she was sullen and resentful, all was lost. He hoped it would be otherwise.

He was not disappointed. The girl who walked towards him had the docility of the recently-whipped, certainly, but there was no anger, no resistance in her demeanour. Nor, he saw, was there defeat. She walked up to him, quietly and demurely, and then without any prompting, dropped to her knees. He reached out and took her chin, lifting her head so that she was looking up at him.

'Hello,' he said. 'Welcome to Mas Gassac. I'm glad you're here. I hope you are too.' She smiled uncertainly, and he let go of her chin. 'Pera has whipped you,' he said. 'Did it hurt?'

'Yes,' she said quietly.

'A great deal?'

She seemed to think for a moment. Then she shook her head. 'No, not a great deal,' she said. She spoke French well, but with a faint English accent which would usually have annoyed José, but which she somehow managed to make exotic.

José nodded. 'So you could bear more?'

'I, I think so.' She looked up anxiously. 'Am I going to be whipped more? I mean, what's going to happen to me?'

José walked round the kneeling girl, admiring the lines the whip had written on

her body. 'She marks easily,' he said to Pera, and the old man nodded agreement. 'She's not used to the lash, lad,' he said, 'no doubt of it.'

'You're right. But she will be!' José turned back to Cynthia. 'The answer is yes, you are going to be whipped more. In different ways, with different things, you will be whipped every day, and probably more than once. We will see that you learn to love the whip as much as you will fear it.' He paused, then reached down and began to unbuckle his belt. 'Now, I'm going to thrash you, plain and simple, just as men have thrashed their women for thousands of years. And after that, if you're a good girl, you'll be rewarded, because I haven't forgotten my promise. Stand up!'

She obeyed, and he pointed to the heavy desk that stood in the middle of the room. 'Go to that, and bend over it,' he told her.

She walked slowly over to the desk, and bent herself forwards.

'Take hold of the far side,' he said, 'and get your legs as far apart as you can. Go on! Open yourself for me.'

He watched eagerly as she did as he had told her. The fine buttocks tightened and parted as she moved her feet, until her sex, visibly moist, was thrust out and opened. To complete the picture, the tiny wrinkled dot of a young woman's anus – virgin, he would bet – nestled at the top of the arrowhead-shaped cleft.

It was a superb sight, and José felt himself growing almost light-headed with excitement. He nodded to Pera. 'Be ready to hold her,' he said, and the older man walked round to the other side of the desk and stood by the bowed girl's head.

José ran the belt through his hands, and then doubled it up to make a heavy loop, grinning as Cynthia flinched slightly at the faint hiss and slap of the leather. Then he drew back his arm and whirled it forwards.

The belt landed across the centre of the taut globes with a sound like a gunshot. For one startled second, Cynthia was quite still, while a two-inch band across her bottom flashed white and then began to darken almost immediately to an angry red. Then she put back her head and gave a single howl of anguish.

José watched as the girl writhed with pain, the muscles in her thighs and bottom dancing and twitching exquisitely. Pera stood ready to seize her if she showed any sign of trying to leave her position, but he was not needed; despite her obvious, and entertaining, distress, Cynthia's hands did not leave the far edge of the desk. José nodded approvingly, and raised the belt for another stroke.

It whistled down in a perfect mirrored twin of the last stroke, sweeping from the opposite side and landing to the millimetre on the same flaming skin so recently scorched by the leather.

This time there was no delay; the suffering girl let out an ear-splitting shriek the instant the blow landed. Once again, her behind twitched and danced uncontrollably. Between the reddening cheeks, her exposed cunt and the little bud above it wriggled and winked in a display of such delicious obscenity that José very nearly threw his belt aside and mounted the bitch there and then.

He mastered himself. It wasn't time, yet. Anyway, if he handled her properly he would be able to enjoy her delights, whenever and however he chose, for as long as he cared to. The prospect gave fresh strength to his arm, and he began to swing the doubled belt down onto her bottom, first from one side and then from the other, taking his time over each stroke and making sure that the fat tip of the doubled leather swung into her exposed crack as often as possible, drawing howls and squeals of pain from her with every cruel invasion. But no matter how he thrashed her, and no matter how she cried and begged for mercy, she did not let go of the desk, and Pera did not have to take hold of her.

Eventually José stopped. The girl's buttocks, and everything between them, were thrashed purple, his arm was getting tired, and besides, there were other things on his mind. He dropped the belt and stepped forward, thrusting his hand roughly into the burning cleft between those swollen cheeks. She was soft and hot and wet, and as he pushed his fingers into her she shuddered and mewed with pleasure.

He leaned down so that his mouth was by her ear. 'Is it time for your reward?' he asked, hoarsely.

Her voice was hoarse too. 'Yes, please,' she whispered.

Keeping his fingers in her, working roughly at her flesh as she shivered and swayed, he loosened his trousers with his other hand. His cock stood out, almost vertical with passion, and he guided it to her threshold and then thrust forward fiercely. She opened readily to receive him, and he drove forwards until he was buried to his full length in her.

She was so hot and so close! José had taken many, many women, but he remembered few that had felt as good as this. He kept himself at full length, feeling the tip of his cock pushing against the tender wall of flesh at the top of her vagina, and savouring the low grunts of pleasurable pain she gave him in return.

He began to rock in and out of her. She had the fresh tightness of youth, and he suspected that she was not that experienced. Some girls of her age, he knew, could seem submissive when what they really were was uncertain, but all his instincts told him that Cynthia was far more than that. He moved faster, feeling her tunnel rippling around him. It was warm, and her skin was becoming damp with sweat. The scent of her rose to tease him, and his shaft felt as if it would burst with passion.

Helplessly, and all too quickly, his pleasure peaked, and he came, growling with triumph and thrusting jets of his seed into her with quick trembling movements, almost as if he was a dog impregnating a bitch. To his delight, he felt her contract around him, and then she was coming too, with little whinnying cries that aroused him even more so that he felt as if his orgasm could last forever.

Eventually he relaxed, and withdrew himself. Cynthia gave a sigh which sounded almost disappointed, and José felt a flash of irritation. He swung his hand down and smacked her sharply, twice on each of her crimson cheeks.

'What do you say?' he asked evenly.

'Ow!' Her surprise was almost comical. 'Sorry! Er, thank you.'

'That's better.' José turned to Pera. 'She shows plenty of promise,' he said, 'but she needs to learn manners. Take her away and teach her some, and bring her back to me in a week.' He paused, and added: 'For now, give her to the girls in the press room. They'll enjoy the task, I'm sure.'

Pera nodded, pulled the girl upright, and led her away. José listened as the door closed, then let a smile cross his face.

Plenty of promise, indeed!

CHAPTER 8

Cynthia followed Pera dumbly down the stairs. Her head was whirling with a mixture of emotions. She was shocked, first of all, at the pain José had inflicted on her, and just as shocked at her ability to bear it and – even inside her head she felt somehow that the words should be whispered – enjoy it. Then, she was just as shocked at the way her body had responded to eagerly to José's abrupt penetration of her. She thought back to the sensation, and to the amazing intensity of the orgasm he had given her, and for a second her eyes half-closed and she almost swayed.

Then she snapped back to the present, and her cheeks flushed with shame, because afterwards it felt as if everything had been spoiled when he said she needed to learn manners! How dare he!

But still, said a very quiet voice from the centre of her soul, what's the point of craving the sort of attention you crave, if you don't get taught some manners along the way? Isn't that your fantasy? Really?

Unconsciously Cynthia nodded to herself. It was true. She wanted to be controlled. Disciplined. Even owned. And that wasn't going to happen if she stamped out of here in a huff.

It was a decision, and it felt right. She nodded to herself again, and then realised with a jolt that she had stopped, and that Pera was looking up quizzically at her.

'Are you coming?' he asked. He sounded amused, almost as if he had guessed her thoughts.

'Yes,' she said. 'Sorry.' And then, after a brief hesitation, 'Sir.'

This time he was definitely amused. 'I'm not Sir, or Master, or any of those names,' he said. 'I'm Pera. Always, and to everyone, just Pera.'

She nodded. 'Yes, Pera,' she said. And she followed him down the stairs, across the hall and out into the warm silky evening. He led her across a courtyard and through an archway into a long low building. 'This is the press room,' he said quietly. 'The girls who work here, sleep here. It's time you were asleep too. I'll show you where.'

They walked along a corridor lined with doors. Pera opened one of them. 'Here,' he said. 'The bed on the right. Sleep well.'

As her eyes adjusted to the dim light in the room, Cynthia saw that there were three beds. Two seemed occupied; the one on the right was empty. She tiptoed over to it, suddenly limp with exhaustion, collapsed on to it as quietly as she could, and was asleep almost as soon as she had landed.

She dreamed she was running through a forest, one of the forests that came close to the centre of Paris, but the trees were getting in her way and she kept having to break off branches. Each time it made a terrible crack and she felt she had to say sorry to the tree. As the sun got higher the forest grew sparser, and she realised she wasn't in Paris any more, but in the hills near Perpignan, and the branches she was snapping belonged to huge overgrown vines. The cracking noises got louder and louder until she woke with a jolt.

Crack!

'Sorry!'

Crack!

'Sorry!'

Cynthia peered blearily out of the covers, and then sat upright quickly. It was morning, although still early to judge by the light. A tall woman was standing by the middle bed with her back to Cynthia. Her black hair ran down the exact centre of her back in a French plait, and she was severely clothed in a plain close-fitting claret dress that came down to her knees, and black ankle boots with high narrow heels. She held a broad wooden paddle in her hand, and as Cynthia watched she brought it down sharply on the already flaming behind of a girl who knelt, naked, on the bed, her rump thrust out.

Crack!

'Aah! Sorry…'

So that had been the source of her dream. She watched the heavy blows landing, as regular as a metronome, while the girl on the receiving end yelped and squealed, her apologies becoming more and more perfunctory, and her bottom swiftly darkening to a blotched field of red and purple, and still the tall woman went on whipping the paddle down over and over again. My God, thought Cynthia. When will she ever stop?

Eventually, the dreadful spanking did stop. By the time it did, the girl on the bed was sobbing uncontrollably. Her bottom was blotched and blistered, and her thighs shone with sweat that had little to do with heat, at this early hour, and Cynthia watched with fascination as the girl's exposed pussy twitched in time with her sobs. She felt her own flesh warm and moisten at the sight.

The tall woman walked over to the wall by the window, and hung the paddle on a hook. Then she turned round. First she looked at the snivelling girl on the bed, and Cynthia thought she was a hint of satisfaction on the cold pale face. Then the woman turned to Cynthia.

'Good morning,' she said, and her voice was as frosty as her expression. 'I am Ariane, and I am the overseer for the press room. You are Cynthia, and you will experience what she has,' and she slapped the kneeling girl's flank, 'soon enough. Work begins at seven. Be ready!'

She turned on her heel and walked out. The door closed behind her with a definite thump.

As soon as Ariane had gone, the kneeling girl slumped forwards onto her bed, and her hands flew to her blistered behind. 'Oooooh,' she moaned. 'God, that hurts. What was she using, a flamethrower?'

Cynthia suppressed a giggle. 'No,' she said. 'A paddle.'

'Are you sure?' The girl turned over carefully, and winced as her scalded cheeks brushed against the bed. 'You're Cynthia, because She said so. I'm Francine, and that,' and she gestured towards the third bed, 'is Amelie.'

The occupant of the bed, who was visible only as a mound of blankets, raised a hand and waved. Cynthia waved back. 'Hi,' she said. Then she turned to the spanked girl, who was still wincing and fidgeting. 'What did you do?' she asked.

'To earn the spanking? Nothing!' Francine frowned, then added: 'Or nothing special, anyway. You don't have to do anything special to get Ariane on your case. You'll be next, I daresay.'

'Why?' The idea alarmed Cynthia, but Francine turned over to give her a direct look. 'Answer me one question,' she said. 'Just to check. Did you come here expecting your arse not to be tanned?'

Cynthia suppressed a grin. 'No, not really.'

'Good.' Francine nodded. 'That means you aren't mad. I was wondering, for a moment.' She reached out and thumped the pile of bedclothes that was all

Cynthia had yet seen of Amelie. 'Come on, Sleeping Beauty,' she said. 'Time to get up. The Jacuzzi awaits, and the servants have got breakfast ready on the lawn.' Then she looked at Cynthia. 'Only kidding,' she said. Cynthia rolled her eyes.

Instead of Jacuzzis, servants and breakfast, there was a chilly shower, some hot rolls and a small pot of jam, with cold water from a tap in the corner. Cynthia felt clean, at least, if not pampered. When they had finished she looked around for clothes; hers were nowhere to be seen.

Francine watched her for a moment. 'Hoping to get dressed?' she asked.

Cynthia nodded.

'Well forget it. You don't need clothes to do what we do, and we don't get them.' She smiled. 'Get used to it, girl,' she said gently. 'José didn't get you here to cover you up. Not to begin with, anyway. He likes arses, and snatches, and nice round tits, like every other man that ever walked, and around here he gets what he likes.' She took Cynthia's hand. 'Stick with me for a bit, The press room's hard work, but you'll be okay.' She half-turned spoke over her shoulder to Amelie. 'Come on,' she said. 'We'd better not be late or we'll all get paddled, and I've had my lot for today already.'

The three girls walked down a corridor and through a double door into a big, dark space more that reminded Cynthia of a barn. There were no windows, but it was brightly lit by rooflights, and the dusty air smelled sweet and a bit musty. There were two big vats, a bit like enormous flat baskets, with frames fixed to their tops. Three other girls, also naked, were already waiting.

Ariane stood between the two vats. She was still holding the paddle, and Cynthia heard Francine mutter:

'Uh-oh!' under her breath, but the tall woman gestured at her and Amelie.

'You two,' she said, 'begin work. You,' and she crooked a finger at Cynthia, 'come here.'

Cynthia's legs tried to turn to jelly, but she just managed to over-rule them. She walked up to Ariane and stood in front of her, her stomach churning. She felt more naked than ever.

Ariane walked round her, studying her closely in a way that made Cynthia squirm inside. She completed one full circuit in silence. Then she said abruptly: 'How old are you?'

Cynthia fought off an impulse to shut her eyes. 'Eighteen, Madame,' she said, hoping desperately that she had chosen the right form of address.

'A good, trainable age.' The tall women pursed her lips. 'And a fair figure, for an untrained girl.' She reached out and cupped one of Cynthia's breasts, hefting it as if it was a piece of market produce, then let the hand fall so that it slid down her hip and brushed round her thigh. All the time her eyes held Cynthia's, as if she was recording every flicker and flinch.

Eventually she stood back. 'A fair figure,' she repeated, 'but capable of improvement. We'll see how it responds to work in a while. For the moment, we'll see how it responds to this.' She held up the paddle. 'Bend over the edge of the press.' She gestured to one of the wide vats, and Cynthia, trembling, did as she was told, parting her legs to imitate the way she had been positioned by Pera. Ariane didn't comment, but merely said: 'I'll start you with ten strokes, so that you understand what'll happen to you if you disobey. Be ready!'

Cynthia was still bracing herself when there was a quick whisper and the heavy paddle exploded against her bottom with a thunderous crack..

Cynthia yelled with outrage. It was agony! The paddle burned and burned as if she was being held against a hot-plate. It was nothing like the sensual pain of the whip. It was just a horrible, smarting pain that seemed never to fade. Just as it finally began to ebb, there was another whisper and the paddle crashed into her again.

Oh God, it had landed in the same place. She stamped her feet and growled, trying with all her might to absorb it, dilute it, do anything to make it fade.

Craaaack!

That one had landed higher, on flesh not touched by the first two, and the scalding smart started afresh. It was impossible; she couldn't stand another seven strokes, no matter how she tried. She heard a voice sobbing and pleading, and realised it was hers. It was ignored; the paddle blasted down again.

She yowled in outrage, she kicked and writhed at the unfairness of it, she begged for mercy. Yet somehow, she realised, she was still bent over. She hadn't let go of the wooden edge of the vat. I'm submitting, she thought. This is what it feels like. And then the wicked paddle detonated against her yet again and she forgot all about everything except the burning pain.

It seemed to be getting harder, impossible as that seemed. The latest stroke had branded her across the tops of her thighs, perilously close to her exposed sex, and the concussion rippled through her, awaking sensations that only a few strokes ago would have seemed impossible, ridiculous – but now they were real.

Another stroke hammered down in the same place. It was almost as if Ariane knew the effect her beating was having. Even as Cynthia yelled, she found herself pushing her haunches back, ready for the next dreadful impact.

The paddle whooshed and landed, and this time there was no doubt. The pain was still dreadful, it would always be dreadful, but now something else was growing through it. Something almost like pleasure.

Another stroke exploded across the upper part of her bottom, further from the traitor flesh that took such pleasure from her pain, but now the distance didn't seem to matter; perhaps her body had bridged the chasm or perhaps – but 'perhaps' had ceased to matter; nothing mattered any more except the next stroke, and the one after.

Cynthia heard her own voice, and now it wasn't a howl of pain, but a moan. Her conscious thoughts were fading as the sensations took over, but a tiny part of her found a second to think: What's happening to me?

Then the last stroke landed. It was the hardest of all.

The paddle landed straight across her lower bottom, compressing her cheeks with such force that the hard wood smacked directly onto her out-thrust quim.

Cynthia gave a single shriek of mixed pleasure and pain. Her muscles convulsed, and she came, panting and moaning as her flesh responded to the lava in her behind.

She didn't know how long she lay over the side of the vat – it could have been seconds or minutes – but when she finally came to she realised that her legs were stiff and trembling, and the muscles in her stomach ached where they had braced against the hard wooden edge. Her bottom felt as if it had been scalded, and her quim burned and twitched with the aftershock of the most unexpected orgasm of her life.

Someone was talking to her. She concentrated, and realised that Ariane had said: 'You may stand up now.'

Slowly, creakingly, she obeyed, wincing as the movement flexed her blistered bottom. When she had achieved an upright stance, she turned to face Ariane.

The tall woman was smiling. 'Well, well,' she said. 'I shall remember the effect the paddle has on you. If you need to be rewarded, I shall know what to do, but if you need to be punished I shall have to think of something else.' She shook her head slightly. 'What an interesting find you are, little Cynthia. And to think I was brought up to believe that the English were without passion.'

Cynthia wasn't sure how to respond, so she just nodded.

Ariane gave her a thoughtful look, then clapped her hands for attention. The other girls turned and listened as she began to speak.

'Our first harvest here begins soon,' she said. 'I can't tell you exactly when, because grapes ripen when they ripen, but soon. Before they do, we have to clean the pressing house, from top to bottom. It must be ready, and you will all work until it is.' She clicked her tongue thoughtfully. 'I'm expected elsewhere. I can't be here all the time. Carla, come here.'

One of the three girls who had been waiting when Cynthia had first entered the press room trotted over to her.

'Yes, Madame?' she said.

'You will take charge. The work for each day is listed here,' and she picked up a clipboard and handed it to Carla. 'See that it is done.'

Even in the dim light, there was no mistaking the gleam in Carla's eyes. 'Yes, Madame,' she said. 'Please, what shall I do if they fall behind?'

'Thrash them until they get quicker.' Ariane gestured towards a stand by the door. 'You'll find several riding crops in there. Use one of those. And you'd better not spare your arm because I'll be holding you responsible.' She leaned in close to the girl's face. 'If we are not ready to press when we should be, Pera will take the skin off my behind. The only thing that will make it bearable will be the memory of me taking the skin off yours. Do you understand?'

Carla nodded, her face suddenly pale.

'Good.' Ariane stood up. 'Well, what are you waiting for? Get on with it!' And with that she turned and strutted out.

CHAPTER 9

Carla waited until the door had closed. Then she sauntered over to the stand and took her time selecting a wicked-looking crop, over a metre long, tipped with a thin knotted thong. She swished it through the air a couple of times, grinning at the sharp hissing sound. Then she picked up the clipboard.

'Right,' she said. 'Jobs to do.' She read out a list of tasks, brusquely assigning girls to each one.

Cynthia and Francine were set to scrubbing the inside of one of the big wooden presses with soda. As they began, Francine leaned close to Cynthia's ear and muttered: 'A slave makes the cruellest master. Or mistress! She's a bitch, this one, and there'll be trouble even if she has to invent it. You wait and see.'

She was right. Carla seemed to be looking for an excuse to lash out, and within a couple of hours all the girls were nursing flaming weals across their bottoms and thighs.

Cynthia was first. Turning awkwardly to wring out a cloth in a bucket she had knocked the bucket over with a crash that rang out through the pressing room. The crash was followed by the nasty trickling sound of lots of dirty water running over a surface that had just been cleaned.

By the time she had straightened up, Cynthia was aware of an angry presence behind her. With a sinking heart she turned and found Carla staring at her.

'Sorry,' she said quickly. 'I'll clear it up. It'll be alright.'

Carla looked as if she was ready to stamp her foot. 'You will clear it up,' she hissed, 'but not before you've had a lesson about being so careless! Bend over the edge of the press!'

Cynthia sighed. 'Okay,' she said, 'but the longer you whip me, the less time I have to clear up.'

'And the more insolent you are, the worse it'll hurt!' Carla emphasised her point with a sharp cut of the crop across Cynthia's thigh. 'You're already due,' and she hesitated as if thinking hurriedly, 'a dozen strokes, and I can always add more!'

Cynthia bent forward hurriedly. She waited for the first stroke.

It whistled in and landed across her lower bottom with an emphatic snap. She drew in her breath at the urgent sting as it re-awoke both the itch and smart of her whipping the night before and the more recent wicked blistering of Ariane's paddle. With an effort she managed not to cry out. If she could possibly manage it she was going to deny Carla the satisfaction of making her howl!

Twice in quick succession, the crop lanced in and scalded the tops of her thighs. The thin stock and the inquisitive tip burned like a hot wire, and Cynthia ground her teeth with the effort of staying silent.

Another three strokes landed quickly, close together on her lower bottom. She closed her eyes and let the breath hiss between her teeth as she took charge of the searing pain and prepared herself for the next stroke.

The whip hissed and landed.

Cynthia let out a short 'Ah!' before she caught herself; whether by accident or on purpose, the whip had landed near the top of her bottom on flesh which had so far been more or less unmarked. The freshness of the pain was shocking, and she felt her feet lifting from the floor, one after the other, in an involuntary dance of agony. With a tremendous effort she stopped them; Carla must not see that she was getting through.

Anyway, she was more than half done. She could survive the rest, surely?

The whip exploded against the middle of her bottom, with the evil loop of leather at its end curling round to sink a fang into her thigh. Cynthia felt herself go rigid with the pain. Her breath rasped in her throat, the muscles in her legs shook, and the blood buzzed in her ears. Surely, it was alright if she cried out now?

No. The tiny voice from inside her spoke through her outrage. Now, of all times, she must keep silent! She was being tested, even if Carla didn't intend it. The other girls were watching, and they would tell others. She breathed deeply, willing herself to relax, to be ready for the next strokes.

They came, hard and fast.

It was like judo, she thought fuzzily, as the crop bit into her flanks. Roll with it, and it's not so bad. And with that insight it really wasn't so bad. It still hurt abominably, but now her mind was in the right place she could bear it, she could let the pain be less of an enemy and – to her astonishment – almost a friend. Now, the burning in her dreadfully thrashed cheeks took on an almost a spicy quality. Like eating a hot meal, she thought, almost dreamily, and with the thought she found herself pushing out those same searing cheeks to meet the whip's last two blows as if they were old friends.

Another stroke across the top of her thighs. Now she was beyond being conquered; the sear of the whip had a rich darkness. It was beginning to light a fire of another sort altogether; one that smouldered between her legs. Another, she thought. I want another!

She wasn't disappointed. There was a longer pause, as if Carla was gathering her strength, and then the whip seethed in and landed right across the middle of her globes.

It landed like lightning.

This time Cynthia didn't resist the low greedy 'aaaahhhh!' that escaped her. Even to her own ears it was much more a cry of passion than of pain. Almost a cry of triumph, she thought, through the sensual pink mist that was somehow filling her head.

Her whipping seemed to be over. She stood up carefully, still a little cautious of the pain from her scalded bottom as she flexed it. Then she turned to Carla.

'Thank you,' she said, pleased to hear her own voice sounding low and steady. 'Shall I go on with the cleaning now?'

Carla gave her a poisonous look. Cynthia resisted a smirk; the other girl was obviously furious at the result of her punishment, and just as obviously helpless to do anything about it. There was a humming silence that grew longer and longer, until eventually Carla thrust out her jaw.

'Yes,' she said, and the words were almost spat out, 'get on with it. But watch your step.' She leaned in close, so that Cynthia could catch the faint scent of her breath. 'You haven't been here long. They've got punishments you haven't even heard of, here.' She stood back, and her mouth twisted slowly into a faint, nasty smile.

'I can't wait,' she added. Then she turned her back and stalked off.

Cynthia watched her for a moment. A touch of worry began to dilute her pleasure; Carla might have been bluffing, but there was no way of knowing. She bit her lip thoughtfully, and then shrugged. Whatever; it was out of her hands. If something was going to happen, it was going to happen, and worrying wouldn't help. It was, she realised, the philosophy of a slave, and the thought pleased her. She picked up her cloth, and knelt down next to Francine to begin the task of cleaning the big vat for the second time.

Before long it became obvious that something was indeed going to happen, but not to her. The two girls had hardly been working for ten minutes when they heard a yell of anger from Carla, and the greedy hiss of the crop, quickly followed by an anguished squeal. Cynthia and Francine exchanged glances, and cautiously raised their heads over the edge of the press.

Amelie was lying on the floor. Carla was standing over her, the crop raised over her head. As they watched, she brought it whipping down with all her strength, laying a viscous cut across Amelie's full behind, where a livid red weal was quickly joined by a second.

Amelie squealed again, but Carla ignored her.

'Stupid girl,' she snapped, bringing the crop down again. Amelie twisted desperately but couldn't avoid the blow, which landed across the tops of her thighs, making her let out another yelp of pain. Another scarlet line swelled across her flesh.

As Cynthia watched, she realised quickly that Amelie had quite a different relationship with the whip from her own. The girl's face was contorted with distress; there was no hint of pleasure, no sign of willing supplication. Poor cow, thought Cynthia. Someone should do something.

Without thinking, she began to rise to her feet. Something stopped her; she looked to her side and realise that Francine's hand was pressing down on her shoulder.

'What are you doing?' the girl hissed. 'No one helped you out; don't put your hide on the line for her!'

Cynthia reached up and moved the hand. 'It's not the same,' she whispered. 'Look at her! We can't leave her like that!'

Both girls looked at Amelie, just as the vicious whip scythed down yet again. Francine winced as Amelie gave another agonised shriek.

'Alright, she hates it,' she agreed. 'But she chose it! No one made her stay here.'

Cynthia shook her head. 'Sorry,' she said. 'I'm going to do it anyway!' She made to stand up, but froze halfway through the action as the pressroom door swung open.

It was Pera. He took one look at the tableau of Carla, who was still standing over the sprawling, sniffling Amelie with the crop raised vengefully above her head. Then he shook his head.

'Stop,' he said. 'Stop now.'

Carla lowered the crop, and Amelie wriggled quickly away from her and stood up, the marks of the whip glowing across her hips.

Pera looked at them, and then around at the other girls.

'Who authorised this?' He looked again. 'Where is Ariane?'

Carla spoke up quickly. 'It was Ariane. She said I could! She put me in charge while she was away.'

'Ah.' Pera smiled, but it was not a cheerful smile. 'You are not in charge any more. All of you,' and he turned to the others, 'get on with your work, and do nothing but work until I get back. None of you has any right to punish anyone.' He lowered his voice. 'Believe me, there'll be plenty of punishment to go round, if I think it's needed.' He looked round the watching girls as if to make sure his message had been heard, then turned and walked out.

Cynthia and Francine exchanged glances. Simultaneously, they said to each other: 'Ariane's for it!' Then, without another word, they lowered their heads and started scrubbing.

CHAPTER 10

After a short search Pera found Ariane in a room off the main courtyard, by the simple technique of following the sound of the paddle - Ariane was the only one of all of the staff at Mas Gassac who favoured that tool over all others. He opened the door and was almost knocked over by a girl with a tear-streaked face and, when he turned to see her, an impressively purple rump. He watched the furnace-hot globes wiggling until the girl had trotted out of sight, then shoved abruptly through the door.

Ariane was standing alone in the small room. The paddle was still in her hand, and she looked flushed. She jumped when she saw Pera, but quickly recovered herself.

'Good morning,' she said. Then she looked at him more closely, and he saw her face cloud with worry. 'What's the matter?'

'You've made a mistake,' he said. 'I found Carla thrashing one of the other girls in the press room. She says it was with your permission.'

The worry in her face turned to fear. 'I couldn't stay there,' she said, her voice rising slightly. 'I had to put someone in charge!'

Pera watched her tongue flick nervously over her lips. She was a fine-looking woman; he was going to enjoy himself. Keeping his voice calm, he said: 'You exceeded your authority. I can't ignore this.'

Now she looked terrified. 'Please,' she said, her voice shaking, 'don't tell José!'

'Ah.' Pera stroked his chin. 'Of course, if I tell José he will punish you in the courtyard in front of everyone, won't he? And all the slaves will see.'

She nodded miserably.

'But you do need to be punished, don't you?'

She nodded again.

'Well, I don't know.' He paused, and then, as if he had only just thought of it, said: 'Perhaps it would be better if I punished you myself, in private. That way you wouldn't lose face.' He let his voice harden. 'That way you would keep your authority, and your chance to redden those bottoms you like so much!'

She nodded again, her face a picture of defeat.

'Alright,' he said. 'I'll save your face. But your behind, and perhaps some other parts of you, are going to pay dearly for it, today and on other days too. Understand?'

She gulped visibly. 'Yes,' she said in a whisper. 'I understand. Thank you.'

Pera grinned. 'Don't thank me until you know what you're getting,' he told her. 'Now, strip.'

Ariane reached down, grasped the hem of her dress, and lifted it up and over her head. Beneath the dress she was naked, as Pera had hoped and suspected, and he felt himself harden at the sight of her. Her tall figure was smooth and trim, with the slight indents of her muscles highlighted against her olive skin by the glancing light from the single window. The dark rope of her plaited hair fell almost to the small of her back, and the colour was repeated in the dense, dark nest of hair at the top of her thighs.

Pera allowed his gaze to linger for a long time, until Ariane was beginning to shift fretfully. Then he held out his hand.

'Give me the paddle,' he said. She hesitated for a fraction of a second, and then turned to pick up the paddle from where she had let it fall. The action of bending, even from the knee, tightened and opened the superb buttocks, and gave Pera a fleeting, winking view of the sex that lay hidden between them. Then the show was over; she straightened and handed him the paddle. He hefted it.

'It's heavy,' he said. 'Well made, too.' Then he turned it over in his hand. 'It seems old. Do I guess right that this is a family heirloom?'

She nodded silently.

'Well, well.' Pera looked into Ariane's face. 'And would I be right to guess that Ariane was once very, very familiar with this paddle?'

'Yes,' she said quietly. 'Yes, I was.'

'Ah.' Pera hesitated for a second, then followed his instinct. 'Have you missed it, Ariane?'

She looked down quickly, but not before he had seen the answer in her eyes. He tapped the paddle against his palm.

'Then bend over,' he said. 'And welcome home.'

She turned, and bent herself over the back of the nearest chair, grasping the seat with her hands. The movement completed the revelation she had begun when she picked up the paddle; her globes parted, leaving her sex slightly open. It was like an offering, with the added spice of the puckered prize above it.

Pera felt himself swelling and throbbing at the sight. He took a firm grip on the paddle, and swept it quickly down on to the centre of the delightful target she had offered. It landed, wringing a wail from Ariane.

Pera watched, entranced. It was like some kind of time machine, he thought; with one stroke, the splendid woman in her thirties had somehow regressed by twenty years to become a teenager. She pouted with pain, and those sinuous buttocks snaked from side to side as she shuffled her feet.

Pera lifted the paddle and struck again with another percussive crack, landing the blow across the top of the tightened thighs. He was rewarded with another husky wail of pain, and a fresh burst of wriggling. He waited until she was still before swinging the paddle down again, this time landing exactly on the sweet spot that lay half on her lower bottom and half on the soft flesh at the tops of her thighs. She gave an 'ooof' of surprise followed by a long whimpering moan, and he knew he had found the key to her. He began to spank her regularly, rhythmically, spacing the strokes so that she had time to experience the swelling burn of each one to the full, but not enough time to recover.

She squealed and writhed as he pounded her bottom, and as her skin darkened to a botched purple centre within a halo of flaming scarlet she began to kick her legs out in time with the paddle. Pera sensed that the natural end of her punishment was getting near – he could have kept going all night but already his victim would be unable to sit for some while. If he took her out of action altogether then José would have something to say about it.

He paused, and waited until the kicking wench had subsided a little. Then he said: 'We are nearly finished with your spanking, and I think it has done you good. No?'

Her voice was quiet. 'Yes, Pa.. Pera.'

Papa, thought Pera. That's what she almost called me. Well, I'll come back to that later.

'Good,' he said, out loud. 'And you have taken it like a good girl, too. Just a little more to go, and then it will be over. Just another six.' He tapped the paddle against the flaming skin, and then said, as if it was an afterthought: 'Of course, they will be extra hard.'

The bent woman gave a moan, and he saw her fingers tighten on the rails of the chair. He tapped another couple of times, enjoying the sight of the scalded curves twitching nervously, and then whipped the paddle down on to her beautiful, tightened lower bottom.

It whistled through the air and landed with an echoing crack. Ariane gave a wordless squeal, and immediately began to sob with pain, pausing only to draw fresh breath as Pera followed the blow with another three. The helpless woman was wailing continuously now, tears running freely down her contorted face as the paddle exploded against her behind. She kicked and writhed, shamelessly exposing herself to Pera's eyes, and obviously in so much distress that Pera almost stopped. But a promise was a promise, he reminded himself. And even if his guess was right, and his victim had for the moment the emotions of a much younger girl, she still had the strong body of a fully-grown woman in her thirties – one whose female scent was rising to Pera's nose on a waft of body heat – and she could take another two strokes. He raised the paddle and cracked it down, twice, as hard as he could.

The job was done. Ariane lay draped over the chair, snivelling with pain. Her bottom, from the top few inches of her thighs to the top of the cleft, was spanked to purple, with the exception of an inch above and below the crease, where the greyish patches of two angry blisters showed.

Pera put down the paddle. 'There,' he said. 'Spanking over. You'll be a good girl now, won't you?'

She nodded, and then her eyes opened wide as Pera slipped his hand down her cleft, brushing the hot skin until his fingers found the wet lips at the heart of her.

'I think Ariane has a secret,' he said softly. 'I think that Ariane was often spanked by her Papa. Am I right?'

She nodded mutely, her eyes half-closed as he probed at her sex.

'How old were you when he last spanked you?'

'Nineteen.'

'And since then?'

She shook her head.

'Nothing at all? Even since you have been here?'

She shook her head again, then corrected herself. 'The whip, sometimes, from Le Mestré. But it's not the same.'

Pera grinned to himself. He knew how José favoured the chicote, and for sure he would have wanted to wrap it round those cheeks.

'Well,' he said. 'Papa is back, now, and he has his paddle, and his girl will feel it as often as she needs to.' He left his finger probe deeper into the velvet moisture of her cleft, and added a second, and then a third. 'But now, perhaps there is something else that Papa will have from his girl.'

She gave a soft whimper of pleasure and pushed her body back against his hand as he worked at her. He mauled her flesh roughly so that she grunted and moaned, and the feel of her clenching round his fingers, the sight of her arching her strong back and thrusting her taut bottom on to him, and the sweetly rank, musky smell of her, sent him wild. Without withdrawing, he used his other hand to release his shaft, so that it stood out as high and hard as a hammer. 'Now, girl,' he said, and in the same instant he whipped his hand out of her, and drove his cock full length into her. She gasped, and gave a low urgent 'aaaaahhhh!' as he slammed into her, his force enough to lift the legs of the chair from the floor.

She was so hot and tight! With few exceptions, Pera had his pick of the slave girls, and he had taken advantage of it often, but it was years since he had felt such a tunnel around him. Or perhaps it was years since he had been so urgent? The blood roared in his ears, and he drew back and thrust himself home again and again, rutting into her like a dog at a bitch. The heat from her blistered cheeks warmed his thighs, and she gave little squeals of pain as he forced himself deliberately against them, emphasising her punishment. He grasped her cheeks and forced them further apart as he speared her, stretching the tender skin between them and drawing the puckered bud of her anus out into a tiny, lewd caricature of a smile.

It was too much to resist. Pera withdrew himself abruptly from the woman's cunt. His shaft glistened with a slick mixture of her juices and his pre-come; enough lubrication for what he had in mind. He rested the head of his cock against the tight little prize, and pushed.

For a moment it seemed as if she would not let him in. Then, gradually, the muscles of her ring began to expand. She mewled and panted as he slipped into her a centimetre at a time, until she had stretched to accommodate the whole width of his glans. Then, suddenly, her resistance seemed to evaporate. She opened fully, and he almost fell into her until the tip of his cock was pushing against the muscles at the top of her tunnel. She yelped with the speed of his entry, but at the same time he felt her pushing back against him as if to extract every millimetre of penetration.

There was nothing like the heat and grip of a woman's arse, thought Pera light-headedly. He pulled back until half his length was free, and then began to thrust in and out of the delicious embrace. Ariane moaned with every movement, and Pera found himself echoing her as he grunted with effort and pleasure. He had been close to the end when he swapped holes. Now he felt his passion begin to build again. He moved faster and faster, taking her savagely so that she squealed with the force of him, until finally his orgasm came and dug its spurs into his guts, and he thrust himself to his full length and spent himself into her belly with a hoarse cry.

Finally, his spasms ceased, and he withdrew his softening cock. Ariane stayed where she was, draped over the chair with her breath heaving. Pera watched her for a moment, then slapped her flaming behind, making her squeak with surprise.

'Well,' he said, 'I'll bet I'm one ahead of Papa.' He paused, struck by a dreadful thought, and added: 'At least, I hope I am.'

She raised her head and smiled. 'Yes,' she said. 'You are.'

Pera laid a hand on her shoulder. 'Well,' he said. 'From now on, Papa is my job, and there'll be plenty of that and more besides. Understand?'

She lowered her head so that he could not see her face, but there was a smile in her voice. 'Yes, Papa Pera,' she said. 'Thank you.'

He slapped her bottom again. 'Right,' he said. 'Time to get dressed. You're needed in the press room.' He laid the paddle down in front of her. 'This is mine, now,' he said, 'so that Papa can blister your bottom any time he likes, but you can look after it for the moment. Who knows what those girls have been getting up to while you've been busy?'

She took the paddle and picked up her dress. As she began to pull it over her head, but he stopped her. 'One more thing,' he said. 'Young Cynthia seems to have a strong taste for the lash, doesn't she?'

Ariane nodded.

'Well then, if she needs punishment you'd better think of something else.'

She pulled the dress down and smoothed it out. 'Oh, I will,' she said.

CHAPTER 11

What those girls had been getting up to, as far as Cynthia was concerned, was work. She and Francine had scrubbed, and washed, and scoured their way round the inside of the big vat until the old, worn wooden staves it was made from were pale with cleanliness. Cynthia's back ached, but that was only fair because so did her knees. And her elbows. And her shoulders. In fact her whole body ached, so much so that she had almost forgotten about the smarting from her bottom, even blistered as it had been by Ariane's paddle and then striped by Carla's crop. She was still scrubbing, head down, when there was a creak of hinges and she looked up to see Ariane silhouetted in the doorway. Next to Cynthia, Francine mouthed 'Uh-oh!'

Ariane stood still for a moment, as if she was taking stock. Then she strode into the room, kicking the door shut behind her.

'Right,' she called out. 'Stop work and stand still!'

There was a clanking of buckets as the girls did as they had been told. Ariane walked – no, thought Cynthia, she prowled – around the room. She came to the vats first.

'What have you been doing?' she asked abruptly. Cynthia and Francine exchanged glances.

Cynthia took a nervous breath and said: 'Scrubbing the vats. See?' She gestured towards the clean timber, and Ariane nodded slowly.

'Good,' she said. Then, to Cynthia's astonishment, she moved on. Cynthia looked at Francine, who shrugged. They watched, increasingly mystified, as the tour of inspection continued, with everyone being given the same short glance and nod of satisfaction, until Ariane got to Carla. She looked the girl up and down for a long time, while Carla grew visibly more and more uncomfortable.

Then she said: 'And what have you been doing, Carla, apart from needlessly thrashing your fellow slaves?'

Carla's face was a study in confusion. 'But, but,' she stuttered, 'you said I should, you told me to!'

'I told you to thrash them if they fell behind!' Ariane's voice was a whiplash. 'I didn't tell you to slow down the work by whipping them whenever you felt like it!'

Carla stood with her mouth hanging open. Cynthia, who had been watching the drama, suddenly understood. She nudged Francine and whispered: 'Payback time!'

Ariane was looking at Carla. She was tapping the big paddle repeatedly against the palm of her hand, while the helpless girl wriggled under her gaze. Then she turned to the watching slaves.

'She'll need holding, with what I intend to give her,' she said. 'You two,' and she gestured at Cynthia and Amelie, 'come here.' They obeyed, and she looked down at their striped haunches. 'She whipped the pair of you. Was it fair?'

Amelie shook her head quickly. Cynthia looked at her feet. She had never liked getting people into trouble and – a little voice inside whispered – it hadn't been all bad. But then, it hadn't been fair, either. She looked up and met Ariane's eyes. 'No,' she said. 'It wasn't fair.'

Was there a flash of humour in the cold eyes? She wasn't sure, and there was no time to check because the tall woman turned away quickly.

'Right,' she said, 'come with me, and bring her. The rest of you, wait.' 'Her' was Carla, and it was an order.

Cynthia and Amelie took an arm each and drew the girl, stumbling and shuffling, after Ariane.

She led them out of the press room, across the yard and through a door into a room Cynthia hadn't seen before. It was lit by tall windows, and it was empty apart from a sort of stand in the middle. It was a strange sort of thing, just a single dark coloured wooden bar on two legs. The bar was triangular, with a point facing upwards. At the sight of it Carla gasped and began to struggle; Cynthia and Amelie tightened their grips.

Ariane walked over to the stand, turned round, and smiled at the three girls.

'Carla knows what this is,' she said, 'but Cynthia, at least, doesn't. Do you?'

Cynthia shook her head.

'I'll explain.' Ariane laid a hand to the top of the thing so that her fingers curled over the pointed top. 'This is called a Pony,' she said. 'Some people call it a Spanish Pony and some people call it a Punishment Pony, but here we just call it a Pony.' She smiled. 'This one is used to punish females, although we have a similar one that has been modified to use on males. It's very simple to use. Cynthia, I'd like you to see this closely. Let go of Carla and come over here.'

Cynthia walked up to Ariane and waited, her heart fluttering. She was beginning to guess just how simple the thing might be to use.

Ariane took her hand and laid it on top of the bar. It wasn't quite pointed, she saw; the very top had been smoothed over. It felt cold and hard, and the wood in the middle looked a bit darker than the rest, as if it had been stained with something. She swallowed, and took her hand off it.

Ariane smiled again. 'I think you have worked it out,' she said. 'The female who is to be punished is placed so that she straddles the bar. Usually her arms are tied behind her back, or above her head, and her legs are fixed to the frame of the Pony. Then, we simply raise the bar using these screws.' She pointed down. 'And it is raised, and raised, until as much of the rider's weight as we desire is supported by the bar.' Now she was not smiling. 'The bar divides the rider's lips and presses on her most sensitive flesh. Even a few seconds is very painful, and if the bar is raised to take the rider's full weight, it is terrible.' She clapped her hands, making Cynthia jump. 'Let me show you,' she said. 'Bring Carla!'

'No!' Carla hauled desperately at the arm Amelie was holding. She managed to pull it free and ran to the door. Her hands scrabbled over it, but it didn't open. For a moment Cynthia couldn't see why – she didn't remember Ariane locking it. Then she understood.

There was no handle on the inside of the door.

Cynthia turned back towards Ariane. The tall woman was holding out something that looked like a car key fob.

'I'll open the door when I'm ready,' she said. 'She can't escape. Now bring her here, unless you want to join her on the Pony!'

Cynthia and Amelie exchanged a quick glance, and then grabbed an arm each. For a second, Cynthia found herself looking into a pair of pleading eyes. She had time to mouth I'm sorry, and then they were hauling the trembling girl over to the Pony. Guided by Ariane they positioned her at one end of the bar and then led her forwards so that she straddled it. They held her while Ariane cuffed her hands behind her back.

'She won't need her legs fixing,' she said. 'Once the bar has been fully raised, she'll cut herself in two if she tries to move.' As she spoke, she bent down and began to turn a handle.

The bar rose slowly. Carla snivelled with fear as it crept up her thighs and nestled into the soft folds of her sex. As it rose higher and higher, she rose with it, until she was standing on tiptoe. The sinews in her calves and thighs stood out as she strained to hold her position.

Ariane stopped turning the handle. 'A strong subject,' she said, 'can hold this sort of position for a long time. It's very good training. It encourages an upright posture.' She looked contemptuously at Carla, who was already sweating and trembling with effort. 'It looks as if Carla would benefit from more training. However, today she's here to be punished.' And she leaned down and began to turn the handle again.

Cynthia watched in horror as the top of the bar began to bite deeper into Carla's helpless flesh. The poor girl could stretch no higher; as the bar forced its way into her she screwed up her eyes and gave a long, miserable wail, on a note that rose as the bar did. Cynthia squirmed as she watched the girl's growing torment; would Ariane never stop?

Eventually, she did. She straightened up, and looked closely at Carla, who was sobbing and keening, her face a tear-streaked mask of pain.

'Good,' she said. 'She has ten minutes to go. Watch closely, you two! Punishment here isn't always the romance of the whip, or the half-pleasure of surrender to a strong man's desires. Especially,' and she looked at Cynthia, 'especially if it seems that you have more of a romance with the whip than most. Do you understand?'

Cynthia and Amelie nodded. Cynthia didn't dare do anything else. She had no doubt that Ariane would find an excuse to put her on that thing sooner or later.

Ariane held her gaze for what seemed ages. Then she looked back at Carla, who was moaning and whimpering with pain.

'So,' she said. 'It hurts, yes?'

'Yeeeesss!' The word was hissed through clenched teeth.

'I'm sure. Well, you have,' and she checked her watch, 'another eight minutes. Of course, you could shorten that. Would you like to?'

'Yes!' The word came almost before Ariane had finished speaking. 'Ahhh! Oh yes please!'

'I thought so. It's easy.' Ariane lifted the paddle so it was in Carla's line of sight. 'This is the alternative. I'll let you off, but for every minute you would have spent on the Pony, you'll spend a minute being thrashed by these two.' She waved the paddle towards Cynthia and Amelie. 'Take your time. Seven and a half minutes to go.'

Cynthia shivered. It was a wicked choice. Several minutes of spanking with that dreadful paddle would leave blisters that would last for days! The flash of guilt she had felt earlier returned, stronger than ever. It was spiced with apprehension. She had never beaten anyone. She had little idea how you did it, and no idea at all if she would even be able to carry it through. She sneaked a sideways glance at Amelie, and sighed. The other girl's face was flushed and eager. She at least would have no trouble.

'Six minutes!' Cynthia snapped back to reality at the sound of Ariane's voice. She looked up at Carla, who was shaking with pain, her legs repeatedly tensing as she tried desperately to raise herself off the bar that agonised her girlhood.

'Five and a half minutes!'

Now Cynthia could hardly bear to watch. Carla's white face was set in a rictus of agony. The muscles in her thighs were slack, now; she had obviously given up the struggle to save the meat between her legs from the slow, tenderizing brutality of the bar.

'Five minutes!'

'Aaahhhh!' The cry burst from Carla's lips. 'Enough! Please! Let me off! Do anything you want, just let me off!' The words flooded out as if the last dam of the poor girl's resistance had burst all at once. For a second Cynthia wondered if Ariane, in her cruelty, would spin out the moment of release, but this time at least she was wrong; the tall woman stepped quickly up to the pony and unwound the screws. As the bar dropped, Carla tipped her head back and gave a single long 'ooohhhh' of relief. Ariane took hold of her shoulder, almost tenderly, and helped her shuffle backwards off the bar, and as she moved Cynthia could see that her sex was red and puffy, and the top of the bar was dark with moisture.

When Carla was fully off the pony, Ariane turned her round and pushed her forwards so that she was bent over it, tightening and opening her bottom and making the engorged state of her cunt even more obvious. Cynthia, watching, began to feel confused. Mainly, of course, she was sorry for the girl – it had obviously been a very painful experience – but there was something else, now. The sight of the dark, swollen, glistening lips was causing an echo between her own legs, and to her surprise it was being compounded by something else. Carla's body was giving off a sweaty, spicy, slightly sour scent, one Cynthia recognized from her knowledge of her own body but had never encountered from another's. It was interesting. No, she admitted to herself, it was more than that. It was exciting. And she wanted more of it.

As she watched through a pink haze of arousal, Ariane tied Carla's wrists and ankles together, fixing her tightly over the bar. Then she stepped back.

'Right,' she said. 'Five minutes with the paddle.' She strode up to the watching girls, hesitated, and then thrust the paddle into Amelie's hand. 'You start,' she said. 'Take one stroke each, in turn.'

Amelie nodded, and walked up to the helpless Carla. She tapped the paddle a couple of times against the girl's buttocks as if taking aim, and had drawn the paddle back for her first blow when Ariane interrupted. 'Just a minute,' she said. 'I've had an idea to make it more interesting. We'll make it a competition!' She leaned down and spoke to Carla. 'Before each stroke, I'll say the name of the girl holding the paddle. When the five minutes are up, you tell me which one hit the hardest.' She straightened up and looked at Cynthia and Amelie. 'The other girl will spend five minutes on the pony. Amelie – begin.'

CHAPTER 12

Cynthia's heart pounded, while Ariane's words echoed in her ears. Five minutes! But how could she avoid it? Amelie was bound to hit harder than her!

Amelie obviously thought so too, if her confident expression was any indicator. She positioned herself for the first swing, and sure enough it was delivered with the full length of her arm, swishing in to land with an explosive crack across the top of Carla's thighs.

'Aaaaahh!'

As Carla wriggled frantically, an area exactly the shape of the paddle flashed white and immediately began to darken to an angry red. Amelie smirked, and handed the paddle to Cynthia with a dismissive shrug.

Cynthia hefted it. It was astonishingly heavy, but somehow it felt better in her hand that she had expected.

Ariane gave her little time to prepare. 'Cynthia!'

Well, this was it. Cynthia took a deep breath, and let fly.

Her aim had been good; there was a squeal, a new patch of skin was blushing scarlet, half-way up the curved mounds, and Carla was shuffling and wriggling as much as her position would allow. Perhaps this was not the foregone conclusion Cynthia had feared. She handed the paddle back to Amelie, who seemed not to be smirking any more, but rather looking determined. She took the paddle, compressed her lips as if to say, if you want a battle, you've got one. Then, even as Ariane spoke her name, she drew back her arm like a woodcutter, and sent her next stroke swooping in.

The force of the stroke pushed Carla up against the bar, and sent a ripple through the soft flesh of her bottom. Her eyes opened wide and she gave a single outraged shriek.

Amelie stood looking at Carla with her back to Cynthia for a few seconds, as if she was admiring her handiwork. Even Cynthia had to admit there was plenty to admire; the latest stroke had landed on the poor girl's upper bottom, which was quickly darkening to a deep, angry red.

The war was on.

'Cynthia!'

'Amelie!'

'Cynthia!'

Time after time, the heavy paddle swept in and scorched the unfortunate Carla's behind. Her skin became blotched, red and purple, and the sinister greyish-white that was the forerunner of some nasty blisters appeared on the curve of flesh just above the topes of her thighs, where both Amelie and Cynthia had concentrated their fire-power. The punished girl howled, and squealed, and moaned, and the scent from her body seemed to grow stronger as her ordeal went on, making Cynthia more and more aroused. She had forgotten her earlier inhibitions. Now all she wanted to do was paddle those delicious globes and drink in the scent from the ever-wetter flesh between them.

She lost track of time; all she knew was the feel of the paddle in her hand, and the impact against Carla's flaming skin, and the poor girl's cries of pain. So this is what it's like, she thought, thrashing someone.

'Stop!' Ariane's voice brought her back to reality. She realized that she was holding the paddle; presumably she had just hit Carla with it, but she could hardly remember.

Ariane stepped forward and took the paddle from her. 'All finished,' she said simply. 'Take a look at your handiwork.'

Cynthia turned to Carla, who was hanging limply over the bar, sobbing quietly. Her bottom was a war zone – a cluster of sullen off-white blisters just above the tops of her thighs, set against a blotched background of blue, purple and scarlet, framing an engorged cunt that looked as if it, too, had suffered some collateral strikes. The sight made Cynthia's heart race. Looking to her side, she saw Amelie gazing at the scalded flesh, her eyes glazed and her cheeks flushed. She looks like I feel, thought Cynthia.

Ariane walked up to the trembling Carla and stroked her hair. 'Time to get up,' she said softly. 'It's finished.' Her voice hardened a little. 'Now you get your chance to put one of them where you were.'

Carla stood up slowly. She winced as the movement flexed her thrashed hind-quarters, so that Cynthia winced a little in sympathy. Not just in sympathy, though. It was crunch time. For all her enthusiasm, she knew she hadn't hit as hard as Amelie.

Ariane was still speaking. 'Tell me,' she said. 'Which one of these two was the weakest?'

Cynthia gritted her teeth. This was it. She was going to end up on that horrible pony. She shut her eyes.

'Amelie.' It was Carla's voice.

Cynthia opened her eyes in astonishment. Had she heard right?

From the look of them, both Amelie and Ariane felt the same way. Ariane's expression was almost comical. 'Amelie? Are you sure?'

Carla nodded slowly. 'Yes,' she said. 'I'm sure.' She pointed at Amelie, who shrank away from her outstretched finger as if it was a flamethrower. 'She didn't hit as hard as the other.'

'It's true!' The voice came from behind Cynthia. She, and the others, spun round as one.

Pera stood in the doorway. He smiled. 'I've been watching,' he said. 'What Carla says is true. Cynthia put more into it than Amelie.' He gestured to Ariane. 'Put Amelie on the pony.'

His tone was relaxed, but there was no doubt it had been an order. Ariane's face froze, but she reached out and took hold of Amelie.

'Come on,' she said. 'On the pony with you!' She pulled the stunned girl round to the end of the bar and roughly bound her hands behind her back. Then she shoved her forwards.

'Go on,' she said. 'You heard him!'

Amelie gave one last pleading glance over her shoulder, but Ariane gave her no comfort. She sagged in defeat, and then shuffled slowly forwards until the cruel bar lay between her thighs.

Ariane stepped back. She made a move towards the handle that would raise the car, and then stopped. Turning to Pera, she said: 'Would you like to begin her ordeal?'

He smiled. 'It's kind of you,' he said, 'but I think not.' He paused for a moment, and then said: 'Perhaps Cynthia would like to?'

Cynthia gasped with horror, but Pera only smiled more broadly. 'Yes,' he said, 'I think it would be a useful part of your education here. Go on,' and he nodded towards the pony. 'Lift her!'

Cynthia gave him a pleading glance, but he turned away. She had no choice. Slowly she walked up to the pony, stooped down, and began to turn the handle. It worked smoothly. The bar rose until it met the soft flesh between Amelie's legs. Then the effort needed to move it began to grow, while Amelie moaned as it ground into her parted lips. Cynthia shut her eyes and went on turning.

'Aaaaaahh!' Amelie gave a soft cry, so heartfelt that Cynthia almost stopped, but she was intensely aware of her audience, and of what might happen if she disobeyed. Instead, she pushed the handle round, feeling the resistance grow as more and more of Amelie's weight was taken by the cruel device, while Amelie moaned and hissed.

Eventually, Cynthia felt a tap on her shoulder. She turned to see Ariane who said, almost gently: 'That will do. She is up now.'

Relieved, Cynthia stood up and stepped back away from the pony and its suffering occupant. As she moved, she let her glance flick to Pera, who still stood by the doorway. For a second she let herself wonder why he had spared her the pony – because it was certainly because of him that she was not up there in Amelie's place, grinding herself to swollen agony. His face was impassive, though. She gave a mental shrug. Perhaps she'd find out one day. Meanwhile, she thought, I owe Amelie and Carla, big time. It wasn't a bad thought, in some ways.

Pera watched the tableau in front of him with pleasure. He always enjoyed watching a girl on the pony, and even though it was less than an hour since he had spent himself so forcefully into Ariane, the site of the sweating girl darkening the bar with juices from her tormented cunt was enough to harden him again. Even more exciting though, at least in some ways, was the interesting dynamic he suspected between the three girls. He prided himself a good judge of character and motive; now he watched the body language of Cynthia and Carla.

Carla was a study in resentment. She'd had the power of an overseer briefly conferred and then snatched away, and on top of that she had been roundly punished for something that was not really her fault. Pera smiled to himself at the thought of how he had manipulated Ariane there, and he had plenty of time for more of the same.

Then there was Cynthia. How to describe her? He remembered a phrase his father had used once – like a bundle of contradictions with a cunt in the middle. The old man had been generalising, but he would have recognized his description in the young English girl, with her superb bottom, her sensual thighs, her high firm breasts and her artless, paradoxical combination of strength and submissiveness.

Pera certainly had his reasons for having saved Cynthia from the pony. Putting her in both Amelie's and Carla's debt was part of it, to be sure, and he would steer that situation to the most interesting shore he could come up with. But he had a much more important reason.

Cynthia was all but untried. True, she was submissive, and also true, she seemed to be a genuine masochist, in that she had gained real sexual pleasure from punishment. So far she had survived her experiences, but Pera guessed that the delights of the pony would be a step too far for her, just now.

He checked his watch. 'One more minute,' he said. Amelie, who had managed to keep fairly quiet so far, gave a despairing whine and began to sob. Next to him, he sensed Cynthia fidgeting, but Carla's face was flushed and her eyes glazed. The sight swelled him further. Soon, he promised himself.

The second hand of his watch shuddered past the twelve, and he signalled Cynthia to lower the bar. As it withdrew from her engorged sex, Amelie let out a long low moan, and he could see that the top of it was dark and slick with moisture.

He gestured to Ariane and Cynthia, and they helped the punished girl to shuffle, bowlegged, off the pony. At first she seemed to sag, but then her legs straightened and she stood upright, her head lowered.

Pera stepped forwards and took hold of her chin, raising her head until he was looking into her face. 'It's over,' he said, 'at least for today. Go to bed. Ariane will escort you. Rest, and be ready for tomorrow.'

She nodded, docile, and allowed Ariane to take her by the shoulder and lead her away. As the door closed behind them, Pera turned to Carla and Cynthia.

'Now,' he said. 'Your day is not over. Carla, why did you lie?'

Carla gasped, but he ignored her. 'You did lie, didn't you?' he said. 'Cynthia wasn't hitting you as hard as Amelie. Ariane knew that, and so did I. So tell me again: Why did you lie?'

Carla bit her lip, and then looked up at him. 'I thought she deserved a chance, because she's new,' she said, with a hint of defiance.

'Ah.' Pera steepled his hands. 'Well, perhaps you were right.' He turned to Cynthia, who was looking satisfyingly terrified. 'What about you?' he asked. 'Do you think you deserve a chance?'

There was a long, aching silence. Then Cynthia lowered her head and said, softly, 'No.'

'No?' Pera feigned surprise.

'No.' She looked up at him. 'It was kind of Carla,' and she glanced for a moment at the other girl, 'but I came here for José. I don't need any chances.'

Pera nodded. 'I expected nothing less,' he said. 'English fair play! Very good. Well, you'll have another chance, in a little while. For the moment, I want you kneeling.'

She blinked with surprise, and then dropped quickly to her knees.

'Good.' Pera turned to Carla. 'Now, girl who gives chances even if they are not hers to give! You will bend over the bar with your legs apart.'

Carla, too, blinked with surprise, but then obeyed, bending herself over the bar until she was holding her ankles, and shuffling her feet apart until her cheeks were widely parted. In a small voice she said: 'Are you going to punish me?'

'Yes I am, in a way.' Pera grinned. 'In fact, in the oldest way of all.' And he reached down, unhooked a button, and let his cock spring out so that it stood before him, twitching in time with his pulse.

Dieu, he was aching for it! The girl was spread perfectly, the lips of her flesh still red, engorged and wet from their bruising on the pony. He reached out, ran his hand down the cleft between her cheeks, and thrust three fingers roughly into the tender meat of her. She moaned, and he felt her body shuddering under his assault, but he persisted, taking her harshly with his hand until he was soaked with her juice. Then he withdrew his fingers, and reached round to hold them in front of her face.

'See what a little rough treatment does to you?' he said. 'Your cunt is like a river. Drink, girl!' And in the same moment, he shoved his fingers into her mouth, and thrust his rigid shaft into her inflamed passage.

She clamped her lips round his fingers as if she was trying to gag herself, while her body snaked and writhed under the assault of his manhood. He loved the sensation of fucking a girl when she was fresh from the pony; all the usual tiny tremors and twitches of an impaled female were multiplied manifold, and the heat and tightness of the swollen flesh were delicious. And the squeals, of course. Carla had certainly warmed up nicely, either as a result of her mistreatment or from watching Amelie suffering the same way. She shuddered and bucked as he took her, grunting and yelping in time with his thrusts, and hissing as he buried himself to the base of his shaft and forced his thighs against her blistered behind.

He ploughed the mewling, panting girl until he felt himself swelling towards his climax. Then, deliberately, he paused at the beginning of a stroke, the head of his shaft just inside her. She growled with frustration and tried to push herself back onto him, but he placed his hands on her bottom – still so hot! – and pushed her away. 'I think,' he said slowly, 'I will finish elsewhere.' She gave a disappointed moan but he ignored her, withdrawing himself fully. He let the tip of his cock trail slowly up her cleft until it rested against the tiny knot of her anus. Then, before she had time to prepare herself, he thrust forwards, forcing her open and sinking himself fully into her tight musky tube in a single motion that shoved her against the bar and wrung a shrill cry from her.

She was so tight it was almost painful! His cock was still sensitised from his earlier use of Ariane, and the strong embrace of her arse was almost too much; he paused at full depth, rocking almost imperceptibly in and out of her until his arousal built to the point where it over-rode his discomfort and he pulled himself almost all the way out and then rammed forward. The speed of his penetration drew a squeal from Carla, and he grinned savagely and did it again.

'Oh...oh...oh...' Each stroke forced another panting gasp from the buggered girl, but all the same he noticed her pushing her hips back to match his movements.

'Does it hurt?' he asked.

'Ye... yes, it hurts!' Her reply was hissed through gritted teeth.

'And?'

'Please... oh... please don't stop... please bugger me hard... oh...'

Her plea was enough to send him mad. He dug his fingers into her flanks and thrust as hard as he could, his breath rasping and his vision clouded as if he was a Viking seized by the invincible rage of the berserk. His thighs smacked into her bottom with the force of his conquest of her, his cock ached and raged and his senses were flayed by the sour smell of her sodomised body as it rose in a heavy cloud round him. As he reached his peak he heard himself growl, and then give a long hoarse moan. The effort of his orgasm, his second in two hours, was tremendous – it felt like being turned inside out, and for a while he lost track of everything.

Eventually he came to himself, and withdrew his softening cock. Carla lay limply over the bar, her body damp with sweat. He turned to Cynthia. Her face was flushed, and her nipples looked hard. Certainly aroused, but how much? How far could he push her?

He shook his head in amusement at his own indecision. Teach her some manners, José had said. Very well; she would be taught. He gestured briskly at Carla's body, still bent over the bar. The gash between her cheeks was wet with her juices, and her sweat, and a trickle of his semen. 'Clean her,' he said.

She turned a shocked face towards him.

'Don't you understand?' he demanded. 'Clean her! Use the tongue you came in with and clean her!'

For a fraction of a second she hesitated, so that he wondered if he had pushed her too far, aroused or not. Then she seemed to steel herself. She went down on her knees behind Carla, shut her eyes and pushed her face into the girl's soaking cleft.

Pera watched, holding his breath. It was a turning point in the girl's training, whether she knew it or not. Which way would she turn?

He watched as she extended her tongue nervously, and allowed it to touch the moist flesh in front of her. It flicked back into her mouth, and for a moment she looked thoughtful and so artless that she reminded Pera almost comically of a kitten trying to work out if it likes a new brand of food. Then she opened her mouth and licked again, and again, beginning with the engorged lips of the open cunt and working steadily, almost greedily, upwards to the abused bud above them. As she did so her eyes, which had started out tightly closed, opened wide as if she was trying to take in the feast in front of her with all her senses.

At the first touch of Cynthia's tongue, Carla had blinked and given a single sharp 'oh!' of surprise. Now, as the kneeling girl worked at her more and more hungrily, she let out a long, breathy sigh of pleasure, and her hips wriggled lasciviously as if she was straining to open herself further to the soft, insistent little muscle that flicked and licked at her. She began to pant and moan, making an accompaniment to the greedy snuffling of the girl behind her.

Pera watched happily as Cynthia went about her task. His instinct had been right – the English girl was bisexual, and not just a little; the act of licking fresh man-juice out of a girl's arsehole needed more commitment than that. She's into men, he thought. She's into women. She comes when you beat her. She was getting the hang of giving a beating with the paddle. To think I was brought up to believe English girls were lousy in bed.

A series of little yipping cries brought him back to the present. Carla was coming. He watched as Cynthia slowed the movements of her tongue, and added another mental note to his list; amazingly, despite all her inexperience, she was guiding and channelling the girl's orgasm.

My God, he thought. What will it be like, the first time I enjoy you? One day, he knew, he would. But not yet. To begin with, she was José's.

CHAPTER 13

Cynthia allowed herself to be led back along the corridor to her room. She followed Pera in a daze. She would never have pretended to have any problem with women's bodies – why should she? She was female too. But the idea of the act she had just committed would not have entered even her wildest reverie. To lick, there... part of her still wanted to shudder. But then, unbidden, her tongue flicked over her lips. The taste was still fresh and clear, that mixture of sweetly salty manhood and something much more musky and primal.

Mmmmm.

She was led to a room. Not the one she had occupied the previous night, but a smaller room with just two beds. She looked at Pera in surprise. 'I thought,' she began, and then stopped, fearful that she would be punished. But Pera's face was mild and inquisitive, so she went on. 'I thought the press room girls always slept where I was last night,' she said.

'They do,' said Pera. 'But you are no longer a press room girl, and no longer an ingenue. The grapes are ready. The harvest begins tomorrow, and so tomorrow you will work in the fields.' He paused, and then added casually, as if it was of no consequence: 'So will Amelie. She will be along shortly. Sleep well!' And before Cynthia could say anything he had pushed her gently through the door of the dormitory and closed it behind her.

Cynthia sat down on the edge of the nearest bed and tried to think clearly. She had come to Mas Gassac knowing that it would involve submitting herself to José. Fine! That, she felt, was a piece of unfinished business; admittedly she had opened herself for him once, but to her mind that was a beginning, not an end.

But so much had happened since that beginning. The paddle and the crop and the effect they had on her. Were still having, in fact – she wriggled a little at the memory of that heat between her legs. The horror, spiced with intrigue, she had felt at the sight of girls on the pony. And then – she licked her lips – the biggest, the most unexpected discovery.

And Amelie would be along shortly. And she was in a room with only two beds. And she owed Amelie. Mmmm....

Pera walked up to the door of José Mestré's private apartment and knocked briefly, using the short staccato code the two men had agreed years before. There was a long pause. Then the electric catch buzzed. Pera pushed through the door.

José was standing next to the old desk, his back to the door. He held something long and pale and thin in his hand, and as Pera walked towards him he raised it above his head and brought it down sharply on something in front of him. There was a whistling crack, and a shrill squeal.

Pera moved to the side and looked round José. Then he smiled to himself. Princess lay on the desk, face down. Her wrists and ankles were fastened by ropes that ran down to the legs of the desk, and a cushion beneath her hips raised her bottom into a neat muscular arc. Her skin was a mass of weals, from the mid-point of her thigh to the top of her globes. He glanced at José.

'Pleasure, or punishment?' he asked.

José grinned. 'Can't it be both?' He gave the girl another lash, wringing another squeal from her. 'Anyway,' he said, 'there's a third way. I'm experimenting. See?' He held out what Pera had assumed was a whip.

Pera took it. 'I see,' he said. 'A cane. The English way, yes?'

José nodded. 'A surprise for little Cynthia. How is she coming along?'

'Very well.' Pera gestured towards a television that stood in a corner. 'If you'd like to take a look, she's in the second courtyard bedroom, and I think she is about to have some company.'

'Ah!' José walked over to Princess and carefully slotted the cane into the deep crack between her thrashed buttocks. 'Hold that for me,' he told her. Then he picked up a remote control and switched on the television. The big flat screen brightened immediately and he flicked through several channels until the image showed Cynthia.

José looked intently at the screen. 'Oh-ho,' he said. 'You were right, old man. How did you know?'

Cynthia was kneeling on the floor. In front of her, kneeling on the bed with her legs spread and her behind level with Cynthia's face, was Amelie. Amelie was talking, and José reached quickly for the remote and turned up the volume.

'…re you sure?'

There was a short sigh before Cynthia replied. 'Yes,' she said. 'I'm sure. It wasn't your fault you ended up on that pony thing instead of me. It's only fair I should, you know, kiss you better. Besides,' and she paused for a second, 'I want to.'

They heard Amelie laugh. 'Do you indeed? Turning you into a little dyke, are they?'

Cynthia didn't answer, but pushed her face into the other girl's cleft.

José turned to Pera. 'Well, well,' he said. 'It seems our little English rose is beginning to flower. Your doing, I suppose?'

'Perhaps.' Pera sketched out the events of the day, while José listened in silence. When Pera had finished, José said nothing for a while, so that that the only sound in the room was Amelie's quiet moans of pleasure as Cynthia lapped at her swollen sex.

Finally José turned to Pera. 'I thought I was getting a shy teenager with a wet cunt and a taste for the lash,' he said. 'But there seems to be a lot more to her than that.' He tapped his fingers, while on the screen Amelie's moans became cries. Both men watched appreciatively as the girl's pleasure peaked; she gave a series of short panting cries and then sagged so that her face was buried in the bed-covers. Then she gasped and arched her back, as Cynthia straightened her legs slightly, raised her body, and began to lick urgently at her anus.

José glanced at Pera. 'A lot more, indeed,' he said again. 'And you say she seemed to enjoy wielding the paddle?'

'More than seemed.' Pera cast his mind back. 'She was scared to begin with, no doubt about it, but once she had the swing of it she warmed up nicely.' He looked straight at José. 'I think you've got yourself a rare one there, Mestré,' he said simply.

'Perhaps I have.' José stared into space for a few moments. Then he seemed to reach a decision. 'Put her in the fields for the next few days,' he said. 'Put her with a strict overseer. Someone who's good with a switch. Let her spend a while being hot and tired and sore and dirty. Then bring her to me.'

'Very well.' Pera nodded, and was about to excuse himself when José gestured to the bound Princess.

'Speaking of hot,' he said, 'I should think she's nicely ready. Would you like a turn?'

Pera looked at the girl. Her body was as splendid as he remembered, and the many weals on her ebony skin added spice to the dark delights between her legs. But he had come twice in a few hours and was still depleted.

'No thanks, Mestré,' he said, a little regretfully. 'I wouldn't do her justice.'

'Never mind.' José did not look unhappy. 'If you won't, I certainly will.' He loosened the girls bonds and pulled her brusquely back towards him along the top of the desk. Then he reached down, set his cock free, and thrust it roughly into Princess's anus. She shrieked.

Pera grinned, and turned to go. As he went through the door Princess gave another shriek. José had certainly broken her silence, he thought.

In the fading light of the bedroom, Cynthia gave a last loving lick to Amelie's musky cleft and sat back, licking her lips. Her tongue ached, but her nose and mouth were full of the taste of the girl, a rich, tart cocktail that reached down through the layers of civilization to speak to something very primitive that lay below them.

On the bed, Amelie wriggled her hips and gave a long, low, satisfied moan.

'My god,' she said. 'I'd ride the pony every day if you promised to do that to me afterwards.' She turned round to look at Cynthia, and her eyes were full of respect. 'Where did you learn to do it like that?'

'I didn't learn it. That was my first time. Or my second, really.' She told Amelie what Pera had made her do to Carla, earlier on.

Amelie's eyes widened. 'He got you doing that, when you'd never licked a girl before? And then you came and did it for me too? Jesus.' She turned over and sat up. 'Why?'

'I was sorry for you. After being on the pony, you know?' Cynthia looked at her feet. 'I was sure it was going to be me up there. I don't know why it wasn't.'

To her surprise Amelie laughed. 'Oh, don't you,' she said. 'It's simple. Carla's got it in for me. She was always going to drop me in it.' Her face clouded. 'I don't know why Pera backed her up, though.'

Cynthia reached out and took her hand. 'Anyway, I'm sorry,' she said.

'Don't worry.' Amelie squeezed her fingers. 'You've more than paid me back. In fact,' and she looked thoughtfully at Cynthia, 'I reckon I owe you something on account.' She let go of Cynthia's hand and let her fingers trail down her belly towards her mound. Cynthia shuddered as they moved lower, and then gave a little gasp of pleasure as they brushed softly against her clit hood.

Amelie kept up the gently pressure. 'What do you say? Do you want your turn?'

Cynthia nodded. Suddenly she felt incredibly aroused. She felt a hand on her shoulder, and let herself be pressed back onto the bed until she was lying on her back, her legs hanging over the edge. She shut her eyes while, for a few moments, the insistent fingers kept up their electric exploration of her clit. Then they stopped. She gave a whimper of disappointment, but then she felt the bed move, and looked down to see Amelie kneeling down in front of her. The girl looked amused.

'You didn't think I was going to repay a licking like that just with fingers, did you?' she said. Then she lowered her head, and Cynthia felt the soft, hot, wet pressure of a tongue against her flesh. She lay back, and surrendered utterly.

In his study, José gave a final powerful thrust into Princess's twitching ring, and then came, spurting and pumping his seed into her tight passage with a satisfied grunt. When he had finished he withdrew, and watched with satisfaction as her abused body expelled thick beads of sperm which ran down her cleft and formed a tiny pool on the edge of the desk. He would make her clean that up, shortly. Meanwhile, he wondered what was happening downstairs?

The television was still on, and he took in the scene at a glance; Amelie, kneeling between Cynthia's legs, her head bobbing as she licked, and Cynthia lying back, her face a study in ecstasy.

José grinned to himself. He would not intervene. The new girl had earned some pleasure, and besides, she was in for a hard few days. He watched a little longer, and then reached for the remote control and turned off the image. Not that the sight was unappealing – anything but – but it was late, and he still had to finish dealing with Princess. He strode over to the desk and loosened her ropes.

'Stand up,' he said brusquely.

She did so, rubbing furtively at her wrists. He pointed to the drops of their mixed body fluids on the edge of the desk. 'Messy bitch,' he said. 'Lick that up!'

She knelt down and her pink tongue flicked out, lapping like a cat at the soiled spot. He watched until she had finished, enjoying the sight of her out-thrust bottom with its dense covering of angry weals. So different from the proud Princess who faced me in the courtyard the other day, he thought. But girls are like horses. They can all be broken in, if you try hard enough.

Soon, it would be Cynthia's turn. José grinned to himself. He liked a challenge.

CHAPTER 14

The next morning brought Cynthia all the challenge she could wish for. She and Amelie were woken early by someone banging on their open door. Cynthia sat up blearily and squinted through the bright, almost horizontal shafts of sun that pierced the blinds of the room. The banging stopped, and someone laughed.

'A bit bright for you, is it?'

The sleepy blur cleared from Cynthia's eyes, and she focused on the young man at the door. Tall, slim, dressed in loose blue jeans and a non-descript tee-shirt. He was leaning against the door-jamb, and he looked amused. As she watched, he bowed sardonically.

'Good morning, your Majesties,' he said. 'I apologise for disturbing your rest, but there are a few things you should know.' He counted on his fingers. 'One, it's past dawn on the first day of the harvest. Two, you and some others will be picking grapes until you wish you had never seen one. Three, if you don't pick fast enough I'll take the skin off your behinds with a vine cane.' He held out a long thin switch and swished it through the air so that it gave a high, angry hiss, making both girls flinch. Then he let it fall to his side. 'Four, I'm called Antoine, and I'm in charge of you until someone tells you otherwise. Now get dressed!'

He gestured towards the back of the door, and Cynthia realized that someone had hung some clothes on it while she slept. She scuttled forwards and took a hanger.

It was a simple dress, knee-length, in light cream-coloured cotton. She pulled it over her head; it fitted closely but well, and felt cool. She turned to watch as Amelie pulled on her own dress. The tight material emphasised her curves, and Cynthia felt an echo of last night's excitement.

Antoine's voice brought her back to the present. 'Don't go looking for more clothes,' he said, 'because you're wearing all there is. Enough to stop you burning in the sun, but easy for me to move aside if I need to light fires in your arses. Like this!' And he quickly hauled up the hem of Cynthia's dress until her bottom was uncovered, and swished the vine cane down sharply across the tops of her thighs.

It stung! A sharp nasty line of pain blossomed across her skin, as if someone had laid a hot wire on her. She clasped her hands over the place, and felt a thin raised weal already standing out.

Antoine was looking at her, still wearing the amused expression which Cynthia suspected she could tire of very quickly.

'Get the message?' he asked.

She nodded, and was aware of Amelie nodding hurriedly next to her.

'Good.' Antoine lowered the cane. 'You'll find hats and sandals in the courtyard, and breakfast of a sort. Now get going!'

They trotted out along the corridor and into the courtyard. A rough table had been set out with plates of rough-looking bread rolls and pitchers of water. Several other girls, including Francine and Carla, were already eating quickly, and Cynthia and Amelie joined them. They were all hungry and no-one spoke.

Cynthia had barely finished eating the one roll that seemed to be her ration when Antoine slashed the cane down on the table, making a high-pitched crack that made all the girls jump.

'Right,' he said. 'Nearly time to get going. I'm not going to ask if you have any questions because they'd all be stupid and I'd have to whip you, but I am going to answer a few of the obvious ones.' He held out his fingers and counted them off. 'One – why don't we use machines to pick grapes, like lots of other places? Answer – because machines can't tell the difference between fair grapes and mouldy ones, or between grapes and birds' nests. You can, or at least you will if you want any skin left on your arses.' He sliced the cane through the air, and then continued. 'If it comes to that, machines don't have arses, or any of the other few strong points of the human female. Another point in your favour. Two – will it be hard work? Answer – yes, that's the idea.'

Cynthia glanced at Amelie, and saw a pair of round eyes in a pale face. Good, she thought. I'm glad it's not just me. She dragged her eyes back to Antoine, who still had his hand out. 'Three – will you be rewarded for doing well? Answer – possibly, depending on what you mean by reward. In the simplest sense, yes, I will reward you by allowing you to keep enough skin to sit on. Metaphorically, then yes, I suppose, because you will have the satisfaction of knowing that some wealthy old boozer somewhere has pickled another bit of his liver with the beautiful product of your labour. He'd probably like to fuck you by way of thanks, but he can't because he isn't here, he's a metaphor, and even if he could he can't get it up anymore because he probably drinks too much, so I might have to do it for him.' He drew in a breath. 'Finally, you might, you might just be rewarded by being promoted.'

Cynthia pricked up her ears. Antoine looked along the lines of girls and continued. 'If you work hard, if you behave yourselves, and if I suspect that you have the potential to be a complete bitch towards your fellow females, then you might find yourself being made up to overseer. Put in charge. Given the whip hand.' He looked at them again as if gauging their response. Then he gave a slight shrug and brought the cane lashing down on the table again. 'Lecture's over, girls,' he said. 'Hats on, sandals on, follow me.'

Picking grapes turned out to be hard work. They began on a long, steep hillside.

'Faces south,' explained Antoine, 'and gets the early sea breeze. Cool in the morning and hot in the afternoon; ideal for this grape. This slope always beats the others.'

The vines were planted in rows, marching up the hillside. Antoine positioned a girl at the bottom of each row, and gave each one a basket.

'Remember,' he said, 'no mould, no flaws, no stems and nothing but grapes. Clear?'

They all nodded.

'Good. Something I forgot; whichever girl has the lightest basket by midday will be whipped, no matter how much she's been whipped already. Whoever has the lightest at the end of the day,' and he paused for a moment, 'will be punished double. Clear?'

They all nodded.

'Good! Then begin!'

They began. Cynthia took hold of the first bunch of grapes and began to pull them from their stems. It was not difficult; they were ripe and ready to part, and she found something sensual about thrusting her hand into the rich black spheres. They felt cool and firm.

She had cleared a handful of vines when she realised that Antoine was behind her. 'Stop,' he said. 'Let's see what you've got.'

He thrust his fingers into her basket and pulled out a fat handful of grapes which he inspected, gradually them fall back into the basket until he had a few left in his palm. He held them out to Cynthia.

'These,' he said, 'are mouldy. You need to learn the difference. Put down the basket.'

She obeyed.

'Now lift your skirt.'

Awkwardly she raised the hem of her skirt, wriggling the tight material up until it was past her hips, where it stayed.

'Now bend over, spread your legs and grab your ankles.'

Cynthia lowered herself into position. She had hardly finished when she heard the thin whistle of the vine cane and felt a searing line across the tops of her thighs. The sharp pain made her gasp, and the stroke was quickly followed by another, and another as Antoine whipped her quickly and expertly.

There was no pleasure in this! Tears sprang to her eyes and she heard herself whimpering and sobbing as the thin, pliable vine punished her bottom, her thighs, her hips and, nastiest of all, her cunt. How long would it last?

It took a while for her to find out. It wasn't until her sobs had turned to wails of pain that Antoine dropped the vine cane onto the ground.

'Whipping's over,' he said, as matter-of-factly as if nothing much had happened. 'Fifty cuts. I'll never give you less, but I might well give you more if I think it'll help you learn. Now, stand up, get your dress back down and get on with you work!'

Sniffling, Cynthia obeyed, wincing as the tight cotton rubbed at her freshly-whipped skin.

It was going to be a long day.

Antoine watched the subdued girl start picking grapes. His arm tingled pleasantly with the exercise of thrashing her, and his dick ached in its captivity. It had been a sheer delight to whip the English girl, with her soft white bottom and her shy expression and her ready tears. Of course, it was a delight to whip any girl, any colour, practically any shape – Antoine hardly cared as long as he could thrash their quivering globes.

But the English girl! What a little piece she was. The way her pale skin, so different from the Mediterranean olive of most of the girls at Mas Gassac, bloomed so quickly to scarlet under the lash; the lascivious, unconscious wriggling of those taut, full buttocks, and best of all the wink and clench of the little holes between them – Antoine's cock had raged and strained as he whipped her, and more than once he had been on the brink of tearing down his trousers and fucking her brains out.

Only on the brink, though. Although he was generally free to help himself to the slaves when and how he chose, there was a harvest to get in, and leaving a trail of well-ploughed females would have been unprofessional if it had meant that there were grapes spoiling on the vine. And, even more important, while his freedom might be general, it had been made quite clear to him that it did not include the English girl, at least not yet. As Pera had told him laconically the night before: 'She's José's.' And that was that. Lucky José.

But, he consoled himself, there were others. He strode up the rows of vines, pausing to lay an admonitory lash on the taut cotton covering a labouring slave's behind, until he came to Carla. She was kneeling by a vine, her hands lost in the bunches of grapes that hung from its lower stems. As he stopped next to her she flinched, but then went on picking.

Her basket didn't seem very full. He tapped it with his foot.

'What's going on?' he asked. 'You should have picked more by now!'

She looked up nervously, and gestured back down the line of vines. 'There were lots of mouldy ones,' she said, her voice trembling a little.

He glanced in the direction of her gesture, and felt a momentary touch of disappointment. What she had said was true; even from here he could see that many of the untouched bunches of grapes had the unhealthy bluish-white bloom of mildew. Then he tapped the basket again.

'It shouldn't matter,' he said. 'It takes no time not to pick them; where are all the grapes you should have picked?'

She looked down at her feet and didn't answer. He shook his head.

'Fine,' he said. 'You obviously need a thrashing. Lift your dress, then kneel down.'

For a moment she looked up at him, her eyes pleading. Then she sighed, took her dress by the hem and raised it to the small of her back, and knelt, wincing as her knees pressed into the rough stony ground of the vineyard.

He let his eyes linger briefly on the curves of her behind. Then he placed his foot in the small of her back and shoved her gently so that she fell forwards onto all fours.

'That's better. Now spread your legs and crouch for your whipping like the little bitch you are!'

She whimpered, but did as she was told, and he watched with pure lust as her posture opened her buttocks to display the dark soft flesh that lay between them. She looked good – the tight neat little sex, and above it the merest dot of an anus, seemed to invite invasion.

He took control of himself. For the moment his job was to discipline her, nothing else. He raised the vine cane and lashed it down, crossing her mounds diagonally from top to bottom. She squealed, and wriggled her hips from side to side as a scarlet weal darkened quickly on her flesh.

Antoine grinned like a wolf and raised the cane again. He brought it lashing down repeatedly across her helpless skin, forcing cry after agonised cry from the suffering girl as the angry stripes multiplied on her buttocks and thighs. Every now and then he shifted his aim, exploiting his position above her body to bring the cane hissing down into her cleft, and every time he did she rewarded him with an especially heartfelt shriek.

He lost count of the strokes, and of the girl's wailing cries and sobs. When he stopped, the whole of Carla's haunches and thighs was a mass of vivid weals, slightly swollen, and decorated with a few dots of blood where the tip of the vine cane had bitten especially hard. Carla was motionless, on all fours with her head touching the ground. She had been punished enough, he decided. For the moment.

'You can stand up,' he told her. Slowly she eased herself off her knees, grimacing as the movement flexed her thrashed haunches. As she lowered her dress gingerly, the material tightened over her breasts and Antoine saw her nipples push it into two proud little peaks. He reached out and took one of them between finger and thumb.

Carla flinched as he began to squeeze, but stood her ground, panting slightly through pouting lips.

'Good girl,' he said. 'Does it feel good?'

She nodded. He pinched harder, until her knees gave slightly and she bit her lip. Then he let her go. Her breath whistled out of her and she stepped back. He was half expecting her to put her hand to her breast, but she didn't. He nodded in approval at the tiny gesture of submission, and made a mental note to spend more time with her. He firmly believed that once a man had thrashed his way through a girl's defences, they would drop for him readily, every time. He liked what lay behind Carla's defences.

He dismissed her abruptly, suppressing his triumph at the flicker of disappointment that shadowed her face. You're mine, he thought. Any time I want you. Then he turned and continued his walk across the field.

He had ten girls in his charge, and by the time the sun had climbed towards midday he had visited, and whipped, all of them, tiring his arm and wearing several vine canes to shreds. The last knelt cowering at his feet, her extravagantly flogged behind pointing upwards.

He stood back and admired her. Her name was Li and she was Chinese, one of the few of her race at Mas Gassac, and her neat muscular body was enriched by pale peach-coloured skin, now lavishly striped with the weals of her thrashing. Her long straight hair was so dark as to be almost black, and he imagined the same colour would curl between her legs if it was given any opportunity. In her case it was not; she was fully waxed, and the bare lips of a small, neat little cunt were framed winked between her smooth thighs. Unlike many girls, there was no darkening of the skin between her cheeks, so that the pale peach-colour continued right up to the tiny pink pucker surrounding her anus, itself crossed by several vivid weals.

The sight was too much. Antoine had been restraining himself all morning, and now he was almost beside himself with arousal. She was for it.

He all but ripped at his trousers, forcing the vent open with fingers that were suddenly clumsy. Released from captivity, his cock sprang out, standing high in front of him. He reached down, seized the trembling Li by the hips and pulled her roughly upright, kicking her legs apart so that she was splayed and ready. Then he rested the tip of his aching shaft against her anus and forced himself up her.

Li gave a single wail of protest, and he felt her muscular ring clenching reflexively around him. It felt good, and he drew back and began to bugger her forcefully, each stroke drawing a high-pitched cry from the impaled girl.

Oh, he had wanted this! His cock felt as if it was on fire. He swung his hips, his legs trembling with effort, his fingers digging into the firm flesh of Li's buttocks as he thrust and thrust. The sensation was intense. She obviously wasn't used to being taken that way, and her muscles twitched and gripped him deliciously, until all too soon he felt himself building to a climax that would not be denied. As he came he forced himself to his full length, dimly aware of a wailing which he assumed was his victim, and which added a piquant spice to the rich dish of sodomy he enjoyed so much.

Eventually his spasms faded and he withdrew, watching appreciatively as a bead of his semen oozed from her hole and began to trickle down towards her thigh. Whipped, fucked and dripping, he thought. What better way to leave a girl?

CHAPTER 15

It was a long day, and by the time it was over, Cynthia was hot and thirsty and hungry and very, very sore. Antoine had seemed to be everywhere, him and his horrible cane. Not content with giving her just one thrashing, he had come back to her twice, and each time he had found fault with her, and each time she had raised her dress for another fifty stinging cuts, so that now, when all she wanted was to sit down and never move again, sitting down was the last thing she could contemplate.

She had eaten a light supper with Amelie, Carla, Li and Francine. They had spoken little and remained standing. Now she lay face down on her bed, her dirty dress hanging, together with Amelie's on the back of the door. The shutters on their room were open, letting in a soft evening breeze which played coolly over her flayed, smarting bottom.

On the next bed, Amelie shifted and groaned. 'Ooooh,' she said. 'What is it you English say?' She frowned with concentration, and then pronounced carefully: 'Bloody Hell!'

Cynthia laughed. 'Very good,' she said. 'Nice accent.'

'Thanks. Probably not as good as your French, though.' Amelie reached round gingerly and patted herself. She winced. 'Yup, still there.' She patted a little more, then brought her arms round in front of her, raised her head form the bed, and cradled her chin. 'I wouldn't mind getting whipped,' she said, and then giggled. 'I mean, obviously I wouldn't mind it, otherwise why would I be here, but it's not the only reason I'm here, if you know what I'm saying.' She looked sideways at Cynthia and raised her eyebrows. 'Were you spying when Li got hers?'

Cynthia nodded.

'Well then. Straight up the arse and no messing about. That's what I like.'

Cynthia sighed. 'I know,' she said. 'Apart from José on my first day here, none of the men have laid a finger on me.'

'Apart from José? Wow!' Amelie rolled onto her side and looked at Cynthia with respect in her eyes. 'Le Mestré had you on your first day? That's some compliment!' She rolled off her bed and sat down carefully next to Cynthia. 'Is that why you're here? Because of José?'

'Yes.'

'Well come on then!' Amelie patted Cynthia's hand. 'Tell!'

Cynthia told. She began, a little hesitantly, with her anodyne relationship with Yves, but as she described her night at L'histoire d'O she warmed to her task. The momentum of her story carried her through to her suspicions about her parents, and then to her journey across the full length of France on the track of her José.

At this, Amelie raised her eyebrows until they almost disappeared into her fringe. 'Your José?' she asked.

Cynthia subsided a little. 'Well, that's what it felt like then,' she said. Even to her own ears she sounded a bit defensive.

'Mmm.' Amelie was silent for a moment. Then she asked: 'What does it feel like now?'

Cynthia sighed. 'I don't know,' she said.

'Well, well.' Amelie's hand stroked Cynthia's cheek absently. 'Let me sum it up. You meet José in an SM club in Paris. He whips your tail, gives you his card and leaves you panting for it. Like a good girl you come running, and he sorts you out on night one and then leaves you panting – again – and so do all the other men in the place.' She stood up, put her hands on her hips and looked down at Cynthia. 'You want to know what I think?'

'What do you think?'

'I think our dear leader's got a thing for you, like he hasn't for anyone else. And you know something else?'

Amelie's face was so mock-serious that Cynthia suppressed a smile. 'Go on then,' she said. 'What else?'

'I reckon José's tired of being king of the hill on his own. I'm guessing he wants a Queen.' Amelie knelt down on front of Cynthia. 'One of these days, if I'm right, I'll be calling you Your Majesty.' She lowered her forehead to the floor in an exaggerated grovel.

Cynthia burst out laughing. 'For God's sake,' she said. 'You'll never have to go down on your knees to me! For one thing, you'll be too busy writing fairy stories.' Ignoring the smarting from her rump, she sat up and swivelled herself round so that she was sitting on the edge of her bed. Then she reached out and took two handfuls of Amelie's hair.

'If you're in the mood for going down, though...' She opened her legs and pulled the other girl gently forward. Amelie's face settled between her legs, and Cynthia hissed with satisfaction as the other girl's insistent tongue began to probe at her girl-flesh.

Life at Mas Gassac might not be too bad after all, she thought.

In his study, José watched as the image of the two busy girls rocked and writhed on his screen. The sound was on, and he could hear Cynthia's soft, luxurious panting. As he watched, Cynthia reached out her hands and took hold of Amelie's hair, pulling her closer in. Amelie gave a squeak of protest, and at first José thought that she would try to escape, but then she wriggled herself deeper into the space between Cynthia's thighs.

How interesting, thought José. The sound had been on throughout the girls' conversation, so he had heard Amelie's opinion of him, and the only reason she was not being flogged for her presumption was that she was absolutely right.

José watched for a little longer, allowing himself a brief fantasy of exactly how he would use, and misuse, young Cynthia when her turn finally came. Then he picked up the internal phone and made a call.

Antoine was lying sprawled on a chaise longue when the call came. His cock was buried in the warm, wet, living delights of Carla's mouth, and he was thinking of nothing more than the next pleasurable second, and the next, and the next.

His pleasure was beginning to peak, and his cock felt ready to explode, when the burr of the phone brought him unpleasantly back to the present. He opened his eyes, looked round at the display, and swore softly.

It was José.

At the sound of the phone, Carla had stopped the fluid movement of her lips up and down his shaft and made to sit back, but he reached out a hand and stopped her.

'Wait,' he said. He picked up the phone. 'Antoine here, Mestré.'

His boss spoke shortly. 'I need to see you about Cynthia.' No room for negotiation there, thought Antoine. Still keeping his hand on the back of Carla's head, he said: 'I'll come right away.'

'Good.' The line went dead.

Antoine dropped the phone on the floor and grasped Carla's head with both hands.

'Right,' he said. 'Finish me. Do it fast!' And he pulled her down onto his cock, fast enough so that she gagged, the tissues of her throat rippled deliciously around him.

He felt her tongue go to work on the underside of his shaft, and he raised his hips from the couch and began to fuck her mouth, grunting with effort and satisfaction as her lips rolled up and down his flesh. He quickly recovered his previous excitement and then went beyond it, tensing his muscles and letting out a long, harsh growl of triumph as his dam swelled and then burst. He knotted his fingers in Carla's hair and jammed her face into his groin as he came, and she 'mmm'd' faintly as waves of his seed pulsed over her tongue.

His orgasm was as quick as it was fierce; he drained himself into her mouth with a dozen heaving jets. Then he let her go. She sat back on her haunches, and he watched her throat ripple as she swallowed. 'Good girl,' he said, and she smiled before flicking her tongue over her lips.

Antoine could easily have gone to sleep, but José wanted him. He shook off his post-orgasmic drowsiness and stood up, buttoning his trousers and straightening his shirt. He turned to check his appearance in a mirror. Then he gestured to Carla. 'You can go,' he said. 'I'll call for you when I want you.'

She curtseyed, and trotted off out of his apartment. He watched her departing bottom flash through the door. I might want you quite soon, he thought. Then he pulled on a light jacket and walked out of the room.

A few minutes later he was standing in José's study. José was looking thoughtful. 'Tell me what you think of the English girl.'

Antoine collected his thoughts. 'She is unusual,' he said. 'Very young, and very inexperienced, but nothing seems to phase her.'

José nodded. 'Go on,' he said.

Antoine tried to recall his own encounters with Cynthia, and what he had heard from others.

'She is submissive, obviously,' he said, 'and she can take pleasure from the lash, as they say so many English girls can, but there is more.'

'More?' José's face was impassive.

'Yes, Mestré.' Antoine sought for the right phrase. 'There is something hard at her core. She has the heart of a slave, there is no doubt of it, but it is as if that heart sits on a pillar of granite.'

José nodded again. For a while he was silent, his face brooding. Then he looked up at Antoine. 'Tell me,' he said. 'Is there anything of the dominant about her?'

Antoine thought hard. 'Yes, Mestré,' he said eventually. 'I believe there is. But it may not stand alone.'

'What do you mean?'

It was a good question, because Antoine had spoken from instinct, not from thought. What had he meant?

'I think,' he said, 'she can rule others provided that she is doing so on behalf on another.'

José nodded vigorously, as if Antoine had echoed his thoughts. 'I understand,' he said. 'You think she can rule, if she in turn is ruled.'

'I do.'

José drummed his fingers, while Antoine waited anxiously. 'Well,' he said eventually, 'let's find out. Tomorrow morning, tell her she is the overseer. Give her a whip, and make sure all the girls know she carries it.' He paused, and then added: 'Tell her she is doing it on my behalf. Let's see how she does.'

Antoine nodded, and made to leave. As he reached the door, José spoke again.

'Tell her something else. If she does well, I will expect her company at the weekend.'

'Yes, Mestré.' Antoine bowed slightly, and let himself out of the apartment. When he had closed the door behind him, he let out his breath with a big 'whoof!' Then he walked slowly down the stairs.

Tomorrow, it seemed, would be make or break time for English Cynthia. He wondered which it would be.

'Me, overseer?' Cynthia felt her heart hammering against her ribs. 'But I can't do that!'

'Can't you?' Antoine was grinning. 'Why not?'

Cynthia almost felt like stamping her foot. 'Because, because… because I just can't!' Tears began to prick the corners of her eyes. She brushed them away angrily. 'I'm not an overseer, am I? I'm a…'

Antoine interrupted her. 'You're a slave,' he said. 'Yes. A sexy little slave girl, with your cute English accent and your wriggles and your moans and your tight wet pussy and your tasty little behind. But you're more than that, aren't you?' He leaned closer, so that Cynthia could smell his masculine scent. 'You're José's slave girl. Oh, in one way all the girls here are José's slave girls, but you're different. Think about it! Why are you here? Because he asked for you. Most girls have to beg to get in through the door, but not you! Why haven't you been fucked since you arrived? Because José said so!' He paused, and sat down on the bed. 'Every other girl here is fair game for me, but not you! To me, you're hands off. José is saving you for himself.'

Cynthia's head swam. 'But then why should he want me to be an overseer, if I'm so much his slave?' Now the tears would not be brushed away. She felt them running down her cheek. 'That's what I want to be! It's why I'm here! How can he be so unkind?'

The slap came like lightening, not hard but astonishing all the same. She raised a hand to her cheek, which was tingling slightly. Antoine lowered his hand.

'I'm sorry,' he said, 'and I doubt if you'll ever hear me say that again. But grow up! If you want so badly to be José's slave, then be his slave! If he wants you to be his overseer, do what you're told and be one!'

He held out his hand and she took it.

'Listen,' he said. 'I'm talking out of turn, but I guess there's a big prize at the end of this. Slave girls aren't much use beyond their thirties, mostly. But a wife, well, she's going to sit by her master for always.' He squeezed her hand. 'Which do you want to be, little English? Queen for ever, or bitch for a day?'

Cynthia stared at the floor. She didn't know what to say; she hardly knew what to think. The truth was, in all her fantasies about José she had never gone beyond what would happen as soon as she walked into his domain. And now she was in his domain, she had been pulled into the life of a slave girl so quickly that she hadn't thought of anything else. What should she do?

There was only one answer. Or rather, there were two answers, but one was not to be thought of. She wiped her eyes and looked up at Antoine.

'Okay,' she said. 'I'll be an overseer.' She took a breath. 'What do I have to do?'

He gave her a big grin and then, to her astonishment, leaned over and kissed her on the cheek.

'There,' he said. 'I reckon that's about as far as I'm allowed to go, in that direction.' Then he stood up, and gestured for her to do the same. 'Now – about being an overseer.'

By the time Cynthia and Antoine emerged into the courtyard, the other girls were standing waiting. Antoine strode out with his usual authority. Cynthia followed, trying desperately to mimic his confidence, and certain that she was failing. In her right hand she held the many-tailed whip Antoine had recommended

– he had called it a chicote – but it felt unnatural, like some sort of weird growth that ought to be removed.

Antoine clapped his hands for attention, making Cynthia wince.

'Ladies,' he said. 'I am happy to introduce your new overseer. As of today you will be under the care of Cynthia!' He gestured Cynthia forwards. 'She has the authority of your owner José Mestré, and if that is not enough for you she has the authority of me! Are there any questions?'

Cynthia had the strong impression that there were lots of questions, but none that any of the girls felt like voicing.

'Good!' said Antoine. 'Then let's get on with our work!' He pushed out his hands in front of him as if he was encouraging a flock of hens, and the girls moved off towards the fields.

Cynthia watched them with a sinking heart. How was she supposed to take charge of that lot? But then Antoine put his arms around her shoulder.

'Don't worry,' he said quietly. 'You've got the whip, and I won't be far away. You'll be okay.' He gestured after the disappearing slave girls. 'Go on. Get after them and skin some arses. Remember, you're doing it for José.'

For José. Yes. Cynthia took a firm hold on the handle of the chicote. She would do it for José.

CHAPTER 16

'**O**ooowww!'
Francine twisted her head round to look back over her shoulder at Cynthia. 'That stung like hell,' she said. 'Why do you have to do it so hard?'

Cynthia drew the tails of the chicote through her fingers, admiring the vivid crimson spray of weals they had just left across the kneeling girl's bottom. It was two days since Antoine, at José's insistence, had made her an overseer. Two long, hard days. 'Because if I don't, there's no point,' she answered simply. And because I still have something to prove, she added silently, drawing back the whip for another stroke that had Francine howling and pawing at the ground in pain.

She had struggled, to begin with.

'No, not like that! Like this! Oh, for God's sake, give it to me! I'll show you.'

She had been an overseer for seven hours and for all that endless time it seemed she could do nothing right.

There was a howl of agony.

'You see? The tails of the whip should straighten out like rods, if you are swinging it hard enough, and then curl round. A flick of your wrist at the last minute makes them bite. See?'

Another anguished howl.

And now the whip was being thrust back into her hand, and it was her turn again. She looked down at the upturned bottom, which this time belonged to Li – but by this time she had almost lost count, it could have been anyone's – and noted sourly the stark difference between the pink marks of her own efforts, and the angry scarlet tracks left by Antoine.

Oh well. Here went another failure. Probably her last, because she couldn't imagine Antoine putting up with this for much longer.

The trouble was, it wouldn't be Antoine she let down. It would be José. He would be disappointed. He would send her home, or something.

Like hell he would! She drew back the whip and flicked her arm round as hard as she could.

The impact made a thud that travelled up her arm and ended in her shoulder. Li squealed loudly and looked round in surprise. 'Hey! That really hurt!'

Cynthia was as surprised as Li. Her surprise grew, if anything, as she watched a group of weals blooming to an almost startling red.

She looked round to see Antoine's reaction. He was nodding slowly, his lips pursed.

'Well, well,' he said. 'At last you've landed one! Well done.' He gestured towards the kneeling Li. 'Let's see if it was a fluke.'

Cynthia nodded. She took a firm grip on the handle of the chicote, swirled it round behind her and launched it with all her strength.

The tails whistled through the air and struck. Li put her head back and gave an outraged shriek of pain, and another set of angry seals flashed quickly into being across her lower bottom.

Cynthia couldn't resist turning to Antoine. She knew she had a smug expression on her face, but he didn't seem to mind. Now he looked impressed.

'Good,' he said. 'You make progress – although it's not before time.' He raised his hand as if to forestall any comment. 'Now, your objective is to cover her entire bottom, from the thigh to the top, dark red. Some blue and black areas are acceptable, as is a little bleeding.

She is being punished, after all.' He paused, and then added: 'It should take you about forty strokes. Begin.'

Cynthia took a breath, and started.

Five minutes later, she sent her fortieth stroke whizzing in to follow its predecessors. The knotted tips curled round the nearer of Li's cheeks and curled in to smack against the soft flesh between them. Li, who was sobbing and hiccupping steadily, gave an anguished moan.

Antoine clapped softly. 'A good stroke to finish,' he said. 'You neglected that area a bit. Never forget to whip a slave-girls sex as well as her bottom. It's more sensitive, and the effects are even better if she is to be taken immediately afterwards.' He reached down and undid his trousers. 'Which she is,' he added needlessly, as his cock stood out high in front of him. 'Hold her. She's going to need it. And give me that.' He took the whip from Cynthia, turned, and went to hang it up.

Cynthia knelt down by Li's head and put her hands on the girl's shoulders. She looked up. Antoine's back was still turned.

'Sorry,' she mouthed.

Li managed a tiny smile. 'Not your fault,' she whispered. 'Please hold me hard. Don't let go!' Cynthia nodded, and then lowered her eyes hurriedly as Antoine returned. Without ceremony he knelt behind Li and entered her, hard enough to push her forwards against Cynthia's hands. Li opened her eyes wide for a moment, and then screwed them shut as Antoine began to pound into her. His thighs made a rhythmic slap-slap-slap against her bottom, and the force of each penetration drew a little gasp from her. Her face flushed and she began to chew her lip.

Cynthia watched the girl's face. It was obvious that pain was giving way to passion, and suddenly she felt incredibly jealous, and then very angry. Why were they doing this to her? Or rather, not doing it? Why was she expected to hold a whip, and then watch as a girl got what she so urgently needed?

Her cunt burned as she watched Li being taken. She imagined that it was her on her knees, feeling a man in her. Her with a sore bottom. Her being satisfied! Her jealousy peaked as Li's eyes opened wide again, while Antoine thrust himself fully home and held the position, gasping with pleasure.

Cynthia had never felt so frustrated.

Eventually Antoine finished coming. He withdrew, and Li sagged forwards into Cynthia's arms. She smelt of sweat and girl.

Antoine stood up, buttoning himself. Looking at Cynthia, he said; 'You've done well, today, in the end, Take Li back to a dormitory. We'll start again in the morning.' He walked to the door and then turned. 'José will be pleased with you,' he said. Then he left.

Cynthia helped Li to her feet. 'Are you ok?' she asked.

Li nodded. 'Yeah, fine,' she said. 'Or, at least, fine considering.'

She gave a rueful smile, and Cynthia grinned in return. 'Yes,' she said. 'You got a pretty good seeing-to, there.'

Li nodded, and winced as she let an exploratory hand fall to her behind. 'God,' she said. 'First you flog me, then Antoine fucks me bow-legged. What's a girl to think?'

Cynthia tried to keep her face expressionless but something must have come thought the mask because Li shot her an apologetic glance.

'Sorry,' she said. 'Tell me to shut up if I'm speaking out of turn, but there's a rumour going round.'

'What sort of rumour?' Cynthia was intrigued.

Li seemed embarrassed. 'Well,' she said slowly, 'some people are saying Master José's keeping you for himself, and you won't be getting any until he says so.' She raised her eyes to look at Cynthia. 'Is it true?'

'It might be.' Cynthia looked away. 'He hasn't said, but it does seem that way.'

'Wow. What a bastard.' Li fell silent for a moment. Then she took Cynthia's hand. 'Does the 'not getting any' thing include girls?'

It took Cynthia a moment to work out what Li meant. 'No,' she said. 'At least, I don't think so.'

Li stood up. 'Good,' she said. 'Then why don't you do what Antoine said, and take me to a dormitory?'

Cynthia looked at her steadily for a few seconds. Then she nodded. 'Okay,' she said.

They walked out of the room, across the courtyard and into the dormitory wing without saying a word. It was early, and they met no-one as they walked down the corridor. Cynthia stopped in front of the door to the room she had shared with Amelie the night before, but Li stopped her.

'I'm not sharing with anyone at the moment,' she said. 'Come with me.'

Cynthia nodded and followed her down to the end of the corridor.

Li's room lay through the last door. It was oddly shaped, obviously occupying the sharp corner between two outside walls that met at less than a right angle, so that the two beds it held touched at their heads. One had clearly not been slept on; Li sat on the other, and pulled Cynthia gently down until they were sitting side by side.

'Now,' she said quietly, 'let's see about this not getting anything.' She placed a hand on Cynthia's belly and pushed gently until Cynthia yielded, allowing herself to be pushed back onto the bed until she was sprawling, her shoulders supported by Li's pillow and her hips digging into Li's mattress. She shut her eyes as soft hands raised her dress, and once the material was out of the way it seemed so natural and comfortable to open her legs so that her sex was splayed in front of Li's face.

The first thing she felt was the same soft hands on her thighs. Next there was a fleeting brush of hot breath over her, and then at last the tiny, overwhelming sensation of a girl's tongue on her, on the centre of her, on the only part of her that mattered.

Cynthia lay back and exulted as Li lapped and probed at her. It had only been a few days since her cunt had known the touch of anyone or anything much except her own fingers, but those days had seemed like forever, and yet what she was feeling now was washing away the memory of that forever as if it had never existed.

She yielded with a sort of joy, unsure whether what Li was doing was a gift, or a tribute, or something far more complicated. Soon she didn't care.

At length, and with no knowledge of how much time had passed, she came, and for a few endless moments time became even less important.

Some time; seconds, or minutes or – how should she know? – ages of the world after her orgasm began, it ended, and all its effects ended with it. Cynthia sat up slowly and wrapped her arms around Li's shoulders.

'Mmmm,' she said. And then, conscious of the inadequacy of the words: 'That was wonderful.'

Li hugged her briefly. 'Good,' she said. 'That was the idea.' Then she lay back on the bed and slowly opened her own legs. 'Now,' she said, 'show me what I get in return.'

Cynthia wondered if she should try to look surprised, but it would have been pointless; she had always been a dreadful actress. There was no doubt what Li wanted, and the exchange seemed fair enough. She positioned herself between the spread legs and lowered her face to the exposed sex.

Even as her nose neared Li's swollen quim she could detect the scent of man, and when her tongue touched the rose-colored flesh the taste was unmistakeable. Antoine had left his mark very clearly.

It tasted good.

Cynthia licked slowly and carefully, half of her attention on the responses of the girl under her tongue, whilst the other half revelled in the strong, sensual flavour of a hot little cunt, freshly topped with sperm.

Li wriggled under her tongue, thrusting her hips upwards onto Cynthia's mouth as her pleasure mounted. Cynthia pushed her tongue further into the offered flesh, sighing with pleasure as she probed the soft delicate folds. She felt Li's hands knotting in her hair, pulling her in so that her face was buried in the girl's soaking quim, until at last Li arched her hips up convulsively from the bed, forcing her vibrating body against Cynthia's mouth as she gave a long, ragged cry of ecstasy.

Cynthia held her position, her tongue buried deep in Li's twitching cunt, until the other girl's spasms subsided. She felt Li's hands relax their grip, and the Chinese girl sighed happily.

'Oooooh, You're good. Are all English girls like you?'

Cynthia sat back. 'I don't know,' she said. 'I haven't been licked by all English girls.'

Li laughed. 'Not a bad ambition, though,' she said. Then she turned over on her side. 'I want to go to sleep,' she said. 'Will you hold me?'

'Okay.' Cynthia lay down next to her and wriggled until their bodies were fitted together. She reached out to take Li's hand, but the fingers did not respond to her touch. Li was already asleep.

Cynthia rolled onto her back and shut her eyes. Within seconds, she, too, was asleep.

CHAPTER 17

The next day was Friday. Fridays are traditionally short working days in rural France, but not where the vine is king. Grapes cannot tell the days of the week; when they are ready, they are ready, and they do not stay ready for long. Too much delay, and the sugar content increases and the mould comes, and for a red grape, mould is death.

Cynthia was woken by the sound of a door crashing back. She jerked upright, blinking in the blue-white light of early morning.

'Good morning, lovebirds!' Antoine stood in the doorway. He held a long riding crop in his hand. The tasselled tip slapped against his boot.

'I let you play last night, but today is for work. Overseer – I need you up earlier than this. Fifty strokes of the crop for you! Kneel on the bed. Legs apart. Now!'

Her head still full of sleep, Cynthia scrambled to obey.

'Good. Now, count the strokes and thank me!'

She hardly had time to take a breath before the crop whistled through the air and lashed across her bottom, and what breath she had left her in a whoosh. It hurt! Oh, how it hurt! Although she had been hit with a crop before – thank you, Carla – Antoine was stronger, and the sharp, burning smart of the thing was astonishing. Biting her lip, she managed not to scream, but instead took a few shuddering breaths and said: 'One, thank you.'

Once again, Antoine gave her no time at all; the crop was hissing through the air almost as she uttered the phrase. He must have moved, as the blow came from the other side and the tassel bit wickedly into her thigh.

This time she was ready. She rode the shocking pain and gave the count, and again the whip was moving as she spoke. The tone of the whipping was set.

The crop burned across her rump over and over, and the pain mounted. It was bad, certainly, as bad as any punishment she had yet endured at Mas Gassac, and there was no pleasure in it, even when the tip of crop nipped in to sting the soft flesh between her legs like an angry bee, but she could endure it. Somehow the fact that it was a summary punishment made it easier. She had failed, somehow, in her duties as an overseer! She was being punished, and it was fair.

The strokes mounted, until the whole of her bottom had been scalded, and then at last it was over. She counted off the fiftieth stroke, and heard Antoine's voice through the pounding in her ears. 'Well done. Stand up!'

She stood, gritting her teeth at the pain in her rump.

Antoine tapped the whip against Li, who had remained on the bed throughout Cynthia's whipping. 'Your turn,' he said. 'Fifty strokes, same position. Move!'

Li shuffled into a splayed kneeling position, and Cynthia sucked in her breath at the sight of the girl's bottom. The marks of yesterday's whipping were still dark and vivid, making a thoroughly erotic picture as the tight cheeks parted. I had my tongue up there last night, she thought. Lucky me!

Antoine had started straight in to thrashing Cynthia, but with Li he seemed to be taking his time. He tapped the tip of the crop against her skin and let the tassel skitter over her cunt, almost as if he was tuning an instrument before the orchestra began. Then he braced his legs and swept the crop in for the first stroke, and sure enough the concert started, with a crisp swish and crack from the crop and a shrill howl of pain from Li. The girl's cry was quickly followed by a gulp, and a trembling 'One, thank you.'

Cynthia watched in fascination as the number of strokes mounted. The dark blotches of yesterday's beating became overprinted with fresh pink and crimson, and Li's bottom twitched and flexed delightfully as the crop did its baleful work.

'Ahhh! Twenty, thank you!'

There was no doubt – the spectacle of Li's behind being thrashed scarlet was a sexy one. Cynthia's loins, themselves fresh from the attention of the crop, swelled and became moist as the heat of excitement flowed through her.

'Owww! Thirty, thank you!' Almost the whole of Li's bottom was now bright with fresh weals.

The girl kicked and wriggled as she was thrashed, all modesty being abandoned to the pain of the whip. The lips of her sex twinkled and winked as she moved, but this only exposed them even more to the searching tip of the riding crop.

At last the whipping was over. The sobbing Li gulped out her thanks as the fiftieth stroke scored her flaming behind, and collapsed in a little heap of flogged girl.

Antoine let the crop fall to his side. 'Now,' he said, almost as if nothing had happened, 'dress yourselves and be in the courtyard in five minutes. Except you, of course.' He tapped the whip against Cynthia's thigh so that she jumped. 'You're the overseer. You need to be there first. Jump to it!'

Cynthia jumped. Two minutes later she was standing in the empty courtyard, her dress pulled hurriedly over her shoulders and her hand grasping the chicote as if it was a badge of office.

Ten minutes after that, the courtyard was full of girls. All of them were blinking in the bright early light, and all of them except Li were directing covert, poisonous looks at Cynthia.

She gripped the handle of the chicote even harder, until her knuckles whitened. It looked as though the job of overseer was going to be a lonely one, today.

And now it was nearly evening of the next day, and the freshly-flogged Francine had scuttled away. Cynthia stood for a few moments and reflected. Her arm was tired. No wonder, she thought. It had been active for hours, almost without a break.

Amelie had been the first. Even after just an hour in the fields it was obvious that she was falling behind the others; the depth of fruit in her basket was far less than it should have been. She had blanched at Cynthia's sentence of fifty strokes.

'Fifty?'

Cynthia nodded, trying to look confident. 'Fifty,' she confirmed.

For a moment Amelie looked rebellious. Desperately Cynthia sought control. 'If you don't kneel down now I'll double it,' she said. And then, as Amelie still hesitated: 'Do you want me to fetch Antoine? Or Pera?'

That did it. Amelie lifted her dress, dropped to the ground and spread herself in the time it took Cynthia to draw two breaths. Cynthia shook out the tails of the chicote, and as she drew her arm back for the first stroke she seemed to hear a tiny voice from within, saying, make her afraid of you, like she's afraid of the men.

Cynthia nodded to herself, and let fly with all her strength.

It was a superb stroke. The tails of the whip had spread a little in flight, and landed in a perfect spray that followed a diagonal from the top of the girl's left cheek to the tuck below her right. Amelie jerked forwards and howled with pain as the knotted tails landed, and the angry tracks of their journey bloomed quickly across her haunches.

Good, thought Cynthia. She raised her arm to repeat the stroke but then changed her mind, shifted herself to the other side of the nervously waiting girl, and sent in a stroke that was the mirror image of the first.

The angry weals crossed in the centre of Amelie's bottom, drawing a fresh outbreak of howling, and the freshly-whipped flesh began to twitch and flicker with tiny muscular spasms.

Cynthia settled into a rhythm, sending in strokes first from one side and then the other. She tried to vary the landing point so that sometimes the tips of the lashes whipped in to nip the girl's inner thighs, or the outside of her hip, or occasionally the sensitive flesh between her cheeks – a target which drew an especially heart-rending squeal from the kneeling Amelie. And she made sure to send in every lash with as much force as possible, conscious that each one could mean authority lost or kept. She didn't know why José wanted her to take this role, but she was determined not to let him down.

Eventually she swept down the chicote for the fiftieth time. She was breathing hard with effort, not helped by the heat which had mounted even as she had whipped the wretched Amelie. Wretched was the word – the punished girl had sagged until she was almost lying flat on her front. Her flogged behind was livid with fresh, angry weals, punctuated by dark spots where the knots in the chicote had bitten. Pain and heat had brought out her skin into a glistening sheen of sweat.

Cynthia thought she looked good enough to eat, but that wasn't her business, at least not at the moment. Perhaps, later on, an overseer's privileges would turn out to include her choice of the girls but she doubted if that would be forgiven yet, especially when the girl in question was supposed to be picking grapes. So she tapped the kneeling Amelie with her toes.

'Up,' she said simply. 'Pick grapes, faster than you were before, and don't make me flog you again.'

Amelie did as she was told, wincing as she straightened up and pulled her dress hurriedly down over her flaming bottom. Cynthia waited until the girl's hand was amongst the vines, and then turned and went to find someone else who needed her authority.

The day passed quickly. The piles of grapes mounted in the baskets, looking like dusty garnets under the flaming southern sun. Every now and then one of the girls would tramp down the path between the vines to dump a full basket into the back of one of the waiting trailers that were dotted around the hillsides. The trailer drivers smoked and chatted, and watched the lithe slave-girls and their overseer with unconcealed male appreciation.

And Cynthia worked. She strode up and down the hillside, checking her girls – they were definitely 'her' girls, she thought – for the quality and quantity of their picking. The chicote dangled from her hand, the knotted tails brushing and tapping against her leg as if they were eager to bite into female skin.

They had plenty of opportunities and eventually, as the sun dropped from the top of its arc and the shadows of the vines began to stretch out across the ground, they came to Francine, whose last basket had contained too many mouldy fruit.

Cynthia was leaving nothing to chance. She used all her strength, and all the skill and affinity with the whip that she had found over the last two tiring days. The harsh thongs lashed and bit.

Francine bawled with pain as her bottom and thighs grew redder and redder.

'Ow! Please! Stop it! Aaahhhh!'

Cynthia paused. 'I said fifty and I meant it,' she said, breathing hard.

'But why?' It was almost the whine of a sulky child, and it earned an extra-hard lash.

'Because if I don't, Antoine will think I didn't check your basket. And if he thinks that I'll be whipped enough for all of you!' Cynthia compressed her lips. 'You're halfway there. Shut up and take your punishment or I'll start again!'

That did it. Francine moaned, and lowered her head to the ground. 'All right,' she said quietly. 'I suppose you've go to. Let's get it over with.'

As Cynthia drew back the whip, it occurred to her that yesterday she had had to invoke the names of Antoine and Pera to assert authority. Not now, she thought. I've whipped some respect into them! Weary as she was, the thought seemed to add vigour to her arm. The lashes whistled loudly, and Francine's screams rang out across the hillside. By the time she delivered the last stroke, Cynthia felt damp with sweat, and with more than that; the sight of the kneeling girl, with her spread cheeks thrashed until there were the same colour as the grapes on the surrounding vines, was highly erotic.

She was brought out of a brief reverie by the sound of applause. She spun round and saw Pera and Antoine standing behind her. They were smiling, and clapping softly.

Pera spoke first. 'Very good,' he said, and nodded at Antoine. 'She has learned well, young Antoine. Well done!'

'Thank you.' Antoine smiled at the older man, and then held out his hand to Cynthia. For a moment she didn't know what to do with it, but he gestured at the chicote. 'You can give that to me now,' he said. 'You won't need it tonight or tomorrow.'

Cynthia handed it over reluctantly. She realised that she hadn't let go of it all day, and now she felt almost undressed without it. Was like being stripped of her authority.

The thought must have showed in her face, because Pera grinned. 'Oh, don't worry,' he said. 'You made a good start as an overseer. You'll get another go at it, for sure.'

'Then what…' Cynthia began.

'Then tonight, and tomorrow, you have another job to do.' He reached out, and this time he took her hand. 'José wants you to attend him,' he told her. 'Good luck.'

Cynthia let herself be led away from the hillside. Her guts were churning, but she felt light-hearted all the same. No one spoke as she was led back to her room. She was left alone to wash and groom herself, and when she was dry she dressed herself in clothes that had been laid out for her while she was washing – antique-looking satin briefs and a matching basque that gripped her belly like an embrace, real silk stockings with complicated suspenders, and a knee-length dress in claret velvet, and black heels that made her feel a bit wobbly. And all the time, while she washed, and dressed, and then while she stood a little unsteadily in front of the mirror and smoothed her clothes and pulled her hair back into a plait, her heart was knocking and a single word kept whispering through her head.

José!

CHAPTER 18

José had taken a lot of care over his own preparations. Part of him was laughing at the rest – to get so concerned about one girl, when he had dozens ready to do whatever he asked and more applying, by various routes, all the time!

But it mattered.

He was waiting in his private dining room when Pera showed Cynthia in. The old man gave her a gentle push in the small of the back so that she took a few steps into the room. Then he withdrew, and silently closed the door.

The girl stood where she had stopped, looking around her. She looked a little uncertain, and José guessed that she wasn't used to wearing formal clothes. Or shoes, from the look of her.

'The heels are sending your weight towards your toes,' he said quietly. 'Don't fight them. Let it happen.'

He saw her shift slightly.

'Good. See how it helps you stand? How does it feel?'

She took a step. 'Better,' she said. 'Thank you, sir.'

He nodded. 'Try walking some more.'

She did so, taking short careful steps, but already her balance seemed far better and she gave him a shy smile. She was like a faun, he thought, a little innocent faun, with her stumbles and her awkwardness and her big young eyes and that smile, and for a second he could have seized her and taken her on the spot. But he restrained himself – there was plenty of time, and the better he handled her now, the better things would be in future.

He gestured towards the wall, where two trolleys stood. One held a light supper.

'Bring that over to the table,' he told her.

She walked over to it. It stood next to another trolley, and he saw her hesitate as she passed it. He wasn't surprised. He had laid it out carefully; on it there was a hunting crop, an old heavy razor strop, an English school cane and a broad plantation paddle.

When she had pulled the supper trolley back to the table he gestured her to sit down.

'Now, you must be hungry as well as tired, yes?'

She nodded, and gave a faint smile.

'Good! Then you must eat.' He reached out and lifted covers from plates. 'Ah! Ideal. To begin with, a little pâté and some of our local bread. And some wine, too. You must be wondering what it tastes like, the wine we make here. This is our best, one we sell only to very special clients. This one is ten years old. The grapes your girls were picking today will go to make the next vintage.' He paused, watching her face. 'It is called Fruits de la Soumission.'

She smiled, more broadly this time, as she took the glass with its deep red-brown charge of the wine called Fruit of Submission. He watched her drink, and then gestured to her plate.

'Now, eat,' he told her, 'and as you do, we'll talk.'

She took a careful mouthful of the pâté. Her eyes widened, and she quickly took another. 'It is good?' he asked, and she nodded, her mouth full.

'Good. Good, that it is good, and good that you appreciate food. An appetite of that sort, usually means that appetites of the other kind are also healthy.' He sat back, grinning. 'But we already knew that about you, little English girl, didn't we?'

She blushed, but nodded, and carried on eating.

José leaned forwards again. 'So,' he said, 'let us talk about the origins of these appetites. Where did they begin?' And over the next half-hour he questioned her gently, sometimes making her blush but more often drawing giggles, until the pâté was gone, and a small fillet de porc, and some late asparagus, and two glasses of wine. By the time she had finished eating he knew that she had been punished only a little as a child, but that the fascination had never left her. That until she had arrived as Mas Gassac she had experienced little and fantasised much. And that she had long suspected something of the same in her parents, and had been proved right by her Mother's confidences only a few hours before she had left home.

José sat back and stared at nothing. From what the girl had said he could easily picture the family – the man in charge, the submissive wife, and this Yolanda, the slave-servant. People he must meet, and sooner rather than later.

Meanwhile there was Cynthia, who seemed an even greater prize, now that he knew of her background, than ever before. She had finished eating, and was watching him expectantly.

He smiled at her. 'Remember when we last met?' he asked. 'It's time to find out if your have learned manners.' He let the smile fade. 'Stand up,' he said, 'and bring the other trolley.'

He was pleased to see that she stood up without hesitating. She walked over to the wall, took hold of the trolley and wheeled it back to the table, complete with its cargo of potential pain. Then she stood next to it, quite still.

'Raise your dress,' he told her, 'and bend over the table.'

She obeyed, and he watched appreciatively as her position tightened the antique satin against her skin. It was like framing a picture, he thought. The satin above, the silk below, and the elastic of the suspenders to either side. And the subject of the picture was quite perfect – firm rounded cheeks, ideally divided by the tight satin, and with traces of earlier weals peeking out beyond the edge of the material.

But still, it was a work in progress. He stood up, and ran his hand over the instruments on top of the trolley.

'I think,' he said slowly, 'yes, I think we will begin with some leather.' He picked up the razor strop. Then he put his hand firmly against her bottom. 'Push yourself back,' he said. 'You need to learn how to make a pretty target, if you are to keep a man's attention.' Quickly, she obeyed, and he felt her bottom tightening under his hand. Once again the temptation swept over him to take her, roughly, then and there, and once again he resisted. Instead, he smacked the tightened cheek sharply, drawing a surprised hiss of indrawn breath. A pink hand-print appeared, and he quickly added another on the other side. Cynthia wriggled a little, and José grinned.

'You're wriggling now,' he said, 'but it doesn't end there.' He raised the strop and let it dangle in the air so it brushed against the pink blotch. 'It ends when I've tamed you completely.' Then, without any warning, he swung his arm back and brought the strop hissing down across Cynthia's lower bottom with a blat that echoed round the room. She yelped and shuffled her feet.

José let the strop dangle again, teasing her. 'Did you ride ponies when you were a child?' he asked. She nodded. 'I thought so,' he said. 'So, think of yourself as a mare. As my mare, in fact.'

Another swooping blow drew a sharp cry from the girl.

'A mare may be proud. She can step smartly, be beautifully groomed. She can be the envy of all around her.' He allowed his voice to harden. 'But first she must be broken.'

The strop whistled home.

'Broken by the hard hands of a Master. Yes?'

At first Cynthia was silent. He shook his head, and whipped the leather down onto her darkening behind, four times in quick succession. Cynthia wailed with pain.

'I'm sorry,' he said, raising his voice to be heard over her noise. 'I didn't hear what you said. Try again! Broken by the hand of a Master. Yes?'

'Yes!' Her reply came instantly.

'Good.' He raised the strop again. 'You, my little English mare, are to be whipped into submission.' He paused. 'And then ridden into slavery.'

The leather flashed down, and down, and down. José concentrated his efforts on the exposed skin that lay below the hem of the satin panties, and the heavy leather strop quickly darkened the girl's dancing rump to purple, with the colour extending down almost to the point where the tops of the stockings bit slightly, and so erotically, into her thighs.

José thrashed the girl until his arm began to tire, and then paused to examine the results. No doubt about it, the girl marked well; her skin darkened readily and, he was pleased to note, had become a little swollen just above the crease, where his hardest strokes had landed.

It wasn't just marks, either; the old satin was noticeably darker where her posture had pulled it up between her cheeks. He probed between the hot globes with a finger, making Cynthia shiver, and found wetness.

'Well, well,' he said. 'It seems my little mare is fond of leather!' He let his finger dip further into her crevice for a moment, feeling her push herself back against him. Then he took his hand away. 'Let's see how you respond to something else.'

He put the strop back on the trolley, and picked up the plantation paddle. 'If the strop was the hors d'oeuvres,' he said, 'then this is the main course.' He rested the paddle against her hot skin, then swung it back and let it fall sharply. It landed across the exact centre of her bottom with an explosive crack.

Cynthia took a single gasping breath, and shrieked. Her writhing bottom flashed greyish white under the blow, and then quickly darkened again to an angry, bruised-looking purple speckled with lighter dots.

José smiled grimly to himself. Now they were beginning! He brought the paddle down twice more, once on each of the twitching cheeks. Then he put it down with an audible click. At the sound, Cynthia raised her head from the table and turned tearful eyes towards him.

'Oh, don't worry,' he said. 'We haven't finished, far from it.' She closed her eyes again and lowered her head with a moan.

José reached out and took hold of the waistband of the satin panties, drawing them gently downwards. 'I want to see more of my property,' he told her, as he eased the bunched material down over her bottom. She whimpered as the satin brushed her scalded hide, and her glowing buttocks squirmed sensuously from side to side so that José very nearly forgot his self-restraint. But only nearly! He would be a fool to end the banquet so early.

He eased the panties down to the girl's ankles and then lifted first one of her feet and then the other so that she could step out of them. 'Now,' he said, 'spread your legs. Show me exactly how much of your body belongs to me.'

Cynthia shuffled her legs apart, making the muscles of her bottom wriggle and dance as she did so. The firm cheeks parted, gradually revealing the twin prizes between them – two neat little holes separated by a couple of inches of pinkish tan skin.

José felt his manhood leap with excitement. What a prize she was, and his to tame! He readied the paddle and swung it forward, hard, and Cynthia howled as her tender skin was forced up into dozens of sharp-edged little holes. The girl was sobbing and pawing at the desk, and her behind twitched and rippled with muscle contractions that were obviously completely out of her control.

José hefted the paddle. This had to be done carefully; the paddle was an extreme measure. He wanted to break her to his hand – and other organs! – but not to break her spirit completely.

He made a decision. 'Two more strokes of the paddle,' he told her, 'and then a rest. Are you ready?'

She whimpered, but nodded, and then screwed up her eyes. She obviously needed some help, so José laid one hand on the small of her back, which was damp with the sweat of fear and pain, and raised the paddle with his other.

The blow fell, its echoing crack being quickly followed by another howl. He kept his hand on her back, pressing firmly as she writhed with pain, and waited until she had settled again before whipping the paddle down yet again.

It was his hardest stroke yet. Cynthia gave a high wordless squeal and lay sobbing, her muscles limp. He had guessed well; the girl was near breaking point, and if he went much further just now he would lose her trust and never regain it.

He put the paddle down in the trolley, deliberately letting it clatter against the metal. The sound roused the bleary girl, and she raised her tear-streaked face to look at him.

'Enough for the moment,' he said gently. 'Time to stand up. Here – let me help you.' He took her by the shoulders and helped her upright, shushing as she whimpered and flinched with the flexing of her bottom. When she was standing he supported her for a moment until he was sure she was steady. Then he took away his hands and walked round to examine her from behind.

It was an astonishing sight. Although she was no longer bent over, she had not closed her legs, and her parted buttocks were blazing with a crop of hundreds of sullen little grey blisters where the holes of the paddle had bitten. Between the flogged globes, the folded skin of the neat little cunt was shining with moisture, and a tiny trickle of fluid – whether sweat, female juice or urine he couldn't tell – ran down the inside of her thigh. He put his hand into the hot crevice, and she shuddered and growled as his fingers entered her. He worked at her for a while, entranced at the wet velvet feel of her, and then abruptly withdrew and plunged a finger into the tight pucker of her anus. She gave a single aaahhh of surprise, and then kept quite still, so that he felt he had control of her whole body through this one tight little entrance. I'll bet she's virgin there, he thought. Never been buggered. Well, that's going to change before sunrise.

He kept her transfixed on the end of his finger for a while, thrusting and twisting it a little to gauge her response. Then he slid it out, feeling the ring of muscle nip shut after him like some blind little sea creature snapping after escaping prey. She made a noise he couldn't quite interpret, that could have been either relief or regret, and he stroked her back.

'You've done well,' he said, 'so far.' She preened a little, and he allowed her a few moments of satisfaction. Then he patted her sharply on the bottom. 'Come on,' he said. 'It's time for some dessert.'

CHAPTER 19

Nine hundred kilometres to the north, David Arundel was also sitting at the table, and by a coincidence he would never know, Yolanda had just set down dessert in front of him. He nodded coldly, and she scuttled away.

David watched the naked body of his slave retreating. Her bottom and thighs were striped with the fading mementoes of a caning he had given her a few days ago, and he thought to himself that it was about time he topped them up, but somehow his mood was wrong. He looked down and toyed with his sorbet, but he wasn't really hungry, and his mind was elsewhere. On Cynthia, in fact.

Put simply, he was getting worried. He was well-connected, and he knew without doubt that his daughter had arrived safely at Mas Gassac because he had paid someone to find out. He also knew quite well what awaited her there. The place had a certain reputation in discreet circles, and it was not a bad reputation; quite the opposite. They made decent wine, too. He looked reflectively at his glass of Fruits de la Soumission and smiled a little.

He had heard nothing from Cynthia. That wasn't unusual. He had sent her to finishing school, and apart from a brief call on the first day and two postcards sent weeks later, she might as well have been on another planet. His then-seventeen year old daughter had earned the last of her very rare spankings for that omission. Or at least, he thought, the last so far. He was half-inclined to add another when he next saw her, as a reward for her latest silence. But perhaps, after all, that job was out of his hands now.

He pushed his plate away and tapped his fingers on the table. He had promised himself that he would not interfere in her choices. Very well, he would hold to that. But just as she was a grown-up now, why then so was he. He could make his own mind up to a course of action.

He sat up briskly. At the other end of the table, Julia looked up at him. 'What is it, darling?' she asked.

He smiled, and clicked his fingers. Yolanda trotted over and stood to attention by his chair. 'Yes, master?' she said.

'Fetch a note pad,' he told her. 'I want to send a message.'

She dashed out of the room and returned a minute later. 'Ready, master,' she said.

'Good. The message is to be sent as a telegram, to Monsieur José Mestré, of Mas Gassac, Perpignan. The office will find his address. Say that I request the pleasure of his company here at dinner, next Saturday.'

She nodded, scribbling, and made to leave. He raised his hand, stopping her. 'There's something else,' he said. 'Tell him I request the company of him and his partner.'

His slave withdrew, and he smiled across the table at his wife. 'It will be interesting to see what turns up,' he said.

She nodded. 'I've been worried,' she admitted. 'It would be good to know what is happening to her.'

'I know. I feel the same way. My instincts are that she is well, and perhaps better than well, but all the same, as you say, it would be good to know.'

His wife smiled. 'What will you do if she turns up on the arm of this Monsieur Mestré, looking safe and well and happy?'

'I will rejoice,' he said. And then, after a pause, he added; 'and then I will put her over my knee, eighteen years old or not, and teach her never to leave us worrying in the same way again.' After all, she is still my daughter, he added silently to himself.

His wife nodded. 'I approve of that,' she said. 'We women need to be shown who's in charge, sometimes.'

David looked at his wife for a long moment. Her eyes were shining, and her face looked a little flushed. Her lips were parted a fraction. 'Tell me,' he said, 'when did I last beat you?'

Her reply was instant. 'Four days ago,' she said.

'Four days?' David raised his eyebrows. 'How remiss of me. Stand up!'

She did so, thrusting back her chair with a loud scraping noise.

'Good. Now strip to your corset.'

He watched as she raised the tight-fitting evening dress over her head. It was like the dance of the seven veils, he thought. Every movement reveals a little more flesh, but the final moment of shame never comes; there is always something left.

His wife wriggled out of her dress, stockings and panties, leaving only the tight wasp-waisted corset with its abandoned fringe of suspenders. He stood up and walked round the table to stand next to her. This close, he could smell the faint, complex floral scent of her eau de toilette, overlying the barely concealed notes of flesh and sweat which meant far more to him. He let his hand rest on her rump, testing her firm rounded flesh. Then he leaned in so that his mouth was close to her ear.

'Go,' he said. 'Fetch the tawse. Be quick!'

She nodded and ran off, almost colliding with the returning Yolanda. The girl hurried up to David and curtseyed. 'Please, Sir, I've sent the telegram,' she said, a little breathlessly.

'Good.' David nodded. Yolanda curtseyed again and turned to leave, but he reached out and hooked a finger in the metal ring of her collar. 'Not so fast,' he told her. 'The Mistress is to be tawsed, and you night be needed. Wait in the corner.'

Yolanda bowed her head and retreated to her accustomed place in the corner of the room.

A few minutes later Julia returned. She close the door carefully behind her, walked up to David and dropped to her knees, holding out a tawse in front of her. David took it with a brief nod of acknowledgement, and examined it.

It was made of a thick, heavy hide, of such a dark brown that it seemed almost black. It was the same length as his arm, as wide as his index finger was long, and more than a quarter of an inch thick – the archaic measure seemed appropriate to the age of the thing because this was no reproduction but a genuine Scottish tawse, at least fifty years old. One third of its length was handle, and the rest was split into two heavy, supple tails, and its soul (if such a thing could be said to have a soul) was soaked with generations of pain and fear.

David tapped it softly against his palm, appreciating the power and weight of the thing, and marvelling at how even the slightest contact with it seemed to sting. With each tap, Julia flinched, and her fear aroused him, just as it always did.

'Stand up,' he said.

She rose from her kneeling position and stood with her hands by her side. David was secretly pleased to see that they were trembling slightly. He reached out and stroked her cheek.

'No need to be frightened,' he told her. 'You women need to be shown who's in charge, remember?' She nodded, and he turned away abruptly. With his back to her he said: 'Turn, and bend over.'

The pat-pat of her feet on the floor and a faint movement of air told him she had obeyed. He waited a little longer, to give her time for her exposed position to sink in, and then turned round.

Tightly bent, with her legs parted, his wife made a superb sight. The position emphasised the curves of her bottom and thighs, already heightened by the unforgiving pull of the corset, and the slightly open lips of her sex peeked invitingly out from between the parted cheeks.

David spent a few seconds admiring the spectacle, while his cock pulsed and complained in its captivity. Then he tapped the tawse once more against the palm of his hand, drew it back, and brought it lashing down across the defenceless target.

It landed with a pistol-shot crack across the crease at the top of the tightened thighs, and a bar of skin immediately flashed white and then darkened, incredibly fast, through red to purple. Julia howled with pain and her heels lifted from the floor, one after the other in a dance of agony, but she stayed in position, her hands grasping her ankles with whitened knuckles.

David nodded to himself, and watched until his wife had absorbed the pain of the first stroke. When she was still he pulled back his arm and sent the tawse whipping home again. The blow landed a little above the first, so that half the width of the tawse revisited skin that had already suffered the first stroke, and the other half landed on the fresh white skin of Julia's lower bottom.

Julia gave another howl, which to David's expert ear sounded a little higher and sharper than her first, and her bottom began another dance of pain as her heels lifted and twitched. It was, thought David, one of the most enticing sights in the world – a woman's behind wriggling and fidgeting under the lash. No wonder men had beaten their women since time immemorial. He waited until Julia had almost settled down and then changed his aim and sent in the next stroke from the opposite side. It landed on the same low track as his first stroke, relighting the fire in an area which had already been scalded, and this time Julia's knees gave for a second and her shriek made the glasses chime on the table.

This time David didn't wait so long. He began to up his tempo, sweeping the heavy tails across from alternate sides every half-dozen heartbeats, so that Julia barely had time to complete one wail of pain before having to draw breath for the next. Her flaming cheeks swayed and wriggled under the onslaught, making the two holes in the depths of her cleft flash and wink lasciviously, and her feet stamped as she tried to ride the waves of fire he was sending through her hips.

After two dozen strokes, David stopped and took stock of the punishment he had inflicted. It was considerable. A broad swathe of his wife's rump, beginning at the top of her thighs and extending about halfway up her cheeks, had been thrashed to a blotchy purple. The punished flesh still twitched and trembled a little in time with the subdued woman's quiet sobs.

It was impossible to resist; David reached out his hand and pushed two fingers quickly into the soaked gash between the cheeks. Julia gasped, but then leaned back a little, pressing herself harder onto his hand, and he felt her flesh clenching around him. 'Good girl,' he said quietly. 'You know your master, don't you?'

'Yes, Sir.' The words were gasped as he pushed his hand deeper, forcing her open.

'Good.' He worked at her until she began to sigh and pant, and then withdrew his hand. He held his wet fingers in front of her face, and her tongue flicked out to lap at her own juices. He turned his hand, letting her clean every drop. Then, when he felt she had done enough, he wiped his hand on a napkin, and took his wife by the hair, pulling her up and out of the bending position so that she was standing in front of a chair.

'Down,' he told her. 'On all fours, and wait.'

He sat on the chair and she knelt in front of him. He kept hold of her hair with one hand, and undid his trousers with the other. His cock sprang up, throbbing in time with his heartbeat. A bead of pre-ejaculate glistened, and he saw Julia lick her lips. She made to lower her head onto him, but he restrained her, jerking at her hair so that she sat up a little, her face surprised.

'Oh, don't worry,' he told her. 'You'll be sucking it in a moment.' Then he reached down and picked up the tawse, which lay on the floor next to his chair. 'You'll be swallowing, too. And the sooner you get to swallowing, the less you'll feel of this,' and he held out the tawse, 'because I'll be thrashing you until you've satisfied me. Understood?'

She nodded, her eyes wide.

'Well then. What are you waiting for?'

She hurriedly lowered her head, and he felt the delicious sensation of her warm lips and her busy tongue. He luxuriated for a few moments, and then raised the tawse. It swept down, landing vertically down her bottom with the tails, if he had judged it right, just biting nicely into the base of her cheek.

A tremor went through her body, and he felt her mouth twitch around him, bringing an unexpected but enjoyable bonus. He lashed her again, and felt a soft humming buzz as she moaned down her nose.

This was a trick worth knowing! David began to whip the tawse down regularly, working blind and judging the result of each stroke solely by the added sensations in his cock. The best result seemed to come when he caught her down the middle, when he assumed those punitive tails were finding the soft, sensitive skin between Julia's thighs. She was certainly reacting – her hips began to weave from side to side, and her face grew wet with tears as she gulped and gagged at him.

Soon, far sooner than he had intended, he felt himself begin to peak. He waited until he was hanging on the brink and then pulled Julia's head a little upwards so that his pumping spurts filled her mouth rather than going straight down her throat. She sucked greedily at him, growling appreciatively down her nose as his seed flooded her tongue. He kept her head in position until he had completely finished, and then released her. She sat back, smiling though her tears, and he watched her throat ripple as she swallowed.

'Well,' he said, 'it seems the incentive worked. I must try that again.'

Her smile widened. 'Yes please,' she said.

David laughed. 'Meanwhile,' he said, 'you probably have some unfinished business?'

She blushed, and nodded.

'Well, then' he said. 'Let's see it finished. Yolanda!'

The slave, who was still standing in her corner, snapped to attention.

'Come and please the Mistress.'

Yolanda stepped forwards. Julia stood up, and turned towards the table. 'May I have it from behind, please?' she asked.

David nodded. 'Of course,' he said, and Julia bent herself a little forward over the table, parting her legs and looking over her shoulder at Yolanda.

David gestured to his slave. 'Begin,' he told her.

Yolanda dropped to her knees and shuffled forwards until her face was just behind her Mistress's open legs. She studied her richly marked target, and then pressed her face into the soaked cleft. David saw her head bob a little as she began to lick.

Cynthia began to mew with pleasure as the slave-girl's tongue worked at her. David relaxed, sat back and let himself enjoy the show.

He wondered how long it would take for the reply to come from Mas Gassac. And what it would say when it arrived. He agreed with his wife – women needed a firm hand.

He hoped his daughter had found a man who would provide it.

CHAPTER 20

José pulled the supper trolley towards him and lifted a cover with the hand that had not entered Cynthia. 'What would you like? There's a tarte au citron, or some cheese. And sit down!'

He gestured toward a chair. She looked at it doubtfully, and he guessed she was thinking about the fire he had lit in her bottom.

'Go on,' he said, and shoved her gently so that she sat down with a little bump. 'You need to learn how to carry on with your tasks, whatever they are and whatever the state of your bottom.'

She winced and fidgeted for a moment. Then she seemed to resign herself. She reached out and, without hesitating, pulled the cheeseboard towards her.

José applauded softly. 'I thought you would,' he said. She looked baffled, and he added: 'I had a bet with myself that you would take the cheese, not the tarte.'

'Why?' She remembered to add: 'Please, Sir?'

'Because I have watched you enjoying plenty of savoury things.'

She went on chewing, her face puzzled, and he took pity on her. 'I'll show you,' he said. 'Look over there.' He pointed to the big plasma TV at the end of the room, pressing the remote. The screen flicked on, and he selected a channel.

Then he watched Cynthia, watching.

After a while she turned to him and said: 'That's Amelie and Li.'

'Yes.'

She watched more, her face expressionless. Then she said, without turning away from the images on the screen: 'Did you watch me?'

'Of course.' He paused, and added mischievously: 'It was very enjoyable.'

She blushed. 'What did you see me... do?'

'I saw you lick, and be licked.' José shrugged. 'I saw nothing I wouldn't expect of a female in this place. I saw that you are bisexual, but that doesn't surprise me because I believe most girls are, even English ones, at least in their minds if not in their actions. I saw that you are not inhibited. I saw that you appreciate the taste of the female, and the male too, at least at second hand. And that you look as pretty on your knees as you do when you are handing out a thrashing.' He spread his arms. 'I make no apology for spying on you, since you have made yourself my property. And what I saw pleased me, if that matters to you.'

She blushed deeper and looked away. 'It does matter,' she said quietly.

'I'm glad.' José stood up. 'Now, if you have had enough cheese, we have some unfinished business.' He didn't wait for her answer, but clapped his hands sharply. A slave girl trotted in and stood to attention. José nodded to her, and she began to clear the table. While she was busy, José turned to Cynthia.

'Stand up,' he said. She did so, and he picked up the riding crop from the trolley. 'As soon as there is room,' he said, 'I want you to lie on the table, on your back, with your bottom close to the edge and your legs in the air.'

She waited until the maid had finished, and then turned round and sat back up onto the table, making a little hopping jump like someone springing her bottom up onto the side of a swimming pool. Then she lay back and raised her legs, her ankles together, until they stood up at right angles to her body.

'Good girl.' José nodded approvingly. 'Spread your arms as widely as you can – it will help you balance. Then spread your legs. Open yourself.'

He watched, barely daring to breath, as Cynthia's legs formed a V-shape that became shallower and shallower. Her muscles trembled and the sinews stood out along the insides of those pale thighs as she fought to maintain the position. She had obviously had some gymnastics training, because she managed to hold herself steady, the lips of her sex opening like a lustful smile. Even so, José clicked his fingers at the maid, who was about to leave.

'Stay,' he told her. 'Be ready to hold her.' Then he turned to Cynthia. 'Over the last week,' he said, 'you have been thrashed, and you have given thrashings. You have licked, and been licked. You have worked in the hot sun, and now you are lying on my table like the lowest whore there ever was. What do you think is going to happen now?'

She shook her head. 'I don't know.'

'I'll tell you.' He tapped the crop against the inside of her thigh, and she flinched. 'I am going to hurt you, more than you have yet been hurt, and then I am going to take you. Do you have anything to say?'

There was a pause. Then she raised her head and said: 'May I refuse?'

José nodded slowly. 'Yes,' he said. 'If you like. You can refuse, and go home, or you can accept, and stay.' His heart jumped in his chest as he heard himself say the words. Before, he had always made such offers to girls when they first arrived, and never afterwards. Certainly not when they had already been at Mas Gassac for a week! What had he been thinking of, and what would she decide?

The answer came quickly, in a low clear voice. 'I don't care how much it hurts,' she said, 'as long as it's you doing the hurting.' Then she lay back on the table and closed her eyes.

José felt the tension leave him like the tide going out. 'Well done,' he said. And then, unable to think of anything better: 'Well done!'

Then he stood back and raised the crop.

It whistled down and landed on the inside of her thigh, raising a sharply defined purple weal barely a centimetre from the soft moist flesh she had opened for him. Cynthia opened her mouth, but instead of the shriek he was expecting – it had been a cruel blow – she gave a long, low moan that could as easily have been a sign of pleasure as of pain.

He raised the crop again and struck at the opposite thigh, raising a second weal that was the mirror image of the first. Again she gave that contradictory moan, full of nuances that could have meant yes or no, but when he looked, the opened lips of her sex were slick with moisture and her chest was heaving.

It was yes, then. He raised the crop and whipped at her, striking at her thighs, at the mound at the base of her belly, and more and more at the parted sex that shone so enticingly.

It was like playing a musical instrument; each target produced a different cry. The inner thighs, quickly darkening to an angry purple, drew short, sharp squeals. Strokes to the belly caused a darker note, and when the leather tip of the crop cracked against Cynthia's cunt the girl gave long, greedy-sounding panting growls. She began to writhe from side to side, and at a nod from José the maid went round to the other side of the table, reached over and took hold of Cynthia's parted ankles. She held them firmly, steadying the girl's lustful rocking and pulling her legs further out and back so that her hips rolled a little upwards off the surface of the table. The movement exposed her sex even more, and brought the little twitching pucker of her anus into view – and within reach of the crop.

José whipped and thrashed at the helpless girl-meat in the ecstasy of the conqueror who has found a willing victim. For there was no doubting that the girl was willing! Even as she squealed and moaned and growled under the lash, her punished sex grew wetter and wetter so that the juices soaked the tip of the crop and ran down her cleft in a shiny trail, moistening the lascivious bud of her anus and collecting in thick droplets on the table.

At last, Cynthia's cries merged into one another so that she was letting out a single, panting sob of mixed pain and pleasure. The pleasure won; her head rolled from side to side, and José watched in awe as the spasms of her orgasm gripped the girl and animated her flesh.

It lasted a long time.

Eventually, Cynthia lay quiet. The maid was still holding her legs, her eyes glazed and her lips flushed, obviously aroused by the drama she had helped create. José clicked his fingers and she snapped out of her reverie. 'You can let her go now,' he said. She took her hands from Cynthia's ankles, and Cynthia rolled over onto her side with a little sigh.

José reached out and took her hand. 'Well done,' he said. 'I'm proud of you.' He squeezed her hand a little. 'Now,' he said. 'There might be something else you want?'

She nodded.

'Can you tell me what it is?'

'I want…' She stopped, and then sat up so that he was looking into her eyes. 'Please, Sir,' she said, 'may I be fucked?'

José smiled. 'Well asked, my girl,' he told her, 'and yes, you may very well indeed. But there is one more thing first.' He pointed to the trolley. 'There is something there that hasn't yet been used.'

Her eyes followed his gesture, and he saw them widen.

'The cane,' she said, in a flat voice.

'That's right, the cane.' José took it from the trolley. Cynthia's eyes were glued to it, he saw, and they widened as he flexed the pale wand. 'I think,' he said slowly, 'that it's time for your last test of the night.'

CHAPTER 21

Julia stared at the cane. Her stomach churned. Hadn't she endured enough? Her bottom smarted and glowed with the punishment José had inflicted on it, and her quim still burned from the explosion of pleasure-pain it had suffered. Besides...

She had never been caned. Girls of her generation just weren't. So it had been a subject instead of breathless fantasy, where its sinister reputation as the harshest tool of all had grown with every secret stroke of her fingers against her clit.

'That's right. The cane.' As she watched, José picked it up and ran his hands along it. 'Such an English thing, isn't it?' he said. 'The formality, the ceremony. So much tradition.' He pointed it at her. 'Time for us to buy into that tradition. Stand up!'

There was a touch of the parade ground in his voice, and she obeyed immediately, keeping her eyes fixed on the slim, pale wand in his hand and trying to control her legs, which were suddenly trembling.

Then, when she was standing, he suddenly flipped it over so that the crooked handle was pointing towards her.

'Take it,' he said.

She looked down at it, baffled. He thrust it at her again.

'Take it,' he repeated. 'You're going to need it in a moment.'

She stared at the cane a little longer, and then reached out a tentative hand and took it from him. She had no idea what her face was registering, but whatever it was must be comical, because José laughed out loud.

'Did you think I was going to cane you?' he asked. 'Hardly! As much as you seem to love being whipped, you've taken plenty already. Always leave some skin for tomorrow, that's my motto.'

She smiled, trying not to look too relieved or too nervous. 'But then,' she said carefully, 'who…'

José took her by the shoulders and swivelled her round until she was facing the maid, who stood cowering on the other side of the table.

'Who do you think?' he asked. 'Not me, for sure!'

Cynthia look down at the cane in her hand. 'I know what you're thinking,' he said. 'Why me, and why her?' He let go of her shoulders and laid a hand on her cheek. 'It's simple,' he said. 'Her, because she is my property and if I say she should be caned, then she should be caned. That's the easy bit. Why you?' He took his hand from her cheek, and began to count off on his fingers. 'Because a slave makes the harshest master. Or mistress, in your case. Because I believe you have it in you, and more besides. Because it would please me to see you thrash her, as I have seen you thrash others.' He gestured towards the big TV, and she nodded and felt herself blush again at the thought of what he had watched her do. 'And because, well, there is one because I'll save until later.'

She nodded again, and tightened her grip on the cane.

'Good girl,' he said. 'For the moment, you're in charge.' He paused, and then added; 'By the way, the maid's name is Chloe.'

Cynthia nodded again and took a deep breath. Then she turned to the maid. 'Chloe,' she said, 'come here.'

Chloe walked slowly round the table until she stood next to Cynthia. She wore a conventional maid's uniform of a knee-length dress of black satin. Cynthia looked her up and down.

'Since I have been here, I have always been punished on bare skin,' she said. 'So will you be. Raise your dress.'

Slowly, the maid obeyed. The material of the dress gathered slowly round her waist, revealing a pair of plump girlish thighs set off by tight hold-up stockings. Her buttocks were naked, and Cynthia shot a questioning look at José.

He shrugged. 'She is the property of the household, to be available at all times,' he said simply. 'Why would she need more clothes?'

Cynthia raised her eyebrows and gave José a short smile. Then she turned to Chloe. 'We will follow tradition,' she said. 'Twelve of the best, in the English style. Bend over, and grasp your ankles.'

Chloe did as she was told. The tight position emphasised a trim pair of buttocks crowning pale, well-shaped thighs. Cynthia studied the skin at the junction of the two, which was a little darker than the surroundings. This time she decided not to ask, but José must have seen her look because he offered an explanation anyway.

'The paddle,' he said shortly. 'A few days ago. She's over it now. Proceed.'

Cynthia nodded and turned to the bending girl. 'In my country,' she said, 'it is traditional to count the strokes, and to thank the punisher after each one. Are you ready?'

'Yes Madame.' Cynthia raised her eyebrows at the word. Madame – a mark of respect. Commanded, she thought, by a girl whose legs you were holding open only minutes ago. Well, well. I could get used to this.

Hoping that José wouldn't notice, Cynthia gave a single gulp of nervousness. She tapped the cane against Chloe's tightened bottom once, twice, three times. Then she drew it back and sent it whistling in to its trembling target.

Whether through judgement or beginner's luck, Cynthia didn't know, but the stroke landed across the exact centre of the proffered behind. The hiss of the cane and the crack of the impact were almost simultaneous. The response came a little afterwards, as the pain of the stroke made its way through Chloe's shocked nerve endings. Then the maid put back her head and gave a howl of outrage.

Cynthia couldn't resist it. She turned to José, and let some of her triumph and relief show in her face. He nodded a brief acknowledgement, and then gestured at the maid.

'She hasn't completed her side of the bargain,' he said mildly.

Cynthia felt herself flush. She turned to Chloe. 'You were supposed to count, and say thank you,' she said. 'That one doesn't count. We'll start again.'

The maid groaned, but Cynthia was already tapping the cane on her bottom. The next stroke hissed in with at least as much force as the first, landing just below the purple bar that had already blossomed on the pale cheeks.

The maid gave another agonised wail. Then she fought herself back under control.

'One, thank you,' she said, in a trembling voice.

Cynthia gave José a look which she fully intended to mean there, you see? Then she turned back to her task. The cane whipped down across the maid's tightened cheeks, leaving stripe after purple stripe on the lavishly punished skin, while the howling maid stamped her feet and swivelled her hips from side to side in the ancient dance performed by females under the lash since the beginning of time. Cynthia watched first in astonishment, and then in frank lust, as the angry weals darkened and spread across Chloe's behind, while the beaten girl panted and gulped out her thanks.

The count mounted quickly – almost too quickly for Cynthia's taste, but the cane seemed to have taken on a life of its own – until the twelfth stroke had fizzed in and landed, and the last sobbing thanks had been given. The bent maid trembled, her hands still grasping her ankles, snivelling with the docility of the thoroughly whipped, and Cynthia turned to José. Suddenly she felt incredibly excited; suddenly she needed to feel him against her, very urgently indeed.

'I've finished, Sir,' she said. 'What would you like me to do now?'

The words seemed to push José over the edge. He took the cane from her hand, and threw it to one side.

'On your knees,' he said, his voice thick. She dropped to the ground in front of him, her heart pounding, and he tore open his trousers. His cock stood out, high and angry.

'Suck me,' he ordered, but even as he spoke she had darted her head forwards in an ecstasy of arousal.

Chapter 22

José had watched Cynthia caning the unfortunate Chloe with frank respect. The ability of the genuine switch, to go from deep submission to outright dominance at a single command, was very rare indeed, but there was no doubt at all that he had found it in Cynthia. And now she had switched back; there she was, on her knees, offering him one of the oldest tributes in the world.

He grunted with pleasure as her mouth embraced him. Her hot tongue busied itself at the underside of his shaft, and he felt her warm breath flowing over him.

It felt good, there was no doubt. She worked at him with the instinctive, untrained enthusiasm of the amateur, in a way that reminded José of earnest teenage blow-jobs in parked cars. He grinned to himself at the memory and took hold of her head, controlling and slowing her movements and pulling her deeper on to him so that the head of his shaft nestled into the softness of her throat. She gagged a little but didn't fight him, and quite soon he felt himself begin to swell towards a climax.

Far too soon; he didn't want to finish yet. He withdrew from Cynthia's mouth, leaving a silver trail of mixed pre-come and saliva that stretched and snapped. He pulled her to her feet.

'Turn round,' he told her. As she turned he pushed her so that she stumbled forward. While she was still unbalanced he took one of her arms and pushed her again so that she fell forwards onto the table, her arm pinned behind her back.

'Now,' he said, and his voice felt harsh in his throat, 'let's try another hole.' He rested the wet tip of his cock against those slick, bruised lips, and thrust himself into her.

Cynthia grunted with the force of his entry, but there was greediness in the sound, and something told him that no matter how rough he was, he would be welcome. That suited him perfectly; he began to ram himself into her, hard enough that his thighs slapped against her purple cheeks in an echo of the punishment that had coloured them in the first place. It must have hurt, but Cynthia's groans and growls sounded anything but complaining. Pinioned as she was, she could barely move, but she still managed to squirm her bottom a little, and the tiny movements added to his pleasure out of all proportion to their size.

All too soon, the heat and wetness and youthful tightness of her cunt began to bring him close to the edge. It took real self-control, but he managed to stop, and pulled himself out of her body with a thick, wet sound. Cynthia moaned and turned her face back to look at him pleadingly.

'Don't worry,' he told her. 'I haven't finished yet!' And without any warning, he aimed himself at the last of her defences, the tight little wrinkle deep within the top of her cleft.

His first stroke took him mercilessly to full depth, drawing a long, guttural cry of pain from the helpless girl. For the first time she tried to struggle, but her held her in place, leaning his weight down to pin her arm into the small of her back, and after a few seconds she quietened to a watchful stillness.

'Not an hour ago,' he told her, 'you said you didn't care how much it hurt as long as it was me doing the hurting. Well, this will hurt, and you'd better believe it's me doing it. I'm going to do it often. If you learn to enjoy it then maybe I'll do it as a reward. If you don't, then I'll do it as a punishment. But either way, I'm going to do it, and you'd better get used to it.'

As he finished speaking he had withdrawn about half way, and now he thrust forwards again, and again, and again, possessing her harshly in the most intimate way he could. It was an act which, if he was honest, he had dreamt of almost from the moment he had first seen her being so ineffectually whipped in l'Histoire d'O, and the reality was easily living up to his dreams. She was so tight! And inexperienced, too – her ring tightened with muscular spasms she had not yet learned to control, and the effect was delicious.

José held off as long as he could, but even before he had entered her last sanctum he had twice been near the edge. Now he was closing quickly; he moved faster and faster, and his thrusting cock hardened and burned within her muscular embrace, until suddenly the pumping extremity of his orgasm was on him and he forced himself deeper yet into her and came as if he had never come before. He heard his own cry of release, and with it came another, and he felt Cynthia's body arching beneath him, and realised that she was coming too.

It took a long time to spend their mutual passion. When they were finally still, he withdrew gently and stood up. As he released the pressure on Cynthia's arm she let herself slide off the table so that she landed in a kneeling position. Then she turned round, put her arms round his waist and rested her cheek against his thigh, looking up at him with drowned eyes. 'Please, Sir,' she said simply, 'I love you.'

He nodded. 'I know,' he said. 'Good girl.' He took her by the shoulders and lifted her gently until she stood in front of him. I could spend my life with this one, he thought. The one girl that old pirate Pera keeps nagging me to find – perhaps this is her. Perhaps I struck lucky in L'histoire d'O, of all places.

Cynthia was trembling a little, and her face looked pale. He wasn't surprised, after what she had been through. He put an arm around her shoulder and guided her to a chair. 'Sit down,' he said. The last time he had said that, she had demurred, but this time she obeyed without question, even though her eyes half-closed in the faintest of flinches as her bottom met the firm seat.

He reached for a glass, and poured the girl a little more wine. She took it gratefully and began to sip. As she did, the colour returned to her cheeks and her trembles quieted.

'Thanks,' she said.

José smiled. 'You're welcome,' he told her. Then he made up his mind. He turned to Chloe, who was still tightly bent, with her vividly striped bottom on display.

'Stand up,' he said. The girl obeyed stiffly. 'Say thank you to Cynthia,' he told her, 'and then leave us.'

Chloe turned to Cynthia and curtseyed. 'Thank you, Madame,' she whispered. Then she turned and almost ran from the room.

José waited until she had shut the door behind her, and then turned back to Cynthia. 'Now,' he said, 'there's something I want to ask you.'

She became watchful.

José continued, choosing his words carefully. 'You have been at Mas Gassac a week now,' he said. 'During that week you have been, how should I put it, a slave of the house. Has it been a good week?'

She nodded immediately.

'Does that mean you have enjoyed your first taste of slavery?'

She nodded again. 'Yes,' she said. 'It just feels… right.'

'I'm glad.' He paused, and then went on slowly: 'I said slave of the house, but tell me – whose slave have you really thought yourself?'

There was no hesitation. 'Yours,' she said, looking up at him.

'Ah.' He smiled. 'Well, that's good. Because I have an offer for you.' She put down her glass and sat bolt upright, but he shook his head gently and stood up. 'On your knees, please,' he said, and quickly she slid off the chair and knelt in front of him. He ran his fingers through her hair, feeling the trace dampness of her sweat. 'I want you to be my permanent slave,' he told her. 'My partner, if you like. You'll join me in the running of this place, and you'll have plenty of chances to indulge your taste for thrashing attractive young females – don't deny it! I've watched you, remember?'

She frowned a little. 'Your permanent slave and partner?'

'That's right.' José looked down at her, and was surprised to see her face crack into a broad smile. 'What's funny?'

She giggled. 'Sorry,' she said, 'but I was just thinking. Slave and partner – it sounds like a really old fashioned proposal of marriage.'

He rested his hand on her cheek. 'But that's just what it was,' he told her. 'Wife, queen, partner, servant, slave. I know you can be all of those. I want you to be them for me.'

She looked up at him for a moment, and he saw her eyes begin to well. Then, rather formally and quite unbidden, she bent her head down and kissed his boot. She held the position, and he heard her whisper: 'Yes, please. Oh, yes!'

His heart raced, and even as depleted as he was, he felt himself harden. He raised his foot a little, pushing it against her mouth, and was gratified to see her tongue flick out and curl against the dusty leather. My God, he thought, as his cock swelled even further, is there anything she won't do – and any effect she can't produce in me? He watched for a while as she licked contentedly, twisting her neck and rolling her head from side to side as her tongue followed the contours of his boot.

His excitement quickly rose to a level that would not be ignored, and he reached down and took her by the hair. He pulled her roughly up until she was level with his waist and forced his cock into her mouth. She plunged her head forward, greedily welcoming his full length, even fouled as he was by having buggered her so recently, and the heat and closeness of her quickly brought him up to a climax that was all the more intense for being his second in a short time. He growled as he came, and held her in position until she had sucked the last drops of sperm from him. Then he let her go, and she dropped to all fours, breathing heavily.

'Thank you,' she said, so quietly he could hardly hear her.

He reached down and patted her head, and he was about to say something (although he wasn't quite sure what) when there was a knock at the door. Not just any knock; two short, one long. It was Pera, and he had something important to say.

José straightened his clothes and walked over to open the door. 'What is it, old friend?'

'It is something unusual.' Pera held out a piece of paper. 'It is a telegram.'

José raised his eyebrows. 'Really? Do we still have them?'

'Apparently we do.' Pera looked amused. 'At least, we certainly have this one.' He handed it to José. 'Even so, I would not have disturbed you, but it is from a

Monsieur Arundel of Paris. It occurred to me that we have here a Mademoiselle Arundel, also of Paris.' He gestured towards Cynthia, who was sitting back on her haunches with her head up and her eyes alert, and shrugged. 'And so I disturbed you.'

José took the telegram. He read it, and then looked at Cynthia. 'What is your address, in Paris?' he asked.

'Avenue Pergolèse.'

'And your father's name?'

'David.'

José read the telegram again. 'It is he, certainly.' He looked at Cynthia again. 'What do you think he wants, this father of yours with his address on one of the most expensive streets in Paris?'

'I don't know,' she said, and her face began to fall. 'Is something wrong?'

José shook his head. 'I doubt it,' he said. 'Otherwise, I don't see why he would be asking me to dinner next weekend.'

Her eyes widened comically, and José laughed. 'He is a formidable man, your father?' She nodded, and he went on: 'Don't worry, little English flower. I am formidable too, and besides I shan't be undefended. Your father asks me to bring a partner. Will you come?' Even before he had finished his question, her face had given him his answer.

He couldn't remember when he had ever seen someone look so relieved, and so happy.

CHAPTER 23

Cynthia had slept like the dead, the long dreamless sleep that is so deep that you wake up in the same position you were in when you collapsed on the bed.

She came to slowly. Her body felt, she was not sure what. Present. That was it. She was very aware of every corner of her. She explored further. Her bottom was definitely sore. It itched and smarted against the sheets, and when she reached down a careful hand she could feel raised tender areas.

She could remember every stroke, and the memory moistened her. She reached her fingers into her tender flesh, found the spot and began to caress herself, very gently. Then she froze.

There had been a rustle of sheets. She wasn't alone in the room.

She turned over softly and found herself looking into Chloe's eyes. The maid was lying on the next bed, the sheet shrugged back to her knees. She was lying on her front, her up-turned bottom still showing the vivid stripes of the caning Cynthia had given her the night before. Her hand was beneath her belly, and her hips were moving slowly.

Cynthia watched her for a second. She remembered the big screen in José's apartments; if he wanted, he could see their every move. Then she shrugged to herself. He hadn't seemed to mind what she got up to with the other girls. Besides, if she did something wrong, well, she would be punished, and then she would know not to do it again!

She took her finger out of her sex and used its glistening tip to beckon slowly to Chloe. The maid climbed off her bed and came to lie down next to her. Cynthia placed her hands on the girl's cheeks and gently pushed at her until she lowered her head to the junction of Cynthia's thighs. A tongue sprang out, and Cynthia felt its soft, hot caress moving up her lips, gently lifting, moving aside her clit hood and – aahhh – sliding over the sensitive centre of her. She pressed her hands against Chloe's face.

'I think you're going to be my little pet, aren't you?' she said, and the girl nodded without lifting her tongue from its place.

Chloe was good! Even as abused as Cynthia's sex had been the night before, and even as sore as it still was today, the girl seemed able to judge her pressure just right, so that Cynthia was caught exactly on the perfect cusp between pleasure and pain. It wasn't somewhere she could stay for long; the quick, intelligent movements of the slurping tongue brought her rapidly to the edge and then over it, so that she arched up from the bed and hissed her satisfaction to the morning sun.

The sun – it was rising quickly. With an effort of will Cynthia wrenched herself away from the diminishing waves of pleasure that rolled over her like a receding tide. She lifted Chloe's face from her hips, and smiled at the sight of a chin slick with her own juices. 'Enough fun for the moment,' she told her plaything. 'It must be time to get on with the harvest.'

And it was; only seconds after she had finished speaking there was a knock – a knock! – at the door, and Antoine's voice said: 'Good morning! Sorry for the disturbance, but Pera would value a word with Miss Arundel before work starts.'

'Coming!' Cynthia sprang out of bed and seized the dress that hung on the back of the door. She pulled it over her head and was still straightening it as she opened the door.

Antoine stood outside. He looked amused.

'Come this way, if you please,' he said. Pausing only to grab the chicote that lay by her bed, Cynthia followed him. Miss Arundel, she thought. My goodness. That makes a change. What's happened, and will I like it?

Pera was waiting for her in the yard. He smiled, and gave a slight bow.

'Good morning,' he said. 'I will spare you a long explanation. I know, more or less, what has passed between you and the Mestré. You have my congratulations.'

Cynthia felt flustered. 'Thank you,' she said, 'but what…' She paused, uncertain how to continue.

Pera smiled again. 'What does it mean?' He sucked his teeth. 'In the long term, it means exactly the same as any other tryst of this sort. Triumph, or disaster, or any point between the two.' He shook his head slowly, and then looked up at her, his face hardening. 'In the short term, it means that instead of answering to me, or to my assistants, you will answer to José and me.' He grinned, in a way was quite humourless. 'You're not off my leash yet! Quite the opposite. I hope you think you got a bargain.'

Cynthia nodded dumbly. She did think she had got a bargain, but she suspected Pera wasn't out to make it an easy one.

'Right. Well, two things. First, we have an important evening ahead of us. The first young wines from last year's pressing are ready to be tasted, and José has invited some of our most,' he paused, and then continued, 'discerning buyers in for the evening. They will expect to be entertained, and you will be part of the entertainment. Understand?'

She nodded.

'Good. But before that, there's a harvest to get in, so take yourself and your whip out into the fields and see that it happens. Because if you don't,' and he narrowed his eyes, 'I'll happen.'

Cynthia turned and trotted out of the yard. The sun was climbing and it was already a bit too hot for running, but she wanted to show willing.

Of course, the opportunity to put some distance between herself and Pera was an added advantage.

Pera kept his face carefully impassive as he watched the girl trot out of the yard, her bottom jiggling pertly through the sleek material of her dress. Then, when he was sure she was out of sight, he allowed himself a long, quiet laugh. No doubt about it, José had found himself a live one! The girl seemed submissive, but there was something un-crushable about the core of her. She would never stop needing a firm hand, he was sure, and no doubt José would never stop being able to provide one.

Still amused, Pera shook his head and walked back to his quarters. He might attend to Cynthia himself later, if he felt like it. For now he had another female to concern him.

He opened the door and stepped into his apartment. It was a single, large, open plan space with a wide bed at the far end, close to a set of French windows that opened onto a private balcony.

There was a mound on the bed. He walked over and looked down.

Ariane was still asleep. She was naked except for a pair of broad leather manacles on her wrists and another on her ankles. Fine grey chains led from the manacles to the head and foot of the bed. As Pera watched, the sleeping woman stirred and turned over on to her front. The movement brought her bottom into sight;

even in the dim light of the shuttered bedroom the pale mounds were still blotched, bruised and striped.

The sight awoke Pera's body. He reached down and tugged gently at the chains that led from the woman's wrists. She stirred, and her eyes opened. Pera smiled.

'Good morning,' he said. 'Papa's here.' He undid his trousers, allowing his cock to stand free. 'Time for breakfast.'

Ariane craned up from the bed, her eyes heavy with sleep but her lips flushing. He tongue darted out and caressed the head of Pera's surging flesh. Then her lips parted and she took him into her mouth, embracing the whole length of his shaft in a smooth, practiced movement. Pera cradled her head in his hands, controlling and constraining her movements, and sighing with pleasure as her tongue and teeth went to work on him, delicately but insistently.

She had the skill of a grown woman; his pleasure was rising faster than he preferred, and he withdrew himself, leaving Ariane's parted lips dripping with saliva and his own pre-come. Wet holes, he thought. That's what a woman should offer. Tight, wet, welcoming holes. Everything else is just seasoning.

His passion was beginning to drive him. He pushed Ariane down on to the bed, hard enough so that her face bounced off the pillow, and reached down to undo his belt. The leather hissed as he drew it through the loops on his jeans, and the woman flinched a little at the sound. The action sent a little tremor through her, making the skin of her bottom ripple. He folded the belt and stretched it out so that the two sides clapped sharply together, and Ariane flinched again.

Pera raised the belt, ready to thrash the cowering girl where she lay. Then he hesitated, and lowered his arm.

'I think we'll have you positioned better,' he told her, reaching down to undo the chains that held her legs. 'Papa wants to see his girl properly spread.'

He unclipped the chains from the end of the bed. 'Up on all fours and stick your bottom out, you,' he said, and she shuffled her hips upwards, her knees picking the sheets up into folds as she crawled forwards. He let the belt lick and snap across her haunches, driving her forwards until he was satisfied with her position. Then he took one of the trailing ends of chain. He threw it under the bed, walked round to the other side and picked up its end, pulling on it so that the kneeling woman's leg was forced to the side of the bed. He grabbed her other ankle and pulled, drawing her legs further and further apart until the sinews stood out tightly on the insides of her thighs and she was mewing with pain. Then he fixed the loose end of the chain to the manacle on the leg in his hand, and stood back, nodding with satisfaction. Ariane was now splayed, her ankles held cruelly apart by the chain, her hips shifting a little as she tried to ease the pain of her position.

The sight of the widely parted buttocks was too much for Pera. He couldn't resist reaching out his hand and burying it roughly in the hot wet gash between the mounds, quickly working the lips further apart until he had four fingers fully inside. He felt the abused flesh clenching around him.

'Squeeze,' he said quietly. 'Squeeze yourself round Papa Pera's hand. Squeeze until it hurts. Hurt yourself for me!'

He felt the pressure mount, and Ariane moaned on a rising note, her head weaving with effort. 'Good girl,' he said. 'It's good exercise as well as good discipline. In fact,' and he paused and considered for a moment, 'it's an idea we might follow up a little, later on. You can let go now.'

Ariane relaxed with a sigh. He withdrew his hand and walked round so that he could hold it in front of her face.

'Does it smell good?' he asked, and she nodded. 'Then lick,' he told her, and her tongue flickered out. He turned his hand as she licked, giving her access to every surface. 'Dirty girl,' he said, and she made a whimpering in her throat, but went on licking. He took his hand away, and picked up the belt.

'Dirty girl,' he said again, raising the belt. 'Dirty girls get whipped by their Papas, don't they?' And he brought the belt whipping down. It landed with a percussion-cap crack across Ariane's bottom, and she put her head back and gave a squeal of pain.

Pera grinned, and began to thrash her regularly, layering his strokes so that a fresh swathe of deepening purple blotted out the weals and smudges of her last beating. The leather slapped and cracked explosively against the poor girl's globes, and she shrieked and howled as the folded tip curled in to brand the soft skin of her inner thighs and the dark, wet sex above them.

Pera kept up the punishment for a long time. At last, though, he began to feel his arm tiring, and he paused to review his progress.

There was plenty to review. Ariane's full bottom was thrashed blue and purple, with occasional greyish blotches flagging where the skin had blistered under the cruel leather. The welts had licked the outsides and the insides of her thighs, and there were signs of welts across the splayed sex and the tight bud above it. A sharp, mineral smell, together with a trickle of moisture down the inside of one of those welted thighs, told him that at some stage during her punishment, Ariane had lost control of her bladder.

It was a delicious, slightly disgusting sight, and Pera licked his lips. Tired arm or not, he could have gone on thrashing the bitch all morning, but he was aware of the whipping fever taking him, like a sexual version of the red mist that took over the mind of a Viking berserker; if he gave it free rein there'd be no skin left on Ariane's arse. Besides, they both had work to do, and before that he badly needed a fuck.

He dropped the belt, climbed on to the bed, and drove his shaft into the soaking, steaming cleft. Ariane hissed as he took her, and he rammed himself home repeatedly, fucking her as fast as he could. His thighs smacked sharply against the roasting flesh of her behind, making the punished globes quiver and ripple exquisitely, and Ariane began to moan, and then to wail, with the force of his conquest.

Anything so vigorous couldn't last; after only a score of thrusts Pera felt himself rising to a climax that would not be denied. He thrust faster and faster, and then with a long, hoarse cry he came, every muscle straining as he pumped himself into Ariane's belly, while she cried out in response and her tunnel clenched around him.

It took a long time for him to finish spending himself. At last he withdrew, and moved round to the head of the bed. Ariane's head was down; he took a handful of hair and made her raise it so that his cock, still engorged, was in front of her face.

'Lick it clean,' he said simply. She flinched slightly, and Pera guessed she didn't like the idea – which was a fact he could use for his enjoyment, and her punishment, another time. Then she put out her tongue and began to run it carefully up and down his shaft, lapping up the mixture of his juices and hers. The sensation of the warm, wet little organ against his sensitised flesh was intense, and he shivered with pleasure as she cleaned and soothed him. It was almost enough to arouse him again, and for a few seconds he allowed himself the fantasy of taking her, just once more. Then he shook himself, and pulled his cleaned shaft away from her.

'That will do,' he told her. 'Much as I am enjoying you, we both have other things to do.' He reached down and loosened her chains, and she stood up stiffly.

'Is the entertainment to go ahead this evening?' she asked.

'The buyers' evening? Yes.' Pera buttoned himself up. 'Our newest queen bee will be there, and I think she will have a few surprises. That is, if you have anything to do with it?'

Ariane smiled. 'Oh, yes please,' she said.

CHAPTER 24

José had taken great care over the preparations for the evening. As a vinier he knew that good wine could sell itself, but as a businessman and a man he knew that it would sell a great deal better in the right atmosphere. And atmosphere was where Mas Gassac could score, over everyone.

The guests, ten in total, were gathered in the hall. Each had been greeted by a girl especially dressed to please his carefully-researched tastes, for José took pride in knowing things about his clients that they barely knew about themselves. Chloe was a schoolgirl, complete with gym slip and knee socks, and her English partner already had his hand firmly on her bottom and looked as if he would never remove it. Chloe didn't seem to mind. Quite the opposite; José suspected that he had accidentally tapped into a hidden fetish on her part. He filed his suspicion under useful facts.

Francine was somewhere between French maid and Mississippi whore, all fishnets and flounces, and was flirting energetically with a cheerful-looking Parisian man with slim hips and laughing eyes. Amelie, on the other hand, had been allocated to a fat Germanic-looking man with jowls that wobbled as he moved, and she was sheathed in a shiny skin-tight, latex cat-suit, so close-fitting at the crotch that the tiny bump of her clit hood could be read through the plastic like an indecent coded message. She looked hot and uncomfortable.

Carla, by contrast, was naked apart from a broad, plain leather collar around her neck. Her companion was a quiet, muscular-looking blond-haired man in a beautifully-cut dinner suit, who barely acknowledged her, but who kept a firm grip on the leash that was hooked to her collar.

The other girls were dressed in a range of styles, from gangster's moll to starched secretary. They had all been well-drilled.

When everyone was assembled, José raised his hands for attention.

'Welcome,' he called. 'Welcome to Mas Gassac, and to the annual tasting of our new releases. The tasting will take place over dinner, and the dinner will, I hope, be enlivened by some entertainments we have arranged and by your companions,' and he swept his arm round in a gesture encompassing both the guests and their girls. 'Please enjoy them exactly as you wish. They are under instruction to deny you nothing.' He paused, and then repeated: 'Nothing.'

There was a short silence and then a quick buzz of comment. José waited until it had subsided, and then nodded to Pera, who stood at the side of the room. Pera nodded back, and struck a gong. 'Messieurs,' he announced, 'dinner is served.'

José led the party through a set of double doors and out onto a broad terrace that ran alongside the courtyard. A large dining table had been set on the terrace; when the guests were seated, each with his allotted girl standing behind him, José gestured towards the courtyard, which was lit with hundreds of tall candles, each in a simple iron holder.

'Gentlemen,' he said, 'may I introduce Mademoiselle Ariane?' As he spoke, Ariane strode into the courtyard. She was dressed as a circus ringmaster, in a silk blouse, a red jacket, tan jodhpurs and tall black boots. She carried a long whip which she cracked theatrically.

There was a round of applause. José waited until it had faded, and then continued.

'Ariane is a slave of Mas Gassac, as are all the girls you see around you,' he said, 'but tonight she will be our Mistress of Ceremonies. You are about to be served pâté, with a merlot from our southern slopes. Ariane, what is to accompany the first course?'

Ariane bowed. 'Mestré, and Gentlemen,' she said, 'we begin with a simple flogging.' She turned and gestured to the side. 'Bring Princess!'

The watching guests drew in their breath as the black girl was brought into the courtyard. She was naked, and her superb muscles glinted in the candlelight as she struggled between two of the farmhands. Ariane stepped up to her and caught her by the chin, forcing her head round until she was facing the diners.

'Gentlemen,' she said, 'this is Princess. She is to be flogged, not for any particular fault, but for your pleasure.' She gestured to the farmhands, and they dragged the girl over to two wooden posts, driven four feet apart into the earthern floor of the courtyard. They took an arm and a leg each and pulled the girl into an X shape, with her ankles and wrists close to the posts. Ariane stepped forwards. She shook out a coil of fine cord and bound the spread-eagled girls ankles and wrists to the posts. Then she stood back and turned to her audience. 'Now we introduce the girl who is to wield the whip. Gentlemen, I give you Cynthia!'

There was a polite round of applause as Cynthia walked into the courtyard. She was dressed in a short plain black dress which emphasised her figure and contrasted sharply with the golden tan her pale skin had assumed. She was carrying a chicote, longer and heavier than the usual pattern, and just for a second José thought she looked a little nervous. Then she seemed to gather herself together. She took up a position behind the bound Princess and well to the left of her, and waited, the tails of the whip hanging casually just above the dust of the courtyard.

Ariane smiled at the reception the girl had been given. As well you might, thought José, since you know what's coming later. But the applause had died down, and Ariane was getting ready to speak once more.

'All females here are slaves,' she said, 'and so is Cynthia, but she has the role of overseer, and the privilege of whipping her fellow slaves. Which she will now do.' She paused, and then said slowly and loudly: 'Sixty lashes! Cynthia – begin.'

There was a murmur from the guests, and José saw some of the slaves exchanging glances. He wasn't surprised – it would have been a stiff sentence as a punishment, but as an un-earned whipping it was harsh indeed. But Ariane knew what she was doing, he had no doubt. He settled back in his seat to watch the beginning of the show.

Cynthia drew her arm back until the whip was almost directly behind her. She paused, as if gathering either her strength or her resolve, and then brought the long lashes humming round through three quarters of a circle. They landed across the centre of the gleaming black globes with a terrible thudding impact, so heavy that it could be felt as well as heard.

The watching diners froze with their glasses in mid air and forkfuls of pâté in front of their open mouths. José froze too; the stroke had been wickedly powerful, and even as he watched a swathe of that superb bottom was flashing into scarlet and purple weals. He remembered the last time Princess had been flogged in that courtyard. She had been stoical then. How would she react now?

The answer was – not at all. Princess stood her ground without a sound, without a twitch.

Her silence seemed to be infectious; for a dozen heartbeats, no one made a sound. Then, the fat German began to clap his hands softly, and one by one the other diners put down their glasses and joined him.

Cynthia looked first baffled, and then angry, at the applause her victim was receiving. For a moment she seemed uncertain what to do. Then she shook her head, drew back the whip, and sent it whistling in to its target.

The second stroke managed to be even harder than the first. Another set of vivid weals bloomed across Princess's bottom, and once again, the flogged girl stayed silent.

The battle was joined. Cynthia sent the wicked lashes hissing in to their target time and time again, and Princess absorbed stroke after stroke in stoical silence, without even tensing a muscle. José realised that he was sitting on the edge of his seat, almost holding his breath, as the flaming weals multiplied on the perfect ebony skin, and as Cynthia grew more and more flushed and determined. He was not the only one; all around him, both diners and slaves were leaning forwards, food and drink forgotten, as they lived the spectacle in front of them, stroke by stroke.

At the twentieth lash, Cynthia paused. She had gained nothing from her victim; not even a sigh. The whole of Princess's bottom was striped purple, and her skin was glistening with a sheen of sweat that had little to do with heat, but she held her position exactly as he had from the beginning of her flogging.

Cynthia stood still for a few seconds, as if she was thinking. Then she gave a slight smile, so transient that José suspected he was the only one who had seen it. She left her place behind Princess, and walked round until she was standing directly in front of the pinioned girl. She moved forward until her body was pressed against Princess's. Then she raised the whip over her head, and brought it keening down in a vicious arc that landed the knotted lashes straight down the girls back, ending in a deadly impact exactly in the centre of the parted cheeks.

At last, she got a response. Princess let her head fall forwards onto her tormentor's shoulders and gave a long, low moan of agony.

Cynthia smiled again, and sent in another stroke in exactly the same place. This time the moan was louder, and now it was accompanied by a scattering of applause from her audience, as if they had been waiting for the silence to be broken.

Now the whipping could only go one way. Cynthia had broken through Princess's resistance, and every stroke summoned a growing cry of pain from the punished slave. As José watched, the girl's bottom, thighs and back bloomed red and purple like a garden of pain, while Cynthia danced round her victim, delivering lash after cruel lash, first with confidence and then, towards the end of the epic flogging, almost with arrogance. José nodded, and grinned, and applauded with his fellow watchers. Go on, girl, he thought. Enjoy yourself while you can – but don't think you're the only one with a strong arm and an imagination!

At last the sixtieth stroke hissed down and landed. Princess's wailing had become almost continuous, broken only by shuddering breaths, and Cynthia's triumph had become more obvious with every lash. Even in the candle light, the dark spots of sweat beneath the flogged girl's body stood out starkly against the fawn dust of the courtyard.

Cynthia let the tails of the heavy whip fall to her side. She glanced at Ariane, who nodded and stepped forward to address the diners.

'Gentlemen,' she said, 'our first flogging is complete, although it is not likely to be our last.' She turned towards José. 'Mestré, shall I have the girl untied?'

José shook his head. 'Not yet,' he said. 'First tell me – is she aroused?'

Ariane smiled slowly. She walked over to the bound Princess, who was till sobbing quietly, and thrust her hand quickly into the dark entrance between the girl's muscular thighs. She kept it there for several seconds, working it in and out and turning it a little, making the girl moan out loud. Then she withdrew it, and held it up. Even in the candlelight, it was easy to see the wet sheen on her fingers. 'She is aroused, Mestré,' she said. 'Moist and swollen.'

'Good! Keep her there for a little while, please.' He turned to the guests. 'Wetness, in a woman, is not something to be wasted. Would any of you like to make use of her?'

Several voices spoke. José looked around, and pointed at the fat German man. 'Herr Glaser, I think you were the first. Feel free!'

Glaser got to his feet. 'My pleasure,' he said. He jumped down the shallow step from the terrace, landed heavily on the packed earth of the courtyard, and walked over to stand behind Princess, where he gave her body a long, appraising look.

José grinned. 'Does she please you?' he asked.

'She looks fine.' Glaser moved a little closer to the girl. 'And smells fine, too. A combination of sweat, and pussy, and fear. Very appropriate.' He opened his trousers and released his cock, which looked to be only of medium length, but exceptionally fat, and so hard it stood up almost vertically. He guided it towards the girl's crack, and then thrust forwards. The speed of his entry drew a squeal from Princess, but Glaser ignored her completely, his fat hips rocking quickly back and forwards like a machine. Each stroke drew a yelp from the spreadeagled slave, but Glaser went on fucking her like a piston, grunting regularly with pleasure and effort.

José glanced at his fellow diners, who were once again rapt, and then called over to the busy German. 'Does she feel as good as she looks?' he asked.

'She feels like a woman.' Glaser was already panting heavily with effort. 'Hot enough, and wet enough, and tight enough. I – aaahhhh…' He stopped talking, gave a single long groan of pleasure, and thrust himself to his full length, his flesh quivering, as he pumped himself into the helpless slave's belly.

José clapped politely. 'Well ridden,' he said, and some of the guests muttered agreement.

'Thank you,' Glaser withdrew himself. 'Most enjoyable.' He turned his back on Princess and stumped back to the terrace, his cock still bobbing in front of him. When he reached his chair, he sat down heavily, and clicked his fingers at the sweating, plastic-clad Amelie.

'Get under the table, girl,' he told her. 'Make your tongue busy, while I finish my pâté.'

José watched as Amelie ducked hastily under the table. A few moments later Glaser paused with a forkful of pâté halfway to his lips, and gave a satisfied growl. Then he popped it into his mouth, swallowed it, and washed it down with a mouthful of wine. He smirked at the others. 'The wine goes well with the pâté,' he said. 'So does a blow job.'

José smiled. The evening had started well.

They finished the first course, while the limp Princess was untied from the posts and led away by Ariane and Cynthia. The men discussed wine and made small talk, apart from Glaser, who spent the time grunting his way to a second orgasm. When they were finished, José signalled for the slaves to remove the remains of the pâté. 'I hope the first course was enjoyable,' and he paused, 'in all respects. If you are ready, we shall move on to something more substantial.'

CHAPTER 25

The guests sat forwards expectantly. José clapped his hands. The waiting slave girls left their places and returned moments later carrying dishes including a large silver tureen. At the same time the two menservants reappeared, carrying a big bulky thing shaped like a school vaulting horse. They put it down in the middle of the courtyard, bowed to José, and withdrew.

José waited until the slaves had set the table for the next course, then stood up.

'My friends,' he said, 'you tasted a red wine with your last course. Now I want you to enjoy a white, and since we are in the south we will try it with bouillabaisse, which as I'm sure you know is the ancient fish stew of the Mediterranean. But with this peasant dish I propose something which is still a little exotic, at least to us French. We know it as la vice Anglaise.' He turned to the Englishman. 'Monsieur Cavendish, I have been told you are an expert with the rod.'

The Englishman smiled and made a dismissive gesture. 'Not so expert as some, Monsieur,' he said, in good, but heavily accented French.

José wagged a finger at him. 'I suspect you of false modesty, my friend. And here we have, not only un Anglais, but also a schoolgirl for him to play with. What could be better?'

Carla's companion, who had remained silent so far, raised his hand. 'A cane?' he suggested.

José nodded in acknowledgement, and clicked his fingers. Ariane stepped forward from the shadows where she had been waiting, and handed him a long, slim cane with a crooked handle. He examined it briefly, and then handed it to the Englishman.

'Will it do?' he asked.

Cavendish flexed it experimentally. 'Yes,' he said. 'This will work very well.' He stood up. 'If I may, Monsieur?'

José nodded. 'Please do,' he said. 'The horse has been provided for you, if you wish it?'

'No, thank you. A chair is more traditional, or nothing at all. Girl, come here!' This was to Chloe, who stepped forwards nervously. Cavendish pushed his chair back a few paces from the table and turned it round to that the back faced the diners. He took Chloe by the pigtail and pulled her sharply along until she was standing against the back of the chair, her face already contorted with pain from the tug on her hair.

'We'll begin here,' he told her. 'Bend over the chair and grasp the end of the seat with your hands.'

She did as she was told, rising a little onto the balls of her feet as the back of the chair dug into her belly. The posture tightened the flannel of the traditional skirt against the swell of her behind, and the hem of the skirt rode just high enough to expose the tops of the seamed stockings that bit a little into her plump thighs.

Cavendish inspected her for a moment, then reached down, took the hem of her skirt and raised it slowly, exposing little by little the girl's full, firm bottom with its covering of tight white panties. Then he turned to the others.

'We all enjoyed the flogging of that slave girl,' he said. 'Now I will show you something different. I will be giving the girl only a dozen strokes,' and he gave a frosty smile, 'but I promise they will have more effect that the whole sixty lashes we saw before.' He turned back to Chloe. 'Are you afraid?' he asked.

'Yes, sir,' she said, in a trembling voice.

'You're right to be. It will hurt very much, and fear is an important ingredient.' He stood back and addressed the others again. 'The first stroke will be over her panties,' he told them. 'We'll uncover it, and re-visit it, later.'

He stood well to one side of the girl, gave the cane the briefest of preparatory twitches, and then sent it hissing in to land across the middle of her tightened bottom. He hadn't seemed to move his arm either far or fast, but somehow the end of the cane seemed to accelerate until it would have been impossible for the eye to follow it. It landed with a blunt, heavy crack, and the force of the stroke threw the bending Chloe off balance for a moment so that she staggered slightly against the chair.

José waited, but for two or three seconds that movement was Chloe's only response. He got ready to be disappointed, but then the girl opened her mouth and let out a long 'ahh' of protest that quickly mounted to a desperate wail. Her hands flew back to her bottom and her fingers kneaded urgently at the spot where the cane had landed.

Cavendish turned to his audience, looking a touch smug. 'Caning is unlike any other punishment,' he said. 'The harder the stroke, the longer it takes for the nerves to register. For the best effect, the next stroke should land just as the pain from the first reaches its peak.' He turned back to Chloe, who was still frantically clutching her bottom and pumping her legs. 'Keep still,' he told her sharply, 'and keep your hands on the seat in front of you. Otherwise I shall add strokes.'

The girl managed a muffled, 'Yes, sir', and reluctantly removed her hands from her behind. Cavendish hooked his fingers in her panties and drew them a few fingers' breadth down her bottom, exposing a pale band of flesh.

'The next stroke,' he explained, 'will land there.'

José glanced at his guests. A few of them shook their heads silently. They were obviously thinking what he was – such accuracy was impossible; the Englishman was boasting.

If he was aware of their looks, Cavendish ignored them. Instead, he took aim and delivered another stroke, just as casually and just as hard as the first. It landed across the dead centre of the band of flesh he had exposed.

This time Chloe had braced herself and kept her balance, but in every other way the effect was spectacular. The skin where the cane landed flashed white, and stayed white for two or three heartbeats. Then, just as the girl began to yowl, and then screech, with the growing pain, the white band darkened quickly to a purple weal with two fine scarlet lines within it, marking the width of the cane itself.

The rhythm was set. After each stroke, Cavendish waited until the suffering girl had begun to howl, and then reached out to lower panties a little more to provide fresh skin, still bearing the fading marks of Cynthia's cane from the night before, for the next. It was a consummate exhibition in punishment that had every watcher leaning forward, poised between astonishment at the extremity they were witnessing, and raw excitement at the ancient spectacle of the female being taken beyond the brink of endurance by the male.

The fifth stroke uncovered the weal left by the first. It was a little less vivid than the weals left by the cuts that had landed on bare skin, but it was still a deep, blotched purple. Cavendish nodded with satisfaction.

'We'll leave that for later,' he said, and lowered the panties a little more.

By the time the tenth stroke landed, exactly on the crease between the base of her bottom and the top of her thighs, Chloe had abandoned any restraint. She screamed and writhed without stopping in response to the glowing weals that marched down her scorched flesh in perfect parallel. Her wriggles kept the soft flesh of her behind in constant motion, making a lewd, flashing peep-show of her cunt, which was winking just above the gathered folds of her panties. Somehow, though, she managed to keep her hands clenched on the edge of the chair seat, and José offered her a silent round of applause. He kept a little satisfaction for himself, too. We trained you well, he thought.

It was almost over. The eleventh stroke landed on the plump flesh at the top of the girls thighs, wringing an even higher cry from her. Then Cavendish paused.

'I said we'd revisit the first stroke later,' he said. 'Now it's time.' And he sent the cane whipping in to land exactly on the weal he had left across the centre of the girl's bottom, minutes ago.

It was a harsh, cruel act.

This time there was no delay. Chloe leaped as if she had been branded. For a second she seemed almost to hang in the air. Then she collapsed slowly to the ground, lying curled up on her side with her hands glued to her tortured bottom.

For a moment the silence was broken only by the sobbing of the prostrate girl. Then Glaser stood up and began to clap. He was quickly joined by the others, until all the guests were on their feet. José walked over to Cavendish and put an arm round his shoulders. 'Please excuse my Latin familiarity, my friend,' he said, 'but you have shown us the way, both in determination and in skill.'

The Englishman smiled, but then gently moved out of the embrace. 'The skill is in knowing when to stop,' he said. 'To beat, as severely as possible, until the subject is broken to the beater, and not one stroke more.' He extended his foot to tap the girl, and to José's astonishment she wriggled close to it, kissed it, and cradled it to her. Cavendish reached down and took hold of her pigtails again. 'Up,' he said. 'You have something to do for me.'

José watched the girl rise unsteadily. Both the school uniform, and something in her eyes, made her seem suddenly very young. The man's right, he thought. He's broken her to his hand.

Cavendish pushed the girl forwards until she was bending over the chair once more. 'Do you object if I enjoy her?' he asked José.

José shook his head. 'Not at all. I expect she is thoroughly wet, anyway.'

'I expect she is, but it is not relevant.' The Englishman unbuttoned his trousers to reveal a long, slim penis with a thick club-like head. 'I have always preferred the smaller entrance. I don't use lubricant, either. Why make them sigh, when you can make them squeal?'

He placed his hands on the girl's flaming buttocks, pulled them forcefully apart, and thrust himself into her. José watched for a second, then turned back to the other guests.

'I don't suppose it will be easy to outdo our English friend,' he said, 'but our meal is not over, and nor is our entertainment. Please; enjoy your bouillabaisse.' There was a murmur of approval, and the guests turned back to the table. The sound of eating and drinking resumed, punctuated by noises from behind them.

As he had predicted, Cavendish was making Chloe squeal.

Cynthia had watched the caning of Chloe with something like awe. Shit, how she wished she could do that! And, thought a small part of her, how she wished he would do it to her! Or not him, exactly. To be honest, she wanted José to be the one who wielded the cane. She had thought he was going to, the night before, but at the last minute he had made her do it instead. A mixture of relief and disappointment, there.

Back to the present. Ariane was gesturing for something else to be brought in. Several somethings – as Cynthia watched, Pera and some of the other men wheeled in half a dozen small three-wheeled carts, each just big enough for one passenger. They looked ordinary enough, but there was no harness she could see; just two shafts that came together to form the point of a narrow triangle, a metre in front of the cart.

While she was wondering about that, Ariane raised her hand for attention.

'Gentlemen and slaves,' she said. 'We have decided to hold a race! You, sirs, will be the passengers, and you will be pulled by your slaves.'

'Pony play, eh?' It was Cavendish. 'Need to get the girls tacked up, then!'

'Not exactly.' Ariane smiled, and pulled one of the carts over towards the table. 'Take a look at the end of the shafts, gentlemen. Tell me what you see!'

The men stood, and craned to look. So did Cynthia, and she felt her eyes widen. There was a short, puzzled silence, and then someone laughed. 'It's like a damn great dildo,' he said. 'My God! Is that how they'll pull us?'

José nodded. 'It is,' he said. He signalled to the slaves, who were watching with round eyes. 'There are six carts. Amelie, Chloe, Francine, Carla – go to the courtyard and stand by a cart.' The girls ran off the terrace. José waited until they were standing next to four of the carts. 'Ariane, bring Princess back. She has good muscles. It will be interesting to see how she compares.' Ariane nodded, and in less than a minute Princess was standing next to a cart. Ariane turned towards José. 'Mestré, there is still a vacant cart.'

'So there is.' José stroked his chin. 'Who do you suggest?'

The woman didn't hesitate. 'Cynthia, Mestré.'

Cynthia gasped. Surely he wouldn't?

But he nodded firmly. 'A good suggestion! Cynthia – stand by a cart and wait with the others.'

Her heart banging, Cynthia bowed her head quickly in assent and trotted over to one of the carts. Seen this close, the dildo, for the want of a better word, looked enormous; a rounded knob almost the size of a tennis ball, mounted on the end of a shaft two fingers thick.

She gulped.

José was still talking. 'Now, gentlemen,' he said. 'Please stand by the cart selected by your companion.' The four men wiped their mouths, rose from the table and walked over to their carts. They stood waiting, their faces flushed with wine and excitement.

José gestured to Pera. 'Old friend, please mount the cart of Princess,' he said. 'As for me, I will drive the little Cynthia.'

Pera laughed. 'No doubt you will, Mestré,' he said, and climbed up on to the cart. Once he was in his seat he raised a hand. 'Ariane – let the slaves be fitted to their carts.'

The tall woman bowed, and signalled to the waiting guests. 'Gentlemen,' she said, 'please insert the fitting on the end of the shafts of your cart into your slave. You may use either hole, as you judge best. You will find that the fitting is already lubricated.'

The men didn't delay. There was a rustle as various clothes were pulled hurriedly out of the way, and then a series of squeaks and squeals as the fat knobs were worked into their tight destinations.

Cynthia felt José's hand pulling her back towards the cart. She moved obediently until she felt the cold, fat bulbous thing pushing against her anus – of course, she thought, it was always going to be that! – and then the pressure mounted, and she felt her ring stretching and stretching. The taut skin smarted, and then stung, and then burned as the ruthless knob distended it further and further, and Cynthia heard herself gasp and wail with the pain. Then quite suddenly, the thing must have reached the halfway point, and the squeezing pressure in her behind forced it in with a rush. She felt herself snap closed around the narrow shaft with a sensation that she was sure should have made a popping noise.

It was in. She tested her sensations. Her bottom still smarted horribly, but less than it had when the huge knob was being inserted. She could feel her body making futile attempts to expel it, but the muscle contractions only secured it even more firmly.

Reassured, she looked around at the other girls. It seemed that they, too, had all suffered insertion in their bottoms. She wondered how that had felt for Chloe, so recently sodomised by the Englishman.

One look gave her the answer. Chloe's face was flushed and her eyes were bright. It seemed that Chloe was developing a taste for the Englishman's touch.

The cart behind her twitched, sending a shock of mixed pleasure and pain through Cynthia's bottom. She looked over her shoulder. José had mounted the cart, and sat with his hand in the air.

'Dear guests,' he said loudly, 'we are almost ready to start. Set as fast a pace as you dare; you will find suitable whips beside your seats. Each time a girl fails to retain the shaft, she will be whipped. The third time, we have another punishment for her.' He nodded to Ariane, who signalled two menservants forward. They took hold of the top of the vaulting horse and lifted.

It came away to reveal something that drew gasps from the watching slaves. Cynthia felt her knees weaken.

Beneath the top of the vaulting horse lay the cruel, narrow ridge of the Pony. As she started at it in horror, she heard José continue.

'As punishment for the third failure, a girl will spend ten minutes on this. She will then be subject to any further punishment that her fellow slaves should decide on.' He looked round the apprehensive girls slowly. 'Any punishment at all,' he said slowly.

There was a short silence. Then José smiled.

'So,' he said, 'an incentive not to come last! Let's begin!'

Around the courtyard there was the crack of whips biting into defenceless female flesh. Cynthia felt the leather cut smartly across her thighs. She took a deep breath and very carefully began to tug the cart forwards.

CHAPTER 26

It was after midnight. The guests had departed to
their rooms, accompanied by their allotted slaves.
The night was hot and close, and the windows
of José's apartment were flung wide open. As,
apparently, were those of some of the guests, to judge
by the occasional clearly heard impact of something
on skin, and the accompanying squeals. It seemed
that people were still enjoying themselves.

Naked except for a pair of stockings, Cynthia lay
face down on the sofa, mewing softly with pain. José
looked down at her with a mixture of affection and
frank lust. She lay with her legs parted a little; no
doubt the abused state of the flesh between them made
it preferable not to close them, for the moment. Her
bottom was liberally blotched and bruised. José, his
own flesh stirring at the sight of her, let his mind play
over the events of the evening.

'Aahh!' It was a cry of disappointment. José's head
flicked round. 'Who was that?'

Ariane answered him. 'It was Chloe, Mestré. She
has let go.'

'Ah-ha! Our first forfeit!' José climbed down from his
cart and marched over to Chloe, who stood trembling.
He took her by the chin and pulled her head round until
she was staring into his face. 'What was the prescribed
punishment for failing to hold on?' he asked.

She shifted nervously, and tried to look away.
'Whipping,' she said, in a whisper.

'Exactly. Whipping.' José reached round and raised
the skirt she still wore, exposing her bottom which
Cavendish had bared, first to cane, and then to insert
the head of the shafts. 'Hmm,' he said. 'Your bottom

is already well marked. Perhaps it's time to show some mercy.'

The girl nodded quickly. 'Oh yes please, sir,' she said.

'Indeed.' José reached down his free hand and caressed the striped flesh. 'Yes,' he said thoughtfully, 'you are well whipped there.' Then he let his hand fall a little lower so that it lay between the girl's thighs. 'But the skin here is untouched. I think we can safely add some punishment here.' He let go of the girl's chin. 'On your back,' he said sharply. 'Legs in the air. Now!'

Chloe gave him a single horrified look. Then she sat down quickly, and lay back, raising her legs.

José signalled to Ariane. 'Come and help me,' he told her, and she trotted over and took one of Chloe's ankles. José took the other and nodded, and he and Ariane moved apart until the girl's legs were spread far apart, making the sinews on the insides of her thighs stand out like cords.

When he had the girl positioned as he wanted, José called out to the Englishman. 'Monsieur Cavendish? Our girl seems to have a taste for your caress. Will you take a chicote and flog her?'

'It will be a pleasure!' Cavendish stepped down from his cart and walked over to the helpless Chloe, collecting a chicote from one of the menservants on his way. He examined the spread girl. 'Hmm. She certainly looks fine like that,' he said. 'Perhaps later on I will let my curiosity drive me into the front entrance instead of the rear, for once.'

José grinned. 'Feel free,' he said, 'but for the moment I hope you will indulge yourself by flogging it, instead of fucking it. I suggest a dozen, to begin with.'

'Of course.' The Englishman swished the chicote a couple of times. Then he raised it, and brought it hissing down to land on the soft flesh right at the top of

Chloe's inner thigh. She rewarded him with a ragged wail, and he smiled grimly and lashed her again.

From his vantage point at the end of one of Chloe's legs, José had an excellent view. With every stroke, the wicked knotted thongs bit hungrily into the suffering girl's struggling flesh, marking it with angry red weals and purple splodges as an abstract artist marks a virgin white canvass. Cavendish was as accurate with the whip as he had been with the cane, and his harsh strokes quickly covered the whole of his target area from Chloe's upper thighs to the rounded base of her belly, and especially the twitching, winking orifice that glistened in the centre.

By the time the tenth stroke had landed, Chloe had ceased struggling and was sobbing continuously. Cavendish paused, looked down at the girl, and then at José.

'Rather a privilege,' he said, 'to be able to break the same girl twice, in two different ways, on the same night.' He stepped back from his position, and walked round until he was standing next to the girl's shoulder.

'I think,' he said, 'a change of angle… If you would please raise her hips a little and pull her legs back?'

José glanced at Ariane, and they drew Chloe's legs up and back, rolling her hips away from the ground and parting her buttocks.

Cavendish nodded. 'Very good,' he said. 'Now, the last two.' And he raised the whip over his shoulder and sent it sighing down.

The vengeful thongs lashed down the exact centre of the girl's parted crack. She convulsed, her ankles almost wrenching free from José and Ariane, and gave a long, despairing howl. José glanced across at Ariane and smiled to himself. Her face was flushed, her eyes glazed, and her lips slightly parted, a classic illustration of female arousal. He looked round to where Cynthia was standing. The girl's eyes were round with awe, but she, too, looked aroused, and as he watched one of her hands wandered towards the base of her belly.

José, too, felt the intensity of the scene; part of him was almost violently excited, while another part was watching the Englishman's torment of his victim with professional appraisal.

It was almost over. Cavendish had taken his time, but now at last the whip was rising for the last stroke.

It landed. This time Chloe struggled less, as if the strength had at last been whipped out of her. She gave a hoarse cry, followed by a moan. There was a hissing sound; José looked down, and then shifted his feet to avoid a spreading pool. Sobbing with pain and shame, the flogged girl was pissing like a horse.

José turned to Cavendish. 'You've made an impression,' he admitted. 'But I'm not sure it will be a good one!'

'Let's see.' The Englishman walked round and stood with his feet between Chloe's parted legs. He tapped the inside of a thigh with his shoe. 'Where are your manners?' he asked.

Her eyes, which had been tightly closed, fluttered open. 'Thank you,' she said, in a voice barely above a whisper.

'Hmm.' Cavendish twirled the toe of his boot in the puddle between the girl's legs. Then he walked slowly back to stand by her head, and lifted his foot until it was against her lips. Unbidden, she put out her tongue and began to lick the drops of her own urine off the wet leather.

José laughed quietly. 'I take it all back,' he said. 'It seems that you are – what is the English phrase? – flavour of the month. In more ways than one!'

Cavendish laughed in return. 'Very good,' he said. 'But I believe the girl and I still have unfinished business, and I don't want to delay your race. Will you allow me to withdraw, and take this,' and he prodded Chloe with his foot, 'with me?'

'Of course.' José patted him on the shoulder. 'As I said at the start, you can enjoy her as you please.'

'Thank you.' Cavendish prodded the girl again. 'Come on, you,' he told her. Unsteadily, she began to rise to her feet, but he put his hand on the top of her head and pushed downwards. 'Crawl,' he said simply, and walked off.

José watched as the girl's wiggling bottom disappeared into the twilight. Then he turned to the remaining guests. 'Shall we continue?' he asked. There was an affirmative buzz, and a swish of whips, and the carts moved off again.

José wasn't surprised to see that a pattern had been set. One by one, the remaining girls earned their forfeits, and one by one their temporary owners decided they would rather conclude matters in private. Only half an hour after the beginning of the race, the field had been reduced to José, driving Cynthia, and Pera, driving Princess. Neither girl had yet let go, and neither showed any sign of doing so.

Eventually, José signalled to Pera. Both carts stopped. The two men looked at each other. Then Pera said: 'Mestré, we need a way of settling this, or we'll still be here in the morning.'

'I agree.' José clicked his tongue thoughtfully, and turned to Ariane. 'Well, Mademoiselle Maitress des Ceremonies, what do you suggest?'

Ariane smiled. 'Simple,' she said. 'I suggest a tug of war.'

José looked at her, and then at Pera. 'What do you think, old friend?' he asked.

Pera was smiling too. 'I think yes, Mestré,' he said simply.

It was done quickly. Some light chain was fetched, and within a few minutes the two girls found themselves intimately tethered, a couple of metres apart on their hands and knees. Between them, a groove scored in the dry surface of the courtyard marked the winning line. José and Pera had retired to the balcony, where they watched whilst enjoying glasses of the powerful country brandy that was the final resting place of the grapes of Mas Gassac. Ariane stood between the two girls, carrying not one but two dressage whips, one in each hand. At a nod from José she raised both whips, so that one hovered over the naked hind-quarters of each of the girls.

'Slaves,' she said, 'we'll have the best of three. Take the strain!'

Cynthia and Princess each moved forward cautiously, and the fine chain rose from the ground. Ariane raised the two whips and winked at the matching men. 'Pull!' she ordered, and at the same time brought the thin lashes down over the girls' tightened behinds.

The fight was on. Both girls wore looks of fierce concentration, and their lips were set with effort. José watched, fascinated, and wondered why he had never thought of this before. It was the perfect training for the muscles of the rear entry, he thought. And elsewhere, too. He leaned over to Pera, who looked just as fascinated.

'We should make them all do this,' he said. 'With their cunts, too. Imagine the improvement!'

The old man nodded. 'Best not overdo it, though,' he said, and grinned. 'We don't want them too muscular.

Otherwise, one day you'll find some floozy's snatch shutting itself on you like a pair of shears!'

They both laughed, and José turned his attention back to the two girls, who had formed a kind of frozen tableau of tension.

'Go on,' he said, gesturing to Ariane. 'Give them some encouragement!'

The woman nodded, and raised her whips. 'Get on with it,' she said, and brought the lashes down smartly on the girls' behinds. 'We haven't got all night. If you don't make an effort you'll both end up riding the Pony!'

The threat galvanised the girls. Both settled themselves a little lower, and the chain that linked them twisted and flashed as the tension increased.

Pera turned to José. 'Who's your money on?' he asked.

José pursed his lips. 'Well, now,' he said. 'Answer me this. How many times have you buggered Princess?'

Pera reflected. 'Dozens,' he said. 'Scores. At least. And you?'

José nodded. 'Not so often as you, but several times, anyway. And Cynthia?'

'Never, as you know.'

'Well then.' José sipped his brandy. 'I suspect experience will tell.'

'You may be right. Look!' Pera pointed to Cynthia. 'She's losing this one!'

He was right. As they watched, the fat plug began to ease out of Cynthia's bottom. The girl moaned, and gave ground for a second. The tension on the chain slackened enough to let the plug slip back inside her, but the movement took her dangerously close to the losing mark. Princess looked quickly back over her shoulder and, as if sensing her advantage, tensed her superb behind and leaned forwards slowly. It was enough; Cynthia's plug began to slip again, and the girl had no option but to fall back further.

Ariane's hand shot up. 'The winner of the first bout is Princess,' she said.

Pera turned to José. 'You're right so far,' he said. 'But only so far. Your little English rose is a tough one. She'll fight back!'

José nodded, but did not answer. The girls were back in place, and he noticed that this time, Cynthia had changed her position so that her knees were together, her body forward, and her thighs made a shallow angle with the ground. José nodded approvingly to himself. Her new posture would make it much easier for her to clench her buttocks around the invading plug. She wasn't going down without a fight.

Ariane swept down her whips in the starting signal. Both girls jumped as the lashes bit, and then the contest was on.

Immediately, the success of Cynthia's new strategy was obvious. Princess looked first surprised, then alarmed, as the plug began to slip from her body. She gritted her teeth and her eyes screwed tight with strain, but Cynthia was inexorable. Within seconds, Princess had been pulled perilously close to the losing line. She lowered her head for one final effort, but the pull was too much and the plug slipped out of her with a soft poff.

Ariane's hand shot up. 'One all,' she announced.

Wordlessly, José reached out for the brandy bottle and refreshed his and Pera's glasses. There was all to play for. The plug was forced back into Princess' behind, and the two slaves took up their positions again, with Princess this time mimicking the posture that had been so successful for Cynthia. The whips slashed down, and the fight began.

It was unbearably close. For what seemed like hours, and was certainly minutes, the two slaves barely moved, their bodies swaying slightly to and fro as a microscopic advantage passed from one to the other. After a while José grew impatient. He signalled to Ariane.

She grinned, and raised her arms. 'Come on!' she said. 'Put your backs into it!' And she brought the two whips hissing down. Fresh weals darkened on the two taut bottoms. José repeated his signal, and the leather bit again, and then again.

Pera turned to José. 'You know what happens to Cynthia, sometimes, under the whip?'

José nodded. 'She orgasms,' he said.

'She does.' Pera watched the two girls for a moment. 'What do you think will happen to her arse, when she comes?'

'I don't know, but I think we're about to find out. Look!'

While the two men talked, Cynthia's face had flushed, and her breathing had become ragged and urgent. As they watched, she lowered her head and gave a long, growling cry. For a moment nothing happened. Then the plug popped from her body, so suddenly that Princess fell forwards onto her face. Cynthia gave another cry, this time of despair, and collapsed.

José stood up. 'It seems we have a winner,' he said. 'And a loser. Girls, stand up.'

The two slaves rose slowly to their feet. The fine chain dangled from the plug that still filled Princess' bottom. Ariane reached round and yanked it out, making the girl yelp with surprise.

José walked slowly over to the girls. He put his hand on the top of Cynthia's head and pressed downwards. 'Kneel in front of Princess,' he told her. Cynthia's face came close to crumbling, but she did as he had told her.

José turned to Princess. 'Well done,' he said simply. 'You won. Now name your forfeit. Anything you say, within reason, will be carried out.'

Princess looked down at the kneeling Cynthia. Her face was stony, but when she spoke her voice was calm and measured. 'Punish me if you want to for speaking plainly, Mestré, but hear me first. I know what she is to be. She will be yours, and so she will be over the rest of us.' She looked up at José. He nodded slightly, and she went on: 'I'll never get this chance again.' She took a breath. 'I want to piss on her, and then see her riding the Pony.'

José heard Cynthia gasp. He ignored her. 'You get your wish,' he said.

CHAPTER 27

Ariane reached down, took hold of Cynthia's arm and turned her over roughly.

'Face up,' she said. 'That's how I'd want someone, if I was going to piss on them.'

Princess nodded. 'Thank you,' she said. Then, without ceremony, she walked forwards until her ankles were level with Cynthia's shoulders, and squatted.

A preliminary trickle grew quickly into a hissing stream of golden fluid which splashed over the breasts and face of the lying girl. Cynthia screwed up her eyes and tried to turn her head away, but Ariane slashed her whip across the girl's thighs.

'Keep still,' she hissed.

Princess held her position, releasing the steaming contents of her bladder until her flow tailed away to a dribble, and then to a few drops. Then she straightened up, swung her leg over Cynthia's body and took a few paces towards the Pony. Wordlessly, Ariane pulled Cynthia upright and shoved the dazed girl after her.

José watched in fascination. He had known that Princess had the capacity for cruelty – she had been an overseer, after all, until his public humiliation of her – but there was something new, here; a cold, detached satisfaction, which he hadn't seen before. Her request had been unexpected, and his first instinct had been to reject such demeaning treatment of Cynthia. He was glad he hadn't. The sight had been astonishingly erotic, and now he felt himself swept along by Princess' taut, harsh body language, by the sharp, rankly animal smell that drifted across from the courtyard, and by his undoubted desire to see Cynthia writhing on the Pony. He glanced to his side. Pera was sitting forward on his seat, his glass lying forgotten on the ground by his chair. His eyes glittered. José grinned to himself. The old man was just as rapt as he was.

There was a whimper from the courtyard. José turned, and watched as Ariane led the unresisting Cynthia on to the Pony. The girl's face was wet, but José couldn't tell if the moisture was tears, or only the remains of Princess' piss. She straddled the sharp wooden bar and meekly raised her hands over her head as Ariane began to turn the screw.

José's cock, which had been aching for most of the evening, hardened even further as the rising bar began to bite into the soft flesh between Cynthia's legs. For a moment she didn't react, and José wondered if she was going to take her punishment stoically. Then, quite suddenly, her face crumpled. She let out a wail of pain which was quickly followed by another and then another, each one higher than the last, and her hips writhed as she wriggled in a futile attempt to escape the agony.

Ariane laughed. 'That won't help,' she said. 'Keep still, or you'll cut yourself in two!'

'I can't!' There was no doubting the tears now. 'It hurts too much. Please! Let me off! Please!'

The seconds ticked by. José glanced at Ariane, and then at Princess. The slave girl remained silent, her face impassive, but José noticed she had a hand between her legs. It moved slowly, keeping time with Cynthia's cries, fingers curled inward. If Princess was truly turned on, he thought, who knew how long she might keep Cynthia up there? The girl must be near the end of her endurance.

He reached a decision, and stood up. 'That's enough,' he said. 'Let her down.'

Ariane reached down quickly and lowered the bar, and then reached up to support Cynthia as she sagged with relief. As she was helped off the Pony, Cynthia looked over at José.

'Thank you,' she said quietly.

He inclined his head, and then pointed at Princess. 'You'll have plenty of chances to thank me,' he told her, 'but now I suggest you thank Princess for punishing you so well.' He paused, and then added: 'On your knees, perhaps. With your tongue out.'

'Yes, sir.' She dropped to her knees as Princess walked up to her. The black girl reached out, took hold of Cynthia's head and pulled the girl's face into her body, and José saw Cynthia angle her neck upwards a little to ease access. At least the girl was doing her best to please, rather than just going through the motions.

José sat back in his seat and stretched. He was tired. The evening had gone well – was still going well, if the occasional muffled sound of passion from the house was anything to judge by – but he had had enough of it. He turned to Pera.

'What do you think, old friend?' he asked.

'Hmm.' The old man stretched too. 'Well, we kept the buyers happy again. I have taken a few good orders while you were occupied,' and he grinned, 'I expect some more tomorrow, when the boys wake up.'

José nodded. 'Good. And?'

'And, you learned even more about your little English plaything.' He leaned forwards and tapped José on the chest with a gnarled finger. 'You learned that she is much more than a plaything, if you didn't know it already. You know what I think?'

'What?'

'I think, as soon as she has finished with the cunt of our severe little Princess, that you should take her away and do some pampering.'

José raised his eyebrows. 'Really?'

'Really.' The finger prodded again. 'You have made her squeal, and weep, and beg. Now, if you want her to be sweet to you for the rest of her life, you have to show her how to sigh, and arch, and soar.' The old man sat back and grinned. 'And give her a bath. Even from here, she stinks of piss.'

José laughed. 'You're wise as always,' he said. 'Anyway, look; I think Princess has about done with her.'

It was true. The black girl's fingers were knotted in Cynthia's soaked hair, and the muscles on her scored behind stood out as she arched forwards, dragging Cynthia's face fiercely into her groin. She held the position for several long seconds, her teeth bared in a rictus of effort and pleasure. Then, almost brutally, she pushed Cynthia away and turned her back. Cynthia sat back on her haunches, looking surprised and licking her lips like a cat.

José signalled for the last time to Ariane. 'Take Princess away,' he told her, and she took the panting black girl by the shoulder and marched her out of the courtyard. As they went, José walked over to Cynthia. Pera was right – she stank, and she looked tired, but her eyes were shining.

'Well,' he said to her. 'You've had a busy evening. Will you come with me now?'

He reached out his hand, and she took it. 'Yes, please,' she said. 'I'd like that.'

He helped her up and led her gently out of the courtyard. As they passed Pera, the old man looked up at them and gave the ghost of a wink.

Adrenaline had carried Cynthia through the experience of the Pony, and all the way out of the courtyard. It had helped her up the steps to José's apartment, and kept her upright while he removed the few soaked clothes she still wore. It had even kept her upright under the first hissing jets of the shower he had pushed her in to. But then, when she had sluiced the salty sourness of Princess' urine from her, José had drawn a bath, rich with scented oils, and she had collapsed into it with a sigh of relief – and suddenly she was nothing, a jelly, more and more aware of the state of her body. The fat plug had torn her bottom; her buttocks smarted with the many strokes of assorted whips, and her sex ached dully from the cruel attention of the Pony. She shuddered a little, and explored herself gingerly with a finger. Hm. Sore, but not so bad as she would have thought.

She had almost drifted off to sleep in the bath. José roused her, and dried her, and helped her put on some stockings but, to her relief, nothing else, and now she lay face down on a chaise longue.

She felt the cushions move, and looked up to see José sitting down next to her. He reached out for her, and she got ready to tense herself against some sort of penetration, but instead she felt the softest of touches on the small of her back. The hand began to stroke her, and through a gathering fog of tiredness she heard José's voice.

'Today was work,' he said, 'and tomorrow will be more work, but now is reward.' And the stroking became massage, and the massage became a sexual touch so gentle and intimate that even her abused flesh could not object, and finally the touch became an act of love that carried her off into a place where she couldn't tell the difference between the present and a dream.

CHAPTER 28

Cynthia awoke, the morning after the entertainment, with a body so sore it would barely do her bidding. Her bottom hurt, her sex – despite José's final gentleness – hurt so much she could barely close her legs without wincing, and her legs and shoulders ached with the strains of the tug of war.

She had slept well, but not dreamlessly. To her annoyance, Princess had stalked through her sleep; Princess, with her taut body poised above Cynthia. Princess, frozen with her legs parted and the beginning of a bitter golden stream issuing from her. Princess, who had made it quite plain that she expected Cynthia to be in charge of her from that day on, which was interesting. She resolved to find Princess, as soon as she could.

Meanwhile, as José had promised, there was work. The harvest was in full swing, and a procession of loaded carts rumbled and bumped down the rocky slopes of the vineyards. The ancient presses creaked, and poured their rivers of dark juice, and when each pressing was done, the crushed remains were dug out by the press room girls and carted away for animal feed and compost.

Cynthia strode across her patch, the chicote hanging ready. Some of the girls working in the fields had come straight from a hard night's use by the buyers, and they yawned blearily. A few looked distinctly sore, and none more so than Chloe. The girl looked distant when Cynthia found her. She was picking grapes like an automaton set to half speed, and Cynthia tutted at the half-full basket.

'You should have more than that, by now,' she said. 'Kneel down and lift your skirt.'

Chloe did as she was told, and Cynthia, who had already raised the chicote for the first lash, lowered it with a gasp.

'My God,' she said, in awe. 'The state of your arse!'

The kneeling girl nodded. 'I know,' she said, with feeling. 'It still hurts.'

'I bet it does!' Cynthia looked closer. The twelve livid purple weals of the cane stood out prominently against a smudged background of reddish-blue bruises, crossed and re-crossed by the angry red scribbles of the whip. The girl's flesh was lumpy and swollen, and the lips of her sex looked puffy.

Cynthia put the whip down. 'I can't do it,' she said. 'I can't flog you over that lot!' She put a hand on the girl's shoulder. 'Are you ok?'

Chloe nodded. 'Fine,' she said. 'Honestly.'

Cynthia stroked her briefly, and then took her hand away. A sudden fascination gripped her. 'What did it feel like?' she asked. 'Being caned like that. I mean, it must have hurt a lot.'

'Hurt doesn't even come close.' Chloe grinned ruefully. 'I'd never been caned before. I didn't think it was possible to feel that much.'

Cynthia reached out and gingerly ran a finger along one of the weals. Chloe shivered, but did not pull away. The skin still felt hot to the touch, and slightly rough. 'What does it feel like now?'

Chloe gave another grin. 'Very sore.' She paused. 'And very, very sexy.' She wriggled a little so that her bottom brushed over Cynthia's fingers.

Cynthia laughed. 'So you'd go through it again?'

'Oh yes.' Chloe joined in the laughter. 'In a heartbeat. Why? Are you offering?'

Cynthia slapped her lightly. 'Well, I will be soon if you don't get on with your work.' She pulled the girl's dress back down. 'Seriously! If you don't get picking, I'll get whipped. So do me a favour?'

Chloe nodded. 'Thanks,' she said. 'I'll try to wake up a bit, I promise.'

'Good.' Cynthia slapped Chloe's bottom just once more for good luck and walked off.

Chloe wasn't the only walking wounded she met that morning. Practically every girl she came across was carrying either the marks of enthusiastic corporal punishment, or the sore flesh that came from vigorous sexual use. Time after time she was shown baskets not nearly full enough, or fruit poorly selected, and time after time she found herself unable to apply her own whip to skin already scalded by others. I'm going soft, she thought, as she fell back yet again on exhortation instead of flogging.

And then she came upon Princess.

She was high up on the southern slopes. It was almost noon, and the sun was nailed to the southern sky like a baleful spotlight, but the girl was working impassively, her basket nearly full. Cynthia stood a little way back amongst the vines and watched her for a while, trying to make up her mind. She could punish the girl if she chose, and for most of the morning she had certainly intended to. The humiliation of the previous night had given her the right, after all. But now something held her back. She crouched down a little to keep herself out of sight, and tried to analyse what it was.

Fair play came into it, certainly. Princess had been given a choice, and one which she had earned fairly enough. She had made her choice, which she had obviously recognised as a last chance, and José had allowed it. By the rules of Mas Gassac, both written and unwritten, Princess had done nothing wrong.

But there was more. As she watched the superb body kneeling and rising amongst the vines, Cynthia replayed the moment when those muscular thighs had parted above her, and realised that the other girl had unwittingly woken an unsuspected part of Cynthia's soul. Even when she had guessed what was about to happen, she realised, she had welcomed it.

The realisation clicked into place like the last piece in a jigsaw, and suddenly she felt at peace with herself, more than she ever remembered feeling before. I'm everything, she thought. All things to all people, and that's not Princess' fault.

The idea buoyed her. She rose from her crouch and strode towards Princess. Then the black girl looked round as she drew closer. Her eyes widened, and she stood up, her arms rigid by her side.

Cynthia walked slowly up to her, stopping only when they were standing face to face. Princess held her ground, her eyes straight ahead. Cynthia raised her eyebrows.

'Is there anything you want to say?' she asked.

Princess shook her head.

'Fine.' Cynthia took a step back, and let the chicote hang where Princess could see it. 'But there's something I want to say.' She saw Princess draw in a breath, as if she was bracing herself. 'I'll whip you if you need it,' she went on, 'but today your basket is full so you don't need it.'

She saw surprise flicker across the other girl's face, and grinned. 'You thought I'd be looking for revenge, didn't you?'

Princess nodded.

'Well, I'm not. You were just doing what José told you, the same as I would have done. Anyway, there's something else I need.' She took a deep breath. 'I need a friend.'

The other girl wrinkled her brow. 'But you've got José,' she said.

'Oh, I know! Or he's got me, anyway.' Cynthia sighed. 'I'm happy being José's slave. Very happy. And I'll be an overseer, and whip lots of girls' bottoms, and José and Pera will whip me, and I do really want that.' She looked straight at Princess. 'But I need one person, one woman, to be strong and straightforward and just a friend.'

Princess' face was expressionless. 'You're asking me?'

'Yes.' Cynthia suddenly felt very anxious. 'Is that okay?'

Slowly, the girl's face relaxed, and then bloomed into a grin. 'Sure it's okay,' she said. She held out a hand, and Cynthia took it. 'So,' she said, 'what are you doing this afternoon?'

Princess burst out laughing. 'What do you think? Picking grapes! What about you?'

Cynthia laughed too. 'Watching people pick grapes!' She let go of the other girl's hand, and looked away over the slopes of the vineyard. 'It's good here, isn't it?'

Princess followed her gaze. 'Yes, she said quietly. 'Very good.' She looked back at Cynthia. 'You will still whip me sometimes though, won't you?'

'Of course! As often as you need it.' Cyntha swung the chicote menacingly. 'Another thing,' she added. 'I'm new to being pissed on, but I think I could get into it. But if you ever do it again without permission, I'll flog the skin off your arse. Deal?'

'Deal.'

CHAPTER 29

By Friday night, the last of the early grapes were harvested and pressed. Some time during the next week, fruit from another part of Mas Gassac would be ready and the hard work would begin again, but for a few days the slaves and their owner could concentrate on cleaning, and mending, and gathering their energy. And celebrating.

Cynthia had made sure all the slaves under her control had left the slopes before she followed them, dangling the chicote wearily. Her arm and shoulder ached from the effort of flogging. She was almost back at the house when Antoine met her. He looked as if he was in a hurry.

'Ah, at last,' he said. 'I've been looking for you! You've got twenty minutes to shower and change. José wants you.'

'Does he?' Cynthia felt her heart bumping. 'Where?'

'In his apartment. He says there are clothes put out for you. Remember, twenty minutes! Pera will collect you.'

Cynthia ran to the dormitory block and bounced into her room. Just as Antoine had said, there were clothes laid out on her bed. She lifted them up.

Ohmigod.

It was as if she had stepped back to the nineteenth century. There was a pair of white silk bloomers, not just panties but actual bloomers complete with ruffles and, when she checked, open at the crotch. There was a matching silk corset with more lace-holes than she imagined one garment could hold. There were silk stockings, also white, beautifully made, with tiny seams up the back, and there was a glorious full-length fitted evening dress in cream satin.

On the table by her bed there was a small black leather box. She opened it, pulled aside a layer of red tissue, and caught her breath.

It contained three identical rings of the sort used by body piercers, plain hoops of metal just a bit too small to fit over her little finger, with a little ball to close them. But where the body jewellery Cynthia had seen before had been stainless steel, these were made of gold, and the closures were pearl.

They were the most beautiful things she had ever seen.

She stood for a while, staring at them. Then she shook herself. The twenty minutes were ebbing fast. The last thing she wanted was to spoil whatever José had in mind by being late! She tore off her working clothes and dashed into the shower, wrenching the tap on to full and forcing herself to stand beneath the pounding water as it warmed up.

As she washed herself, she wondered for a moment why there were three rings. Then she shrugged. She would find out soon enough.

José was waiting in his apartment when the knock came.

'Come in.'

The door opened, and Pera ushered Cynthia in, then withdrew wordlessly. She advanced a couple of steps into the room, and then stopped, looking nervous, while José looked at her with frank awe.

She looked superb. The dress clung to every curve, and pulled in sharply at the waist. She must have noticed his gaze, because she glanced down at herself and smiled uncertainly.

'It's very tight,' she said. 'I had to get Pera to help lace me up.'

'How does it feel?' José asked.

'Okay.' She patted herself. 'Sort of – safe.'

'Good.' José nodded. 'I'm glad. Did you find the jewellery box, too?'

'Yes. They're beautiful,' she said, holding the box out, 'but I didn't know how to wear them. My ears aren't pierced.'

'Don't worry.' José took the box. 'We'll soon fix that. Now, sit down. I've got some things to tell you.' He gestured her to a chaise longue, and she perched herself on it. When she was settled, José went on. 'You are going to be mine,' he said. 'Is that what you still want?'

She nodded.

'Good. And tomorrow night we'll be meeting your parents. But before then I want to do something to make it formal. To put my mark on you, if you like.'

She looked up at him with wide eyes. 'What do you mean?'

'These rings.' José held out the open box. 'From tonight, you're going to wear them permanently.'

Her eyes didn't flicker, but he saw her run her tongue quickly over her lips. 'Where?' she asked.

José pointed. 'One in each nipple,' he said, 'and one between your legs.'

Her hand flew to the base of her belly. 'Between?'

'Yes.' José took the hand and pressed it. 'Through the hood over your clitoris. It will press on you; you'll be just a bit aroused, all the time.'

She gulped, but then nodded. 'Alright,' she said. 'When are you going to – do it?'

Her fear aroused him. He felt himself swelling at the thought of her, and of the little pearl winking from her sex.

'Soon,' he said. 'Very soon. But first, I want to see you out of that dress.'

She stood up, a little unsteadily, and her hands reached for the double row of buttons that ran down the front of the tight satin. He watched as she loosened the dress and slid it down over her hips. She stepped away from the pool of satin and stood looking up at him.

His cock ached at the sight of her. The effect of the corset was even more obvious without the dress; it pulled her in dramatically to an exaggerated hourglass shape. It pushed her breasts up, too, leaving her nipples peeking out just above the top. Below the corset, the tops of the stockings bit slightly into the soft flesh of her thighs. The effect was intensely, gloriously erotic.

He realised she was smiling. He raised his eyebrows. 'You seem to like me like this,' she said.

He reached out and ran his hand over her bottom, making her wriggle.

'I was just thinking,' he said, 'if Victorian women dressed like this, I'm not surprised they had big families.'

She laughed, and then drew in her breath as he pushed his fingers through the opening in the bloomers. He found hot, moist flesh.

'Bad girl,' he said. 'I think, before we pierce you, we'd better punish you.'

'Yes please!' Her voice was husky. 'How will I be punished?'

He pushed harder, opening her. 'I think,' he said, 'given how you are dressed, it had better be the cane.'

For a moment she stopped wriggling. He kept his hand inside her, and took hold of her chin with the other hand, pulling her round to look straight into his eyes.

'I'm going to cane you,' he said firmly. 'For one thing, I guess you've never been caned before, and for another, I was watching you when Cavendish thrashed Chloe. You wanted it, didn't you?'

She nodded slowly.

'You want it now, don't you?'

There was a pause. Then her head dipped, just once. 'How many strokes?' she whispered.

'Twelve. Just the same as Chloe.'

He took his hand out of her sex and held it up to her face for her to lick. Then he turned and walked over to a cupboard in the corner of the room. He could feel her eyes on him as he opened it and took out a long, slim cane, the twin of the one he had given to the Englishman.

Still with his back to her, he said: 'Take your knickers off, and bend over. Grasp your ankles.'

He heard the rustle and swish of the silk being lowered. He waited for a second, then turned round to see Cynthia's bottom, tightly bent, and framed by the corset above and the stockings below. Her sex glistened flagrantly between her thighs, and he felt his lust rising. He swished the cane through the air, making the girl finch.

'Are you ready?'

For several breaths she said nothing. Then she said, simply: 'Yes.'

'Very well.' José tapped the cane against the taut swell of her bottom. On Cavendish's advice he had practiced for hours, directing blow after blow at a cushion until he had thrashed his way through to the stuffing. Now, at last, it was Cynthia's turn. He raised the cane, took careful aim, and brought it lashing down across the base of her cheeks.

It landed true, leaving a bright white bar that quickly darkened to an angry pair of tramlines, first red and then purple. José waited for the howl.

It didn't come. Cynthia's knuckles whitened as she gripped her ankles fiercely, and her legs trembled, but she made no sound at all.

José tightened his lips. If the girl was going to put up a fight, fair enough. He'd win in the end, he knew. He was the one holding the cane.

He lashed it down again. He had meant to land the stroke slightly above the last one, but his aim was not yet perfect, and it landed across the top of her thighs, just below the crease. She still didn't cry out, but he heard the breath hissing through her teeth, and her bottom began to weave slightly from side to side as the fresh weal darkened to the colour of old wine. The movement animated the lips of her cunt in the ancient, lewd dance that women have performed for their men, whether willingly or not, for thousands of years. The sight hardened José's cock even more. He raised the cane again.

This time his aim was right – the stroke landed just a little above the first. The girl lifted a heel off the ground as the pain bit, and now she couldn't keep back a groan of agony. José waited until she had settled again, and then brought the cane hissing down. He was getting the measure of the job, now. It was his hardest stroke yet, just a little higher up the trembling bottom, and so close to the last that it was almost touching. Cynthia moaned and lifted her heel again, and then the other, her hips rotating as she tried to escape the pain of her punishment.

But there was no escape. José whipped her tightened cheeks, stroke after measured stroke. The livid weals climbed higher and higher, and Cynthia gasped, and then cried, and then finally howled with pain as the evil cane scored her flesh.

After the eleventh stroke, José paused and took stock of the damage he had inflicted. It was considerable – weals covered every inch of the suffering girl's behind, from the top of her thighs to almost the top of her crack. Her hips bucked gently back and forwards as she writhed with pain, and the engorged lips between her thrashed cheeks were swollen and slick with moisture.

It was time to finish the ordeal. José took careful aim and brought the cane down one last time. It lashed diagonally across the girl's extravagantly punished behind, crossing every one of the previous eleven strokes.

Cynthia screamed as if she had been branded, and broke into loud hiccupping sobs. Her hands flew to her bottom, grasped the flaming globes and began to knead them desperately. José put down the cane and took hold of her hands.

'I don't think so,' he told her. 'Take your pain like a good girl, and keep your hands off.'

Through her sobs, she said: 'Yes, sir. Sorry, sir.'

'Good. Now, stand up.'

She straightened slowly, and he saw her wincing as the movement flexed her swelling bottom.

He studied her face. Wet with tears, and red-eyed, but there was no resentment. She had accepted her caning and, he guessed, would accept what was to come after it. He picked up the jewellery box. 'Are you ready for your rings?' he asked.

She wiped the tears from her cheek and nodded.

'Then lie down.' He pointed at the chaise longue, and she walked over to it obediently. She sat down, flinching a little as her bottom touched the leather, and then swung her legs off the ground and lay back.

When she was in place, José reached down and eased each of her breasts a little further out of the top of the corset. Her nipples stood up, high and hard. He turned, opened his desk drawer and took out a packet of needles. He opened one, and rested it against the base of her left nipple, pushing so that it indented the flesh a little.

'This will hurt,' he told her. 'Be grateful.' Then he thrust the needle through her with a single swift motion.

She started slightly and gasped, but didn't try to pull away, and she held her position as he pulled out the needle and replaced it with one of the gold rings.

'There,' he said. 'One done. Only another two to go.'

She nodded, and blinked as a fresh tear welled in her eye.

José pierced her other nipple as quickly as he had the first. This time she was prepared; she didn't start, and made no sound as the needle burrowed through her. Seconds later the ring was in place.

José leaned down and kissed her cheek. 'Well done,' he said. 'I think you have earned a break. Sit up.' While she did, he walked over to a side table, picked up a decanter and splashed a measure of brandy into a glass. He handed it to Cynthia and she sipped, and then coughed, and then smiled gratefully.

'Thanks,' she said, in a voice that shook slightly. She sipped again. 'I'm okay,' she said.

'I know you are.' He took the glass from her. 'Save a little of that for when it's all over,' he said. 'You're going to need it. Now, in a few moments I'm going to pierce your sex. You'll need to be held down so I'm going to call Pera and Antoine.'

He had turned and was walking over to the bell when she said: 'Please, José, if I've got to be held can it be someone I ask for?'

He paused. His first instinct was to refuse, but there was something in her voice. 'Alright,' he said slowly. 'Who?'

'Chloe, please' she said, 'and Princess.'

José turned, and raised his eyebrows. 'Really? The pet, and the friend?' He turned the idea over for a moment, then nodded. 'I'll send for them,' he said, and rang the bell.

A few minutes later the two girls entered. They curtseyed to José. 'You're here because Cynthia has asked for you,' he told them. 'Cynthia, explain.'

She took a breath. 'José is going to pierce me, here,' she said, resting a hand on her mound. 'I want you to hold me still, please.'

Chloe gave a little gasp, but Princess was impassive. 'Okay,' she said, and then to José: 'How should we hold her, Master?'

'Let her sit down,' he said, 'and then each of you take one of her legs. Raise them and spread them so that her sex is opened.'

Cynthia sat down, and the two girls did as he had said. José watched, his heart racing, as the moist folds of her sex opened like a flower. When she was in position, he took a fresh needle, reached down, and felt through her labia until his fingers located the shy button of her clitoris and the soft hood above it. He pinched the hood between finger and thumb and drew it out and away from Cynthia's body, making her moan. He nodded to the two slaves.

'Hold her well,' he said. Then he pushed the needle through the tender flap.

Cynthia convulsed, and gave a long, high squeal of pain that only ended when she had emptied her lungs. Then she took a shuddering breath and moaned.

José nodded to the two girls holding her. 'You can let go,' he said. They took their hands from Cynthia's legs, and she lowered them slowly. José reached out and stroked her cheek. 'Is that good?'

She nodded, her eyes glazed. 'Very, very good,' she said softly. Then she smiled a little. 'With this ring, I thee wed,' she said, and squeezed his hand.

'Exactly.' José kissed her. 'Now, it's time to consummate the marriage. Chloe, Princess – leave us.' They obeyed, and when the door had closed behind them José turned back to Cynthia. 'Turn over!' he told her.

She did so, arranging herself so that she was kneeling on the chaise longue with her hands on the back of it. Her legs were parted, showing the diamond-shaped gash between them with the pearl of the fresh ring nestling in the wet folds of flesh in its centre. 'Like this?'

'Like that.' José opened his trousers, stepped forwards and rested the tip of his aching cock against the bud of her anus. Then he thrust forwards, not hard, but firmly, rocking himself deeper into her so that she growled and gasped, and moving faster and faster until his dam burst and he pumped himself into her while her moans of pain and pleasure caressed his ears like music that was too beautiful to end.

EPILOGUE

A nd then it was Saturday.

Because the French are used to depending on their railways, which run beautifully unless there is a strike, there are few scheduled flights between Perpignan and Paris, and even those are not heavily used. José and Cynthia had been almost alone in the little Air France Régional aircraft, which threw them into the air on a sultry late afternoon at Rivesaults and landed them into the cooler, but even closer, Parisian evening less than two hours later.

Orly Airport, by contrast, was horribly crowded, and José put his arm round Cynthia's shoulder and guided her quickly through the scrum and out to the taxi rank. He pulled open the door of the lead car, guided Cynthia in, and threw himself in after her. The driver pulled away from the rank even as he turned round to ask: 'Where to, Monsieur?'

'Avenue Pergolèse.'

'And the number?'

José looked enquiringly at Cynthia.

'Twenty,' she said.

'Twenty it is.'

The taxi lurched forwards, and José looked at Cynthia. 'Don't worry,' he said gently. 'It will be okay.' The taxi gave another lurch, and he added: 'If we survive the journey.'

She smiled nervously, and looked away.

In his way, David Arundel was also nervous. In his rational moments he knew there was little point. Cynthia was legally an adult, and anyway it was not as if her desires were unexpected – if she was submissive then she was only following in her mother's footsteps.

But still, he was nervous. He wondered what this man Mestré would be like.

The bell rang. He was about to find out. He signalled to Julia, and together they walked down the broad staircase and stood in the hall as Yolanda opened the door.

Cynthia felt her heart thumping against her ribs. Although she had bid her parents goodbye only a couple of weeks ago, she felt as if she had lived a whole life since then. She took a deep breath as the door began to open.

And suddenly there was Yolanda, and there behind her were her mother and father, looking a bit stiff and awkward, but still – them! She ran forward and threw her arms around them, and felt them hug her back.

She savoured the embrace for a few moments, and then remembered herself. She stood back a little, and said, rather formally and feeling a little foolish: 'Father, Mother, this is Monsieur José Mestré.'

José stepped forwards and held out his hand. Her father took it, briefly looking very English. Then her mother made up for it by reaching out, taking José's shoulders, pulling him towards her and performing a thoroughly French air-kiss to either side of his face.

'Monsieur Mestré,' she said. 'We are so happy to meet you.'

And suddenly Cynthia knew it was going to be alright.

The story of Cynthia, José and their families continues in Circle of Submission, to be published by Silver Moon Books.

continues the Circle of Submission, to be published by Silver Moon Books.